T0149229

In the
CROSSHAIRS

In the
CROSSHAIRS

Locked and Loaded

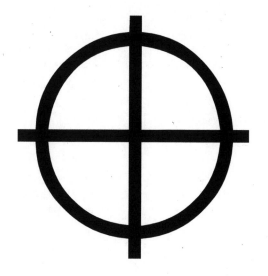

RJ DEMERS

In the Crosshairs
Locked and Loaded

This is a work of fiction. All of the characters, names, incidents, organizations, and dialogue in this novel are either the products of the author's imagination or are used fictitiously.

iUniverse books may be ordered through booksellers or by contacting:

iUniverse
1663 Liberty Drive
Bloomington, IN 47403
www.iuniverse.com
1-800-Authors (1-800-288-4677)

ISBN: 978-1-4917-7106-8 (sc)
ISBN: 978-1-4917-7105-1 (e)

Library of Congress Control Number: 2015911408

Print information available on the last page.

iUniverse rev. date: 09/16/2015

Contents

Chapter I

D-DAY

My sights are set and my trigger finger is itchy waiting patiently. I feel my heart begin to gradual slow down and my breathing starts to become tranquil. I feel the gun in my arm, it's almost like an extension of my body, it knows what I'm thinking and now it's anticipating the command to destroy whatever is in its crosshairs. The wind is peaceful, it brushes my skin ever so gently, the sun is out and warms my face with its sweltering glow. I'm not the most educated man on the face of this earth but I instantly transform into an astute genius when a firearm is put it in my hand understanding the physics and science behind a perfect shot. I sit perched on a hillcrest of trees overlooking a small crescent of seven houses in a quaint little peaceful neighbourhood. There is nothing in my way and nothing blocking me from a clear shot at my target who will soon be sauntering out of his house eventually meeting his ultimate demise. I envision the kill in my head and have replayed this moment over and over again for the last two weeks, there is no way I will fail this contract, it's not even an option. The target has no idea that he is mere moments away from dying as a result of a bullet to his head that will be soon be exiting my gun. My gun, my precious, is locked and loaded just waiting to do my bidding, ready to strike down a man that I have never met, or even spoken to. Still, this is what I do, this is my life, this is my job.

What is the one objective that all humans on earth strive for? Prosperity? Distinction? Long life? No. The ultimate objective for anyone on this earth is to live a sin free life. It is said that in order to truly purify your soul of sin, you must not only repent the words to the messenger of God, but you must also believe in your repent and truly forgive yourself, only then can you truly purge yourself from your sins and atone for your mistakes. Simply put, the words are not enough, one must want to rid himself of the sins that he has bestowed upon his soul. Forgiveness is what I truly pursue, but forgiveness is not attained until I seek it with repentance and forgiveness. For the sins that I have committed in this lifetime of mine are menacing and sinister, I am not sure if I can really be forgiven, perhaps my soul is decaying and cannot be resurrected or become untainted and pure again, but that never stops me from coming in to Church on Sundays to try. Evil is defined as something or someone that is the cause of suffering, injury, or destruction. The best way liberate yourself of evil is simply to confront it head on, look at it in its demonic eyes and command it to disappear. Does that really wash away the blood on my hands, or take the blackness from my heart, or the take away the maliciousness from my soul? Only in the afterlife will I be privileged to that kind of information. Everyone on this earth sins, next time look up at the night sky and count the stars, each one is a single sin that someone has committed in their lifetime, but since sins are repented and cleansed, those stars are now millions of miles away.

Earlier that day...

I am in my bed slowly waking up and look around to see the sun peeking through the window with an elegant awe inspiring mahogany glow. I feel my chest and it is damp from sweat and I know it is the result of another nightmare, images and thoughts that I just cannot escape from no matter how fast I try to run from it. The horrible incident that happened in Russia five years ago that has rocked my very soul. I lay there now trying to get the gumption to get up and start my day, that moment we all feel when we first open our eyes and look around contemplating whether to get up or not. I finally sit up, rub my face and run my hands through my hair trying to wake up. I look over and there she is, still half covered, sleeping like a queen as if she never heard the alarm go off. She is Trina, my girlfriend of four years and the love of my life. I look her up and down, her skin so beautiful and perfect, eyes a piercing blue color and her hair the color of the sun still and looking like heaven and after a full night of sleep, she is perfect. She is the best thing in my life and there is nothing I would not do for her, she is my world, my soul mate. She kind of moans almost ready to get up as an instant grin comes to my face, she still makes me smile and my heart skip a beat when I look at her. I stand up sporting my nice white Calvin Klein underwear against my trim robust body. I walk to the mirror and take a good look at my entire face and the expression I currently have on it, a grin that is telling me that I am happy to be alive and I think I may have the perfect life. A beautiful girlfriend, a mansion for a house, seven cars, and a great job, how can anyone complain right? I can't. Beginning of a new day, each new day is a blank page in the diary of your life. The secret of success is in turning that diary into the best story you possibly can and living that day to the fullest filling up those pages with as much detail as possible.

"Hey you" Trina says in that waking up voice as she looks up at me with her big beautiful blue eyes.

"Hey baby, how did you sleep?" I asked her as I turn my head to her.

"Mmm, great. Had a wonderful dream that I got caught up in" she says semi sitting up "You ready for today?" she asks.

I gently nod and say "Yep, ready as I'll ever be, it's go time, D-day."

She turns back in her bed almost disappointed. I look back in the mirror knowing exactly how she feels. "It'll be okay babe, I will be okay" I say trying to reassure her and myself for that matter.

"I know, it just seems to get harder every time, you can't blame me for getting apprehensive, I mean over time that worry grows and accumulates" she says still not looking at me. She then sits up "What if you don't make it home one of these days, you don't exactly work in a nice cozy office surrounded in bulletproof glass. The world is so unpredictable and nobody is invincible, God can only protect so many people at once leaving so many others susceptible and vulnerable."

I move towards her, sit on the bed and look deep into her eyes "I'll always come home to you baby, nothing, I mean nothing will keep me from doing that. Heaven and earth can't stop me from seeing that beautiful smile of yours that warms my heart and brings an instant smile to my face. After this one we will start our new life in Mexico and leave everything behind us. This is my last, the very last, I promise you, I'm done with this after I get home.

There is no fear in love; but perfect love casteth out fear; because fear hath no torment. He that feareth in not made perfect love" I say to her, a quote from *John 4:18."* I take my religion serious and put all my faith in the Lord who watches over me.

I look at her and a single tear runs down her cheek, I gently kiss her lips then get up and put a shirt on. I suppose I should tell you what I do for a living. I am a contract killer, better known as a hitman. Shocked? This is how I make my money, most punch in and out of time cards, I punch out peoples' lives. Between Angels and Demons you'll find me Chris SLAUGHTER, trained assassin, lethal killer. Trina knows what I do, I've never hid that from her since day one. I was scared, almost petrified at first when I told her what I did for a living figuring she would freak out and call me a murderer or something, but she had almost no reaction as she computed it for a few minutes. I couldn't lie to her, I mean how could I explain the money I had, never actually punching in at a job? She'd probably think I was having an affair or cheating on her, and I didn't want to start off a relationship with a lie, she'd either accept it or leave me, and I can deal with whatever she chooses. To my surprise, Trina came to the conclusion that a hitman was the sexiest manliest job on earth, but after four years and a couple close calls, she is terrified every time I do a job. It's not like taking a picture where you simply just point and shoot, I study my target, I practice daily, and do tons of research. I work alone and perform long-range hits or sniper shots to reduce the risk of getting spotted or caught. Some long-range sniper hitmen use a spotter, I don't. What's a spotter you ask? A spotter works side by side with the shooter calculating everything for him and watching his back allowing the shooter to focus on only one thing, the target. I just don't have enough trust in anyone, I do the calculations myself using an electronic anemometer to calculate exact wind speed, my cell phone calculates the humidity with a SHTC1 humidity and temperature sensor. I also bring a little device called the XA1000 all in one, it calculates temperature, and air flow which is also vital for the perfect shot. All these calculations need to be accounted for, computed and analysed in order to get the job done right, there is no room for error in this line of work, mistakes in estimation compound over distance can cause a shot to miss the target completely. Any given combination of firearm and ammunition will have an associated value known as the circular error probable, defined as the radius of a circle whose boundary is expected to contain the impact points of half of the rounds fired.

D-day, this refers to the day that I will be putting a bullet into my targets' head, killing him dead and eliminating him from this earth. I'm twenty seven years old, I've been doing this for just over five years, I have 8.7 million in the bank and I have killed twenty two people. How did I get into this line of work you ask, I'll tell you all a bit later.

I walk down the stairs into the kitchen which is all made of stainless steel, the fridge, the stove, the sink and even the huge island in the middle and all accented with picturesque chestnut brown wooden cabinets and marble floors. I'm not really hungry as I am anticipating Jimmy's call which is a ritual on D-day, Jimmy is what you would call my middle man, my handler sort of speak. He is the one that does the deals and then gives me the 411 on the next assignment, who he is, who he's associated too, his history and stuff like that. Assignment, target, victim, hit, contract, whatever you want to call him or her, those are the people that I am paid to eliminate on behalf of someone else. I never speak to the client directly, nobody knows who I am and the only way they know how to get a hold of me is through Jimmy. The less people in this world who know who I am and know my face, the better. So here's how it works; say a client wants some low life or backstabber or whoever offed, majority of time it's a gang hit put on by either a rival gang or a gang wanting a potential snitch eliminated. The client will get in touch with Jimmy and inquire to have this job done and how much it would cost to do it. It's not like he's listed in the phone book or anything, you need to know somebody who knows somebody who knows somebody way up in the thug world who's got the right connections. Jimmy will then get a background on who exactly the client is and who the target is, the bigger the risk, the higher the price, that's the deal, client can take it or leave it. Jimmy will then run it by me and get my opinion, then call the client back and give them a price, they want the job done right and no trace leading back to them, they'll pay what we say, it's that simple. I don't care why they want a person killed, what their motives are, what they did wrong or anything of that nature, all I want to know is, where he or she lives, what his or her daily routine is, where the easiest place to take them out is, and what would be the best time to get the job done. All in all I take about a week or so to figure out who this target is, where he or she works, what their daily routine is, where they live, and scope out a suitable spot to snipe the target. Why do people call me? Because plain and simple, I AM THE BEST!

"Jimmy call yet?" Trina says while promenading down the stairs wearing a stunning purple satin robe and her golden hair neatly placed in a ponytail.

"Not yet babe" as I drank my orange juice, astringent taste. "He'll call soon, countdown is on, he'll give me his game day prep talk, tell me to stay focused blah blah blah." I take another sip "it should be soon." I get butterflies in my stomach knowing a contract is coming up, like a kid waiting to open presents on Christmas morning. Pulling off a perfect hit is like, well like almost having an orgasm, when I know I did my job perfectly and a big pay day is coming up, well, not gonna lie, it tingles down there a little bit. These violent delights have violent ends, ice in my veins, black is my soul.

"Sun's out, looks like another beautiful day" she says.

"Promise of a new day. My favorite time of the day, everything is waking up and looking magnificent and inspirational to start the day off" I say looking at her with flirtatious eyes.

Trina smiles and says "Smooth talker today are you?"

"As silk" I respond with a wink.

Just as I was in that thought, my phone rings. Instantaneously Trina looks at me and I look at her knowing that Jimmy is most likely on the other end. I look at my phone "It's Jimmy." Trina then marches upstairs. Dunno why she's upset, this ain't new.

"Hey Jimmy" I answer my phone.

"Christopher! You doing it today huh? You ready?" Jimmy says with enthusiasm in his voice.

"Ya, gonna head there in a bit before he goes to work, everything should go down as planned, no foreseen issues" I respond in the calmest of voice. I didn't have the heart to tell Jimmy that this is my final hit and I'm calling it quits. Not sure how he will react to that news, and to tell you the truth, I was afraid to tell him.

"Be safe out there, stay focused, remain calm and composed, and know you are the best. I'm praying for you" Jimmy says in a more concerning voice.

"Thanks, pray for MYERS too" I say. I always say a little prayer for the victim before I pull the trigger. Why? Well it's like this, I have nothing against this guy, don't know him, he's never done anything to me, I have no beef with him, nothing. But I have a contract to kill him and that is what I am going to do, nothing personal, this is just my business.

"I will. Good luck, call me when it's done so I can let the client know" Jimmy says. "Remember, you be safe my boy. Let the sun open your eyes, let the thunder strike the person down, let the rain wash away your sins, and the night help you rest."

"Will do Jimmy" I say as I push the END button on my phone and walk upstairs. I open my massive closet and pick out a sophisticated navy blue suit with a light grey shirt. I put the shirt on, then my pants, do up my tie, put my shoulder holsters on, then slip on my blazer. I always dress to the nines when I am going to do a hit, it's for respect of the victim, he will be losing his life today by my hands, so this is the way I show respect for that person, kind of like going to a funeral. Put some gel in my hair, two small blast of my cologne, and do a once over in the mirror to make sure I haven't missed anything. Nope, I am dressed to kill, bad joke.

After I get dressed, I amble into my garage filled with exotic cars and open my cabinet, that has all my necessary tools, tools being my weapons, guns, knives, trip wires, binoculars, night vision goggles, you name it. I reach for the other lady in my life, Charlotte. She is my stunning M4OA3 sniper rifle with a night vision scope on her complete with silencer and trimmed in flawless chrome.

I adore her as much as I do Trina and that ain't no lie. As soon as I touch her my heart beats faster and I get goose bumps all over, like a young man on prom, ready to have sex for the very first time. As I look Charlotte over up and down like I was going to make love to it, Trina walks in with two shiny brass plated pistols. She walks up to me with them, one in each hand without saying a word and puts them in my side holster as sexy as anyone could possibly do that. "Don't forget these, and know how much I love you. Do you know why I love you?" she asks as she looks deep in my eyes.

I grab her around her waist, pull her in and say "remind me again."

She gazes into my soul and says "because every day you seem to find a new way for me to love you. You amaze me all the time and seem to always wake my heart up when you look at me and touch me."

I look at her passionately and respond "and that is what keeps me coming home to you every day. Knowing that I have someone as amazing as you waiting for me and loving me as much as I love her."

"Please be safe."

I gently nod and say "I will" I say, kiss her on the forehead and turn to my car. I get into my black beauty, my jet black Porsche 911. "I will call you when it is done, I will be home later" I back up out of my driveway, look at Trina one more time, then off I go.

8:17 a.m

My contract is for a Joseph MYERS. I've been studying him and everything he does the moment we got the contract to eliminate him. The contract for Mr. MYERS was put out by three of his long time work partners slash former gang members turned businessmen who claimed that MYERS took or stole one of their ideas and made a fortune on it, quit, then went into business for himself and made millions off the idea behind their backs. His partners, who are related or were related to the Nazi Low Riders, a criminal organization primarily based in southern California are the ones who ordered the hit two weeks ago. They were obviously miffed that MYERS is now a millionaire on an idea that they all came up with and who could blame them, they got screwed big time. They lost the argument in civil court so I guess they said they can't continue to live a normal life knowing that MYERS is making money hand over fist with their idea while they are busting their asses all day trying to come up with the next big thing. What was the idea? Who knows, who gives a shit, they want this guy dead for $225,000, that's all I need to know. So, once I got the call from Jimmy telling me that these guys want MYERS eliminated, I got all the information for MYERS and studied everything he does. Joseph Woodward MYERS, born December 14th, 1969, former gang member of the Nazi Low Riders of L.A, has the letters N.L.R inked on the back of his neck, drives a 2010 silver BMW, works for the Union Wholesale International Trading Company for seven years, convicted twice of aggravated assault, spent three years in jail for it back in 1998, and got divorced last year from Melisa Stewart Anderson. How did I get all of this advantageous information on MYERS you ask? From the streets as well as my best friend Detective Anthony BECHERELLI of the L.A Gang Unit. Yes I said detective, so yes he is a cop. I've known Tony since I was five years old and we have been best friends our entire life. I was his best man at his wedding, and he will be mine when I marry Trina. Hitman and lawman, best friends, always amuses me when I say that in my mind. Tony knows what I do for a living and helps me out, keeping the heat off me, redirecting one of my victims to a gang hit or random drive by shooting. So why does he do this? Because I give him the low down on crime that the LAPD would never know about. I know all kinds of shit bags, low lives, gang bangers, and mobsters, who do you think most of my clients are? Not one of them know what I officially do for a living, they think I'm some lone wolf gangster with a big bank account that is piggy backing my Dad. I get my weapons from these thugs and pay them handsomely I might add, and when we all get chatting, they spill some stuff to me or I overhear things. Who would suspect a pretty boy white dude like me would be snitching to the cops about their criminal activities and working hand and hand with a detective from the L.A Gang Unit. They have never suspected me as being the person to be a so called informant, in fact, unknowingly, one busts that the Feds did on The Red Rider gang was on account of my information, which eventually lead to one of the largest gang sweeps of 2012. The Feds with the LAPD were led by Tony and simultaneously raided and arrested thirty core members of the Red Rider gang based on some hot information of mine and as a result, they all served a wide range of prison time. The remaining Riders became apprehensive of each other eventually which led to a hit on one of their own who they thought was the snitch that was working with the Feds leading to the big bust, then they ironically hired me to do the hit on the suspected snitch. Talk about a win win for me on that one, I rat them out and then they turn around and pay me to take out one of their own. Anyway, Tony is one of the very few people in this world I trust, I never worry that he will one day turn on me, we're brothers for life and that's as solid as steel. We have a good thing going, I get to do my contracts with the heat being deflected from a loan sniper, and he comes off as a super cop busting all these drug dealers and wanna be gangsters thanks to my information. I do have morals in case you're wondering, I don't kill kids, husbands or wives who want their significant other eliminated, or wealthy business men that benefit the community. MYERS may be a wealthy businessman, but everyone knows him as the former gangster who beat a man with a pair of brass knuckles almost to death in 1997. I'm talking about Casino owners, sports team owners, Politicians, Wall Street big wigs, or anyone of that nature, public figures in other words. And of course, I never kill anyone who I do not have a contract for no matter what, because if I ever do that, I go from a hitman to a murderer.

Sun is almost fully up as I look at the stunning skyline, a luminous piece of art painted on a canvas for all to admire. I then take a glance at the clock, 8:26 a.m., five minutes from MYERS house. For the past two weeks I have studied MYERS daily routine, and everything that he does including when he goes to work, what time he gets home, where he goes for lunch, and so on. Every morning like clockwork, he heads out to work at 8:50 a.m., dressed in his nice suit which is tailored I imagine and strolls to his fancy car parked in the driveway. He's got a long concrete driveway leading to his house, so if I do it right, MYERS body won't be noticed until later in the day due to the shadows of the sun. The plan is to shoot him as he walking in front of his car towards the driver side. If I get it exact, he'll land right between the front of his car and his garage which is shaded by a big tree that over hangs his driveway which will provide the perfect cover. My hopes is that he won't be noticed until later in the day when the sun moves and will expose him a little better. I would do it at night, but over the last two weeks, MYERS has come home at various times from 6:00 p.m. as late as 11:30 p.m., maybe he's a playboy, maybe he goes to the gym, maybe he goes to gamble, who knows, who cares, either way, I can't work with erratic times like that. The only thing for sure is that ten minutes before nine he always steps out of his house, sets the alarm, puts on his sunglasses, then struts in front of his car to the driver side.

As I drive closer to the spot where I'm going to set up, I visualize the kill in my head, glimpsing in slow motion that bullet passing through each side of his skull with a small splash of red on each end. I never listen to the radio, not because I want to stay focused or anything, I just can't stand the bullshit on the radio today. It's like television, nothing ever good on, so I hardly watch that either. Besides, it's soothing just listening to my car's engine, enjoying the beautiful day outside and the sound of peace and quiet. As I approach my heart starts beating a little faster, adrenaline starts flowing, palms getting clammy, and I let out a deep breath, today, MYERS dies! ....

8:38 a.m.

I arrive at my destination. *"For this is my blood of the covenant, which poured out for many for the forgiveness of sins" Matthew 26:28*

CHAPTER II

MIND OF A MECHANIC

How does it feel to take a human life? You think it's easy? Do you think that you could do it? It's not easy to be responsible for the death of another person no matter who he or she is or what the justification may be. It's not like taking a photo where you simply just point and shoot, because after you snap a photo, there are no ramifications that need to be dealt with. When you pull that trigger, you will begin a ripple effect of many people that will be affected by your action including yourself, your loved ones, the target's friends, family and significant other and of course you must answer to the good Lord and justify to him what you have just done. Most people say that they would be able to pull the trigger if they or a loved one was in imminent danger which I truly believe, but, even after a person has taken that life, over eighty percent of those people will be affected by that for the rest of their lives. This means having consistent nightmares, feeling constant remorse and guilt, and replaying the kill over and over in their head before they either go insane or simply just end it all and take their own life. Before you judge me as a stone cold heartless killer, let me tell you that I take all of that into account. That being, who I'm killing, the ripple effect of the kill, the remorse that I will feel afterwards and having to face God and justify the reason to him why I just killed another human being for money. As I assemble my gun, those are the thoughts running through my mind, understanding that with a simple pull of my trigger, that person in my crosshairs will never live again and he may never understand why in his afterlife. As I get ready to take my shot I get into this weird kind of trance where my whole body just goes numb, my mind is black and is empty with no thoughts, and my heart and lungs just appear to stop for a second. I don't hear anything and I see nothing accept for the picture in my crosshairs. The only thing that moves during this trance is my trigger finger as it instinctively retracts when it sees the target come into focus. After the shot is made I instantly come out of the trance, I hear the wind, I smell the air, my heart beats again, and my lungs take in a breath of air. I then take a few moments to confirm a good shot and the target is eliminated and then my mind begins to race with thoughts as I see a person in my crosshairs lying motionless in a pool of blood knowing that I am the one that was responsible for it. I then go through a range of deliberations like, what will their significant other's reaction be? What will their friends feel? How will the community react to this act of violence? Then I reflect on my emotions and deal with the remorse, the guilt, the responsibility and ultimately how with I be judged by the good Lord. So what makes me different from anyone else when I just finished telling you how hard it is for a person to deal with taking the life of another human being? That I really have no answer for. I have asked myself that very question for years and I can't come up with a rational conclusion. Did God forget to put that little piece in me that has an overwhelming guilt that weighs on one's conscience until it becomes unbearable? People have different views about what it means to kill, I mean some people believe that if you kill a few men you are a serial killer, if you kill a couple thousand men then you are a conqueror, and if you kill everyone you are God. Why if you kill one person you are locked up in jail for the rest of your life, but if you kill and slaughter a mass amount of people in battle you get a purple ribbon pinned to your chest? Conflicting idealisms yes but I don't use these rationales to justify my actions at all. I don't have the mind of a psychopathic killer at all where I think one less person in this world out of seven billion, who really cares? I understand that human life is precious and no one person's life of this earth is more valuable or less valuable that anyone else's, but I also realize that there are people in this world that need to have someone else die for various purposes; that being, revenge, justification, vindication, financial motivation, or simply just to make things right. So ask yourself this, do the people that hire me have the same amount of guilt after the target they paid me to kill is eliminated? I suppose they can try to justify to themselves that they will have no blood on their hands because they did not actually perform the act, but in the same breath if it wasn't for them paying me to eliminate the target, the target would still be alive today.

How does one become a hitman you ask? You certainly don't think as an eight year old that this is the profession you want when you grow up. No, at that age you aspire to be something distinguished, someone who people can be proud of, a police man, a fire man, a doctor, or a baseball player, not someone that stops the beating of another's heart in cold blood. Hitmen are glamourized in movies and television and sure we've all thought "what a cool job", living the high life, working once every few months, sniping people like a ninja and always getting away with the perfect crime. But nobody in their right mind would actually ever follow up on that notion and become a hired assassin, it's just a fantasy, nothing more.

I couldn't do math, I couldn't do science, I wasn't good at sports, but man oh man, I COULD SHOOT. It came so natural to me, it's like God was telling me something, not really sure what that was exactly. I often wonder if maybe I may have misinterpreted God's true intention for me, like maybe he meant for me to be a cop, or a sniper in the army, or a soldier gleaming with pride for the country he serves. I don't know why, but I could shoot, I just got it, I understood the physics and the science behind a perfect long range shot. I loved going to the range with my Dad as he thought it was important that everyone should at least know how to handle and shoot a firearm. I remember at age 17, I astonished the entire range when I laid down in a prone position with a M40A3 sniper rifle and struck a target almost dead center just under 500 meters away without any real training. From that instant, I loved it. I loved the feel of the gun, the cold steal in my hands, I loved the challenge of having to account for wind speed, wind direction, temperature, barometric pressure, the angle of the target from you and the projectory that the bullet will take. I kept studying all the time and kept practicing, kept getting better and better, hitting targets further and further away. At age 20, I sniped a target 1614 meters away, some of the best snipers in the world can't make that shot with years of training. Then came the day that made me a legend. At age 22, I hit a target that was 2125 meters, that's 2324 yards, that's over two kilometers away. Try to let that distance sink in and think about how far away two kilometers is. Before I even laid down, before I was about to prone out and make my shot, I did my calculations; the wind speed was 3 km south west, the temperature was 72.2 fahrenheit, the humidity was 69.5 percent, and the barometric pressure was 101.325 kPa. After that I was ready to take my shot, as I laid down I became deaf, I heard nothing as I looked through the scope, lined up my shot, then waited to pull the trigger. I usually on average lay motionless for nearly five minutes before the gun goes off, there isn't a thought that goes through my mind as all I see is the spot I want to hit. I never know when the gun will blast as I slowly begin retract the trigger and just let the gun go off when it wants, my fingers do all of the thinking and when they are ready, they ever so gentle put a little more pressure on the trigger with each passing second until the gun goes off. After I shoot, I remain motionless in that position for another two minutes because I feel paralysed with gratification, like I had an orgasm and just need a minute or two to take it all it. 2125 meters, there isn't too many people on earth this can make that shot. "You just shot a fucking target from over two kilometers away!" my Dad said in utter amazement and pride after I made that shot, I've never really heard him swear in front of me either. "How the hell did you do that"?

I never responded, I just answered in my head "I have no idea, but that's dam impressive." Not really cocky, but just the unbridle fact that I know I have a God given gift. I felt that the beam from God shined down on me and gently touched me with this gift and probably intended for me to use it for good. Now, I wonder if it was more of a curse from hell rather than a gift from the heavens.

I became later infatuated with shooting, not just long range shooting, everything. From 9 millimetres, to 45 millimetres, to twelve gauge shotguns, I just fancied the feel of cold metal in my hand and seeing the target that I set out to destroy get obliterated by my hands.

A few weeks after my infamous shot, I was at the gun range and a big dark skinned gentleman approached me with seeming interest. When I say dark skinned I don't mean an African American or Native American, I mean a guy with a very deep tan like a Mexican or something. He had slick back hair blacker that coke, a scar under his right eye, a dirty little mustache and was a tall as a basketball player. His name, was Cedric Kolov Jones. I didn't know who he was at the time, but Jones was a big time player in the Russian Mafia, extremely wealthy, extremely powerful and extremely violent. "You" he faintly says to me in a Russian accent "you shoot good, I've heard about you" as he approached me. I started to get a little intimidated by this man now, not knowing what his intentions were, DTA my Dad always said. He now stood so close to me I can smell his cologne. He grinned in a sinister way and said "You know boy, you can make some good money with that shooting of yours" Jones said to me almost in a whisper now.

I was unsure exactly of what he meant so I just said "Uh, thanks." Now staring into his eyes I ask "Do I know you sir?"

He again grinned and said "No, you don't know me personally, but you don't have to meet somebody to know who they are. Their legacy and reputation will make them known to people everywhere and they will not have to introduce themselves to anyone for that person to know who they are."

I am still did not clue in to who this daunting son of a bitch was and at that point, I had no clue what to say to that man. He leaned into me and whispered in my ear, "I am Cedric Ruthless Kolov Jones of the Russian Mafia." My eyes widen when I heard that voice "I take it by that reaction that you do know me after all."

I was petrified at that moment as my heart sunk and started beating faster. What the hell does a Russian mafia guy want with me? Does he want to kill me? Did I do something wrong? Shit, I've heard stories about these guys, they are straight up malicious people and do nasty unspeakable things to you. Hang you upside down, cut your forehead, tie a bag around your face and wait until the bag fills up as you drown slowly in your own blood. But, why me? I try to control my fear and act like I'm not afraid and say to Jones "I know who you are Mr. Jones, what do you want with me?"

He smiled at me and reached into his jacket, my heart almost stopped with fear. Was he grabbing a gun? He wouldn't pop me here at the gun range would he? To my relief, he pulled out a cigarette pack, took one out, put it in his mouth and lit it. He took a puff and pointed at me "You my friend are one of the best shooters I have ever laid my eyes on. I've seen you, you have nerves of steel, ice in your veins, focused as a lion hunting his pray. Dam boy! I don't say this to many people, but you have impressed me beyond belief." He stopped and looked at me. I'm not sure if he was waiting for a response from me or if he is just pausing.

"Thank you sir. I don't know, it just comes naturally to me." I said a little more calm knowing that he didn't want to kill me, at least not yet anyway. I was still not sure what he wanted, and I wished he would just get to the dam point of why he was here as my nerves are getting stressed out. Maybe he just saw my shooting and wanted to shoot the shit with me. Heck, he said I impressed him so, maybe it is one of those things where somebody impresses you so much, you just have to come up and talk to them.

"Comes naturally does it?" he smirked. Then in a more stern voice pauses and said "My God, what in the world did I just find? Diamond in the rough, needle in a haystack?" he chuckled.

Find? I thought in my head, was he, was he wanting what I think he wants?

He whispered in my ear and said "How bout we talk about how you can make some serious money for me, as a result you will be protected by us for as long as you live and will become a part of the family. You need a favor, you name it, you need money, you ask us, you... you know what, why don't we discuss this somewhere else. Your choice of course, if you are not interested, then allow me to shake your hand and I will be on my way. If you are interested, then come with me."

I knew in my head I should have just say I wasn't interested, he'd leave and be out of my life. But do I really want to say no to the Russian Goddam Mafia? I had to think fast, what was I going to do. "How much are we talking about" I said just out of pure curiosity. I was still unclear of what he wanted from me, but the curiosity in me had a burning desire to know.

He started to chuckle, put his arm around me and guided me towards the exit "That means you are interested. Come with me and we'll talk some more." He was a strong man, I could tell by his arm on my shoulder, the way he walked, the way he conducted himself.

We exited the place and approached a magnificent black and silver Rolls Royce, something like a modern day Al Capone would drive around in. He opened the back door and waited for me to get in. He got in after me, shut the door and said "Drive" to some dude in a suit in the driver's seat. He then rolled up the silent window separating us from the driver. He put his cigarette out in an ashtray and said "How would you like to make $100,000 for one day of work? No risk, in and out, $100,000 cash?"

I was thinking of all kinds of crazy thoughts of what that could possibly mean. Was he talking about a bank job? A hit? Place a bomb? Distract somebody while he wacked him? What the hell is he proposing? Why me? I asked him "What do I have to do?" I couldn't believe I had just asked that. My heart started to race and I felt sweat building on my forehead, hands getting clammy, and started to get really hot under the collar.

"Make an example out of someone who is stealing money from me. I own the Silver Dollar Casino as you may know or not know. My business partner is a fellow mafia family member Dimitri Volkov, and by God, I know he skims the book and has been embezzling thousands if not millions from me. Thieves I just cannot endure, worst scum on earth if you ask me, and it is my partner of all people who is one of them. Taking money out of my fucking kids mouth, filling up his bank account, dressing up his whore with fancy jewelry, all with my hard earned money" he said visibly upset looking out the window. "What I want from you is to take him out, make his heart stop beating, take the soul right from his body. He lives on a piece of property north of town, isolated, but has a tight as tight can be security system. There is no way I could ever get near him, he probably suspects that I know what he has been up to and is taking extra security precautions. Sure I could do the cliché thing and rig a bomb to his car, poison his drink blah blah blah, but I need this done quietly. Killed at his house for his wife to discover him in a pool of blood with a bullet right between his fucking eyes. You, you my friend can pick this gluttonous bastard off while he's on his balcony drinking his fucking rum and coke, wearing his satin robe, with his dam fake hair plugs. You will be so far away, nobody will ever see you, none of my men are capable of making such a shot. I will be at the casino and so will my boys, so I won't be questioned by the cops about his untimely death. You will then be $100,000 richer" he opened a safe under his seat, pulled out a roll of money, and plopped it on my lap."

"You know what a lone wolf is?" he asked me. "They are not killers or ruthless monsters, but when provoked, they can rip out your throat and leave you to die while you are trying to calculate in your head what has just happened. The lone wolf amazes me at how thoughtful and intelligent these animals are. There has never been a documented attack against a human by a wolf that wasn't provoked by the human. I am that wolf, and Volkov is that human who is provoking me and my patience, I want his throat ripped out."

I stared in absolute astonishment at the wad of money that was on my lap. I had never seen that kind of money before in my life, I knew I couldn't have said no to him, but at that point, I think I kind of wanted to accept the challenge. How much bigger of a challenge was there ever going to be? I thought for a second before I answered. If I said yes, there was no going back, I really had to put some thought into a decision like that and not be overwhelmed by the money that was in my lap. "I'm not sure what to say sir, I…" I said very confused not knowing exactly what to do.

"My boy, I am giving you an opportunity with the promise of bigger paydays in the future and an opportunity for you to build a legacy for yourself. Have you ever heard of the story about the farmer and five grains of rice before?"

I had no clue what he was talking about and simply said "no sir"

He inclined on his seat and began "A rich man had four sons. As he grows old, he decides to give his property to the son who would value the wealth the most that he had earned over the years. He calls his four sons and gives them each five grains of rice. He tells them that he shall ask for these grains at the end of five years and he would give his property to the son who would value these grains the most. The first son throws away the grains, he decides to show his father some other grains when he would ask for them after five years in anticipation that his father would not be able to see the difference between the two sets of grains. The second son eats the grains, he too decides to show his father some other grains when he would ask for them after five years, in anticipation that his father would not be able to see the difference between the two sets of grains. The third son preserves these grains in a silver box and keeps the silver box at home, and offers prayers to the box while offering his prayers to God for five years. The fourth son sows these grains and cultivates them in the backyard of his house. They grow into crops during the harvest season and he keeps sowing the grains from these crops for the next five years. In due course, he has a vast plot of land cultivated with rice. So at the end of five years, the father makes his decision and gives his property to his fourth son, as he was the most deserving among his four sons and truly understood the value of wealth and prosperity. You see Chris, the moral of the story is making the most of every opportunity when it is offered to you. When you have anything in your hands don't look at the mere size of it right then and there, look at opportunity that it may be one day. Don't feel sad if you have less money today, know that you have it and you can grow it. You understand my boy?"

"Yes sir I do," the story was truly inspirational and made a lot of sense which helped me make up my mind right there on the spot, "I can do this for you sir if you want."

"If I want? No son, it's what you want, don't do this to try to appease me."

I paused and replied "I do want to do this sir."

Jones looked at me like a proud father, smiled and said "Good my son, very good. This is off the record, nobody knows, just between me and you. Understood?"

"Yes sir" I said.

"I want you to use this" he reached for a box, opened it up and revealed the most exquisite sniper rifle I had ever seen. Chrome gleaming looking like it was straight from the gun store or a museum. "This is my pride and joy, I call her Charlotte. The best sniper rifle money can buy. M4OA3 sniper rifle, infer red telescopic scope, sniper silencer, hand crafted stock and barrel, 14.5x114 mm round, effective range of 1800 to 2300 meters. I love this gun, this is my baby, use it well" as he handed me the case.

There I was, sitting in the back of a Russian Mafia's vehicle with $100,000 and a sniper rifle on my lap. For some strange reason at that moment, it felt....right and I wanted to make a legacy for myself just like Jones said I could. Funny how Mr. Jones never asked me what my name was. Maybe it's better that way, less he knows about me, the better. I touched the gun like I was petting a dog, I felt that my hands had become clammy, my skin felt all tingly, and my heart seemed to have slowed down. "I won't let you down sir" I said while I was still admiring the gun in my lap.

"You do this job right, there will be bigger and better cash coming your way. You are part of the family now. What, what is your name my son?" He finally asked me.

"Chris, Chris Slaughter", I said unsure if I should have stuck out my hand to shake. No, I was pretty sure Mr. Jones isn't that type of guy.

Mr. Jones then pulled out a cell phone and handed it to me "Here Chris. Open the map up on the screen, that is the GPS co-ordinates to Mr. Dimitri Volkov's house. It will take you there. Next, in the folder, there is a picture of him" as I opened the folder and looked at his photo "So you don't shoot the wrong guy. I want this done by the end of the day, he flies to the Dominican for a few weeks starting tomorrow or the next day or something. Anyway, I want his blood spilled by the end of this day, I will be at my Casino the whole time with my boys, you do your thing, and call me on this phone when it is done. My cell phone number is in the directory of the phone under Red Russian. Once you have made that call to me, destroy this phone. You understand Chris?"

"Ya. I got it. Won't be a problem Mr. Jones" I said.

"Ha ha, excellent. You know, I truly have never seen anyone shoot the way you do, Goddam gifted you are. So, tell me a little bit about yourself Christopher" he asks. We talked for nearly three hours while we drove around aimlessly. I couldn't believe it, only a few hours ago, I was a nobody just having fun at the gun range, and all of a sudden with the snap of the finger, I was in the back of a Russian Mafia's car about to kill somebody for him for a hundred grand. I felt like a movie star in a weird way, I was a hitman for the Russian Mafia, had a nice ring to it and sounded cool. I never once thought about "what happens if I miss" or what happens if he doesn't die" because, that was how much confidence was spewing and coursing through my veins, not to mention the fact that If I fucked it up, I may be the next to get buried six feet under by the Russian Mafia. I mean, I'm use to shooting at targets, not humans, but I just had to do what I always do, stay calm, stay focused, know my surroundings, breath slowly, and clear my head. I got this.

Mr. Jones dropped me off at my house, shook my hand, and drove off. I sauntered up to my door with Charlotte in one hand, and $100,000 in the other. I felt enthusiastic, alive, overjoyed almost. I am still unsure what I have got myself into, It's like diving into a pool, you can't see how deep it is until you dive right in, so how deep is this pool that I am going to be diving into then? I sat on my couch and opened Volkov's picture. I studied it, every detail on his face, every line, every crease, every freckle, every hair on his head. I then looked at the GPS to his house, I calculated it should take me just over an hour to get there. It was one o'clock and I decided I had better get going soon before it got too dark out. First, I needed to spend some time with my new girlfriend Charlotte, admiring the way she looked, the way she felt, I was so intrigued by that gun I just couldn't wait to hear how she sounded. She was just so simple, yet so beautiful, she didn't need the glamour because she was beautiful and perfect as is. Don't get me wrong, I admire elegance and have an appreciation of the finer things in life, but to me, beauty lies in simplicity.

I turned on my computer as I needed to check the weather and all the details associated to setting up for a perfect shot. I played it over again in my mind how it will all go down and visualized my bullet penetrating Volkov's skull. Jones said there was a great little perch I could set up on where nobody would be able to see me for miles and it's a direct sightline to Volkov's backyard. The perch was about 700 yards away give or take which wasn't be too much of an issue for me. I kept replaying it in my head visualizing Volkov's face and what he looked like and how he would die. I wasn't sure how exactly Mr. Jones knows that Volkov would even step foot onto his balcony. What if he didn't, then what? Was there a plan B? That thought panicked me a bit as my temperature started to rise with thoughts of this potentially going sideways. I didn't dare call Mr. Jones and ask him "What is plan B if Volkov doesn't go out on his balcony?" You know what, I would just have to figure it out on my own I said to reassuring myself lowering my temperature. I took apart Charlotte and put her in her box "Well, it's time to do this. Treat me right girl, we can't fail Mr. Jones. I am about to go take someone's life, I'm going to be responsible for the death of another human being. A person that I had never even met before and have no ill will towards" I spoke to Charlotte as if she was listening. "$100,000 though, that ain't no joke."

I wondered to myself if I was in way too deep with something that I had never done before, or even thought about before. I just had to think of that nice wad of money that I just stuffed under my bed and remembered the smell and feel of it. As I walked to my car it felt like time is just slowing down and I had a surreal moment. "Gotta stay focused Chris" I told myself as I got to my car. I took a deep breath, cleared my head, and got in. I punched in the

GPS co-ordinates on the phone, 2:13 p.m., off I went. *All unrighteousness is sin: and there is a sin not unto death. John 5:17.*

GPS is showed me almost at my destination, I could see the house, mansion that is, very sequestered, no neighbours for miles. My anxiety now turned to eagerness, like a challenge that I needed to conquer, like a test I needed to pass. I saw the little perch that Jones spoke of, a little grass hill pointing towards the house. I parked my car near some bushes so it wouldn't be seen, I took Charlotte out and walked towards the perch. No turning back, I had come way too far, I didn't want to turn back anyway, I wanted to see it through. My hands started to get clammy again "Not now" I said to myself "don't get nervous, I can't have clammy hands for this." I reached the small hillcrest, assembled Charlotte, and proned out like a sniper waiting for his target to appear. I looked through the scope and I saw the balcony. Distance 717.45 meters, calculated wind speed, wind direction, elevation, temperature, humidity, and projectory. I laid motionless, looking through the scope waiting, waiting, waiting. 2 hours and 47 minutes now passed and I hadn't moved a muscle, locked on, ready for that moment. Finally, movement! Holy shit, Volkov just stepped outside and onto the balcony. "Slow your heart rate Chris, it's show time" I said to myself "relax, easy breaths, stay loose." I tracked him through my scope, waiting for the moment he stood still, I felt perspiration building on my forehead. He was on his phone and wouldn't you know it, he's was sporting a satin robe too, just like I pictured this would play out in my head. "Steady Chris, wait for your shot" I reminded myself. He stopped and rested his forearm on the balcony, this was it, this was the shot I had been waiting for. My heart almost seemed to stop as I ever so tenderly started to retract the trigger towards me. *"Forgive me Father for this righteous sin that I am about to commit. Please find forgiveness in your heart and wipe the sin that will pray upon my soul"* I said to myself, no bible quote, that one is my own which just came to me at that moment.

Then, almost as a surprise, the gun went off! I looked through my scope and saw the spot where the bullet met Volkov, right between the eyes, absolute flawless shot. I laid perfectly still and watched, admiring my work. Volkov looked almost stunned, staggered around a bit with eyes as wide as could be, looked towards the heavens, and finally, with blood streaming down his face, collapsed to the ground in a thud. I still waited for a few minutes as I felt paralysed, not sure if it was from pride, shock at what I had just did, or a sheer sense of being over whelmed of what has just taken place. I finally began to hear the wind, smell the air, and feel my body. I got up, calmly disassembled Charlotte and laid her in her case, then ever so smoothly, walked towards my car. I got in and just let it sink in for a moment. It started to hit me that I just took the life of another human being, a thought that should have made any person crumble with guilt, but surprisingly, I felt more proud of myself for accomplishing this challenge. Mr. Jones is going to be happy, proud, welcome me into the family and all that jazz. I grabbed the phone, found his name under the directory and dialed. It rang and rang, then went to voicemail. Odd. I tried again, no answer. Again, no answer. I kept trying this for nearly ten minutes, nothing. What was I going to do now? I finally called 411 "directory assistance, for what city please" the automatic voice said.

"Los Angeles" I said.

"For business or residential."

"Business" I said

"For what name please"

"Silver Dollar Casino."

"One moment please. Your call is being connected" as the phone rang.

"Hello Silver Dollar Casino" the voice said in sort of an anomalous tone. Not normally the welcoming type of greeting one would expect.

"Ya uh, Mr. Jones please. Is he available?" I asked. Not quite sure if I should have been calling him like that, but I needed to let him know.

"I'm sorry sir." There was a pause "Mr. Jones is, is not really available" the woman said. Sounds like her voice got a little emotional.

"Uh. Hmmm. Do you know when he will be back by chance?" I asked a little perplexed now.

"Mr. Jones passed a few minutes ago" the woman said now almost crying.

Did I hear that right? Passed, as in dead? My heart kind of skipped a beat at that point "Dead?" I asked just to be sure I heard her right.

"Yes. Were you a friend or business partner of Mr. Jones?" she asked as I could tell she was trying to hold herself back from crying.

"Uh, friend, no, business partner. How, how did he die if you don't mind me asking" I asked not sure how to react. Should I have been sad? He wasn't really what I would call a friend, so should I have been upset? My emotions were a little bit confused.

"Heart attack. Just right on the floor, couldn't revive him. I can call you back if you leave me your number and let you know when the funeral is, I'm sure all of his business partners will be there" she said.

"No. No that's fine. Thank you" I responded as I slowly hung up almost in shock of what I had just heard on the other end. I paused for a moment to collect my thoughts about everything. I said to myself "He's dead. Nobody knows me or what I just did. I'm $100,000 richer and there is absolutely no ties to me and Jones or me and Volkov, I am one hundred percent in the clear. Holy shit!" I said as I felt the enthusiasm building up inside me as I produced a huge smile that I just couldn't contain.

I leisurely drove away, looked around me, and realize, I was home free. I threw the cell phone out the window, I turned on the radio, cranked up the volume then sung along to the music all the way home. What a rush I felt at that moment, like nothing I had ever experienced before in my entire life, more intense than skydiving or bungy jumping put together. I kept looking in my mirror, just so proud of myself for being able to make that shot under extreme pressure like that. I mean when I was at the range, there was no pressure at all, if I missed the target, who cares, reload and try again. But here and now, there is zero room for error or mistake, one shot, that's all I had, one chance to either make the perfect shot or screw up royally. So proud of myself, a new beginning, a new life, new challenges, new things.

Corinthians 5:17 *"Therefore if anyone is in Christ, he is a new creature; the old things passed away; behold, NEW THINGS"*

Chapter III

THOU SHALL NOT KILL

8:45 MYERS residence...

I pull up to my location, a great little inconspicuous bushel of trees with a bird's eye view of MYERS place approximately 900 metres away. Perfect spot to conceal my car from public view, and no worries of anyone passing through as it is remote so I'll have no unexpected visitors. I was slightly on a hillcrest looking down at MYERS small crescent, nobody in the street of this little seven house semi circle. I have an unobstructed view through the trees at MYERS place, and I am perched up high enough so that no roof tops come into my field of vision either, this spot was made for me. I take Charlotte out and swiftly assemble her preparing her to go to work. I take my position, pull out my anemometer to go through my routine, check wind direction, calculate and factor in the barometric pressure and humidity, checking elevation and seeing the temperature at a balmy 79 degrees. Very little wind, low humidity, normal pressure, slightly on an incline, should be routine if there is such a thing in this business. I glance through the scope and see the exact point where MYERS will meet his maker. His house is facing me so I have a beautiful clean shot directly at him and I am elevated enough so that nothing will come into play. I only have one shot, if I miss, I risk either not being able to reload and make another shot, or getting a second shot off and risk MYERS ending up in a less desirable spot where he will be noticed instantly, meaning I would need to make a quick getaway which also is not ideal. 8:49, "Come on MYERS, show yourself, I have things to do, people to see" I say to myself still looking through the scope. I stand perfectly still like a statue, you wouldn't even be able to see me breath, stealth and focus is the key. My mind goes blank, not a thought running through my head as I try to decelerate my heartrate. 8:53, a little unusual for MYERS to be late, maybe my watch is slow, maybe he's running a tad late. 8:56. Now I start to get a little anxious as I feel my heart sink. "Why MYERS, why of all fucking days do you choose this one to break your routine. You have to get to work man, let's get going. Show yourself Goddammit!" I say to myself trying to my best to remain calm. I can feel the panic racing through my blood as I think to myself "This can't be happening, not today, not on my last contract." Finally he appears, MYERS steps out of his house. I quickly refocus and get ready for the shot, my mind goes blank now, my heart slows, everything is in slow motion as I carefully watch every move he makes and grasp the gun tight. As MYERS walks from his door to his car, he walks like he is in slow motion and the world just slows down in my head. I have my kill spot marked by a little hole in the fence, and in two more steps and MYERS will be in my crosshairs. "Forgive me Father for this righteous sin that I am about to commit. Please find forgiveness in your heart and wipe the sin that will pray upon my soul", I ever so gently squeeze the trigger as the world around me goes silent and just halts for a brief second. I see the force of the fired bullet cock his head to the right as he goes down in a hurry. Some blood splatter on the fence but it's in the shadows so nobody will see it. He lands almost under his front bumper which is even better that I anticipated. I don't move, I remain calm and frozen for a while. Slowly, I release the trigger, smell the gun smoke, bring Charlotte down, and stand observing my work, making sure that MYERS is truly dead and not trying to get up. Last thing I need is for him to start crawling around with blood dripping from his head wound catching the eye of all the neighbours. "Nope, not moving, he's laying perfectly still, dead to the world. In the shade, nobody will see him for hours." I say to myself in my head.

I know what I have just done is wrong, it is a sin, but the bible even acknowledges that all men have committed sin and I quote "I*f we say that we have no sin, we deceive ourselves, and the truth is not in us*." John 1:8. I am not trying to justify to myself that taking another's life is morally okay, and I don't even know if God will truly forgive me for these acts of death that I have bestowed upon my fellow man, but I will never stop asking God for forgiveness and mercy on my eternal soul.

I feel a sense of accomplishment, a goal that I have set out and have now conquered, like a lion finally catching his prey after a chase. I truly believe that I am so good because of the work and dedication that I put forth in every job with knowledge making me stronger all the time. Nothing stops the man who desires to achieve. Every obstacle is simply a course to develop his achievement, it's a strengthening of his powers of accomplishment.

I now put Charlotte away, look at MYERS now terminated corpse, say a small prayer *"For if we live, we live to the Lord, and if we die, we die to the Lord. So then, whether we live or whether we die, we are the Lord's."* I slowly without thought walk to my car, get in and take in in for two seconds to reflect. You may ask, do I regret or feel bad about taking the life of another human being? Here is my answer. Let's take MYERS for instant. Somebody wanted him dead so much they were willing to fork over a ton of money to have this done. Now in my opinion, if somebody wants someone dead that bad, that person one way or another will die, if not by my hands, then someone else's, and so forth. Once a person concludes that a person needs to die, he will not stop until that person is gone from this earth, therefore, you might as well call him dead right at that point. Dead while walking around breathing air living his life not knowing that the grim reaper will soon be knocking on his door in the form of an execution. So I figure, why not cash in on it, I mean if I don't kill him, someone else will and will get paid handsomely for it. I know I can do it better than anyone out there because of my astonishing God gifted long range shooting ability. So, I will get the job done quick, efficiently, painless, and without any paper trail leading to me or the buyer since I will have not ever communicated with him or her. Again, I am not justifying this in anyway, I'm just telling you how it is.

I drive away and my heart starts to beat normal, my body is relaxed and my mind is at ease. I take out my phone and dial Jimmy.

"Hey, all done?" he asks softly.

"All done. Flawless as planned, went off without a hitch. I'm driving away now." I say still in a remorseful sounding voice.

"Great job. I know you're feeling guilty as usual, but think of this my son, you have your life, you're living it. It's twisted, exhausting, uncertain, and full of guilt, but nonetheless, there's something there and nobody can take that from you. Free your mind of the guilt and live your life. It's short, so live it care free and at the end of it, God can judge you" Jimmy says with his inspiring words.

"Thanks Jimmy boy you're right." I pause before I drop the bomb on him "Jimmy, what if I was to say that this is it for me, that MYERS was my last hit? I am done with this for good, I don't want this anymore. For me, for you, for Trina, this needs to end."

A long silent pause. "Wow" he simply says. He takes a deep breath and says "Well Christopher, that is a shocker to say the least, but it's your decision. All good things will come to an end eventually. I am disappointed, but we can commence a new chapter in our lives I suppose. My Dad once told me that ends are not bad things, they just mean that something else is about to begin and there are many things that don't really end anyway, they just begin again in a new way. Many ends aren't really an ending; some things are never-ending like our friendship. I can tell that you have thought about this a lot and know the people who it will affect?"

"I have" I simply say.

"It's your life therefore your decision, and you are aware that your choices will not affect only you, but also those around you who care and love you dearly even if you aren't aware of that. So make the right decisions and choices in life to make not only yourself proud and happy but also those around you" he says.

"I have, I've taken all that into account. I want to live a conventional normal life, I'm done with this, the passion is gone and I just don't want to do this any longer, it just doesn't feel the same anymore. It gets to you after a while, I'm not quite sure exactly when that moment hit me, but I know something is my mind is telling me that it's time to close this book."

"Then I gladly accept your decision" he says now more cheerful. "You always have my number, never hesitate to use it if you need to, you hear me?"

"Loud and clear Jim boy. And you have my number" I pause "Promise me you'll take care of yourself."

"Will do Chris, don't worry about me. You going to see your brother now?" he asks trying to change the subject.

My brother is in the hospital and has been there for the past year battling ALS, better known as Lou Gehrig's disease. I visit him every week. "Ya" I simply say.

"Tell Nathaniel I say hi and I pray for him every day. He is a shining star" Jimmy says.

"I will, and he knows that, he knows how you care about him, you are a good person" I say.

"I'll talk to you later buddy, well done" he says and simply hangs up.

"Well done indeed" I say to the dial tone "well done indeed."

I glance at my watch, still got a bit of time before I see my brother, I need to relax anyway, get out of this dam suit, have a coffee. I always bring a change of clothes, don't really want to prance around all day in a tailor made Armani suit. I spot a local coffee shop, looks good, not too busy, think I will pop in and have a coffee.

I take off my jacket and put on a long sleeved shirt and some running shoes and walk into the coffee shop. I approach the counter to a pretty young girl, no more than

17 years old. I look at her name, Athena "Hello sir, what can I get for you today" she said in a perky cheerful voice.

"Oh, I haven't decided yet" I say and now look at her deep rich coffee colored hazel eyes. "Athena? Very pretty name, know what that name means?" I ask in my most flirtatious voice.

She gives me a pretty smile and says, "Uh I think she was like a Goddess or something."

I smile back and say "Ya that's right, she was the Greek Goddess of Wisdom and courage, half-sister to Hercules and daughter of Zeus and one of the most breath-taking women in Greek mythology."

She grinned at me as if in awe "Wow, guess my parents were pretty cool."

"Ya, they put some thought into your name" I said. I now snap back to reality and say politely "Sorry, not sure what I want quite yet, can you gimme two secs?"

"Sure, just let me know when you are ready" she says walking away giving me a flirtatious look.

I study the board then hear the door creek open behind me. I glance in the mirror to see in back of me, two bigger guys walking in, dressed nice, wearing dark sunglasses and looking very daunting. I start to get a little nervous and get a little sweaty as I focus on their every movement in the reflection. Could these guys be cops? Hired thugs? I see them look at each other, then kind of look at me and nod. "Fuck sake" I think to myself "who the fuck are these guys and what do they want with me? How would anyone even know who I am? I have been flawless, where is the leak?" I start to panic now as one of the men approach me and try to look at my face while he lowers his sunglasses to his nose. "Excuse me sir" he says to me.

I'm thinking, "What do I do, how do I stay calm? They have nothing on you, right?" "Yes" I say trying to stay calm.

"Are you Christopher Slaughter" the same gentleman asks in a stern voice. They both sure fit the bill of cops, tall, athletic, clean shaven and short army type haircuts.

I glare at him then at his buddy. I need to stay calm, and get ready for a possible war right here in this coffee shop. Do I let them know who I am? I mean, if these guys are thugs, they want to know that they are beating up the right guy right? If they are in fact cops, do they just wish to confirm my identity? I figure I'll go with the typical Hollywood movie answer "Who wants to know?"

The one gentleman meticulously looks at me and says "you dropped your wallet from your jacket when you were taking it off outside, your ID fell out" as he hands me my wallet.

I try to act casual without showing them the immense relief that I am feeling right now "Oh, thanks. I didn't even feel it fall out" I say as I take the wallet from him.

"Have a good one" the other gentleman says as they both turn and walk away. Nothing like a good scare and panic attack to wake me up then watch them walk out the door.

"Have you decided yet sir?" Athena asks startling me a bit.

"Ya. Ya I'll have a large coffee double double to stay please." She turns to pour the coffee, nice little body she has on her wow. I leave her five dollars, take my coffee and sit down in a quiet corner.

I take my phone out and text Trina "All done. Job went well without any issues. Gonna go see Nate, be home in a while. Love you." I didn't feel like talking, just wanted to text for now. I sip my hot coffee as it slowly touches my lips waiting for her to text me back. I feel like I haven't a care in the world right now, as free as a bird who can fly anywhere he wants with no fears or hesitations. My phone beeps, must be Trina as I open my screen and see "I'm so happy that we are done with this, I can't wait for Mexico and start a new life. Wipe the slate clean and leave our old life in the rear view mirror. See you when I get home, tell Nate I say hi and to hang in there, love you." I have a slight grin on my face as I read it. Just then a voice from behind me yells "Hey!" as he grabs me startling me.

I turn around and it's Tony. He's sporting that all too familiar black leather jacket with a necklace dropping down and his badge at the end of it. He has the look of a cop, clean shaven and brush cut bistre black slick hair with that chiseled jaw bone. And of course, I can always smell that aftershave of his that I have told him to ease up on numerous times. "Shit Tony, you almost gave me a heart attack" I say

Tony snickers at the fact that he scarred me and takes a seat "How ya been brotha? Saw your car out front, thought I'd pop in" he says laughing.

"You want to know if I did MYERS already don't you?" I say in a whisper.

"Oh shit, that was today? Jesus Christ, I totally forgot, my mind is everywhere now days. Well, I should be getting that call soon maybe if they think it's gang related." Tony says also in a whisper.

Tony is in the LAPD gang unit division so, he gets to investigate (if you can call it that) my handy work a lot of the times because majority of my hits are gang members or former gang members. I always give Tony a heads up on any job I do to let him know that it's me and not some other hitman out there whacking people. "Went perfect, and what did I tell you about using the Lords name in vein around me." I pause for a bit not knowing what to say next, time to change the subject. "How'd it work out with Lil Alonzo?" Alonzo is a low level gang banger, or so he pretends to be, rolls with the Azusa 13 gang. The 13 in the name stands for the letter "M", indicating its affiliation with the Mexican Mafia. The gang is known to tax drug sales in the area and funnels money to the Mexican Mafia. I met Alonzo on the streets through a mutual friend. Sometimes when I need some background on a contract, I go to the street for the information, especially if it's a hit on a street thug or gang banger. Anyway, I found out he was selling crack cocaine near a local High School, making some decent money on the side off of susceptible High School kids. I gave this information about Alonzo to Tony stating that he hangs around the school in a beat up old yellow car and Tony of course acted on it and busted Alonzo.

"Went good. He didn't have as much as I hoped, but it was a good bust. Tried to flip him but he wouldn't do it, probably doesn't know much anyway." Tony whispered. He leaned back and looked at me with concern "You doing all right Chris?"

I look down and say softly "I'm done man. That was my last one, I don't want this life anymore, shows over. I just can't do this anymore, live this life, live this lifestyle."

"Done?" He whispers as he leans forward and looks me in the eyes. "Wow Chris. When did you decide this bomb was going to be dropped?"

"A while ago" I say with my head still lowered. "I made my money, I've had my fun, it's time to get out before my luck runs out. I just can't do this no more, I don't want to live this lifestyle any longer. I want to start a family, be a Dad, be a good husband and live like a normal person" I explain.

Tony pauses and puts his hand to his mouth. "I'm in shock. I am shocked. What will you do?"

"Go and live the ordinary life like a regular Joe. Cut the grass on weekends, see my kids school plays and ball games" I say standing by my decision. It kind of felt like Tony was judging me on this. "Live my life, get out of L.A, leave this all behind and start from square one, clean slate."

Tony now runs his hands through his hair, pauses and finally smiles "Well good for you Chris." He then leans into me with a devilish grin "You wouldn't be tempted by one more payday or anything?" he asks.

Weird question to ask I thought but said "Nope, I'm done. I have enough in the bank to be happy, no need to get greedy. Gonna head down to Mexico with Trina and just disappear ya know, get lost in the crowd."

Tony smirks and whispers "Ah, I think if the right payday came up, you'd think about it. It's in your blood man, a leopard never changes his spots am I right?"

"I ain't a leopard anymore, I'm a tired old dog that shed all of the spots from his body. You'd never even know I was a leopard, and I wouldn't even miss my spots" I say in response.

"You can't get rid of the spots dude, they're in your soul. No matter how much you try to cover them up, no matter how much you try to tell yourself they aren't there, you know deep inside, somewhere those spots are perpetually stained on your body. One day you may have to face the consequences for your actions" he says almost incensed now leaning into me almost whispering.

"Thought you'd be happy" I say trying to lighten the mood as I sip my coffee.

"I am Chris I am. Look, don't perceive my words as judgemental or anything, I wish you and Trina the best of luck, I'm just saying it's hard to quit anything cold turkey that's all" he says now leaning back in a normal tone. "Hey, you are my brother man, I love you and I'll miss ya. Speaking of brothers, how's Nate doing? I haven't seen him in over three weeks."

"Good" I sip my coffee again. "Well, good as can be. I'm going to see him in a bit if you wanna tag along?" I ask.

"Nah, besides, I expect a call about your handy work showing up soon anyway." Tony stops talking right away, seems like something is wrong.

"How's Georgia?" I ask in a concerning voice. Georgia is Tony's wife of six years. I know they have been having problems, maybe even divorce kind of talk. I hate to say this but I'm not sure if Tony treats her right. I mean I love the guy to death, but I'm not too fond of the way he treats her or any woman for that matter. Kind of demeaning, like he feels men are superior and women are just objects, almost objectify them.

"Ah man, it ain't good, not good at all. I think it's done and over with." [*Shocker I think to myself not surprised*]. "It's just too far gone to repair the damage you know. Braydon will take it hard I'm sure, he's only five and may not fully understand the ramifications of a divorce and the impact that it will have on his life." He grins while shaking his head "On television divorce seems so easy, nobody gets hurt, child loves seeing mom then dad, but in the real world, you can't really just split a family down the middle, mom on one side dad the other with the child equally divided between them. It's like when you rip a piece of paper in two, no matter how hard you try, the seams never fit exactly right again. It's what you can't see, those tiniest of pieces that are lost in the severing, and their absence keep everything from being complete. I was never one to patiently pick up those broken fragments and glue them together again and tell myself that the mended whole was as good as new. What is broken is broken, and I'd rather remember it as it was at its best than mend it and see the broken pieces as long as I lived. "

"I'm sorry pal, I really am. Maybe it's for the best though in a way. Letting go will never been easy, but holding on can be just as difficult. Strength is measured not by holding on but by letting go, and maybe it's time to let go" I say trying to add my two cents.

"You're right Chris. Heck I knew this wasn't working for a long time now. I just don't want to put my son through a divorce, it'll be taxing on him, but on the other hand I don't want to have him hear all the fighting and bickering either, so, it's time to move on accept it and continue with my life. It's always important to know when something has reached its end. Closing circles, shutting doors, finishing chapters, it doesn't matter what we call it, what matters is to leave in the past those moments in life that are over. I love my son, heck I love G, but it's time to move on, be a good Dad, a good friend, and live my life" he says now trying to smile.

I smile back "Good for you brother. Hey you want a coffee or something?" Athena over heard me say that and started to walk over to us.

Tony looks at her and greets her with a flirtatious smile "Well, I've have an order of you sugar pie" she grins with amusement as Tony looks her up and down. "Okay, since you ain't on the menu, I'll have whatever he's having, what is that a mocha? Expresso?"

I smile and look at Athena, "Just a coffee."

Tony smirks and says "Good enough." Athena walks away with a cheerful smile as Tony ogles at her ass as she struts away. He then quickly looks back at me, takes a deep breath and says "You know, I've thought about getting out of L.A too, not too far away, just out of the big city. It's starting to get to me. Here in the big city people spend their time thinking about work and about money; they don't give any value to friendships and the truly important things anymore, and it can be depressing. People don't appreciate privacy or quietness or nature or things like that you know. Here it's all about money, police and ambulance sirens, pushy commuters, crowd rage, crime, traffic and on and on."

"You always told me you could never live in a small town" I start to laugh "you said because in a small town they are all hillbilly red necks who have sex with his cousin every night and his sister every other night."

Tony giggles "Ha ha, the good ole red neck hicks talk with Bubba Joe brushing his single tooth living in his trailer with his momma who bakes him cornbread daily wearing a shirt that says WHERE'S THE BEEF. Ah yes, I remember the thoughts we use to have about small town folks. But, I have changed my thoughts after living in the big city, I envy the small town folks now. Heck, living next to Bubba Joe may not be so bad" he says as he bursts out laughing again. I was laughing so hard I had to put down my coffee.

Moments like this I can get lost in. I forget my past, my job, my victims and just enjoy the fact that I have a great friend like Tony who I can call my second brother. "Well I wish you the best of luck man, hope you like getting it in the ass from the hillbillies, oh ya Big Bubba will like you" I say laughing again.

"You're an idiot" Tony says giggling at me. "Ha ha, Bubba." He says collecting his thoughts. "You know, I wonder in another life if we made different choices, what that future would be? Where our paths would have led us? I just want a glimpse to what that future may look like and maybe just live in it for a while and test it out."

"You're talking about me aren't you?" I say as if he was judging me again.

"No, not just that, I mean about living here, choosing the roads we both chose, walking through the doors that we have opened."

I look at him sternly and say "You know I didn't choose this path Tony. I didn't wake up one day and say 'oh geese, let's see what I want to be when I grow up, oh I know, how about a contract killer?' I say sarcastically. "Come on man, this chose me, I wish I never got into that car that day, but you know what, I did, nothing I can do about it."

"Ok relax bro, I'm not busting your balls. Here take a chill pill" he says gesturing giving me a handful of pills.

I snicker and push his hands away "Smartass."

"You know what I mean, everyone envisions an alternative life, that 'what if' life you know? And then you can't help wonder what that path would have led too, that alternate life."

"I hear what you are saying, maybe I'd be your partner and we'd be busting bad guys and shit huh?"

Tony laughs again and then stops as his phone goes off. He looks at the name and number and says "Shit, here we go."

I think to myself, "No way someone found MYERS this soon. It was perfect, who would even see him unless you actually walked up to his house?" Tony talks on the phone, conversation was short.

Tony hangs up and whispers "Joseph Woodward MYERS, former gang banger found dead on his driveway with a bullet to the head. Mailman found him, gotta go buddy." Tony gets up, takes one last sip of his coffee, points to me and says "stay outta trouble" then walks away.

"Will do" I say. "The mailman! Fuck sake, why didn't I think of that!" I say to myself frustrated. I pride myself upon perfection, the perfect shot, covering all bases, knowing every last detail no matter how small it may seem "How the fuck did I forget about the dam mailman?" Oh well, it's done and over with and it didn't hurt me as I take a sip from my cup accepting my potential error.

I sit for a few more minutes and ponder that alternate future. It's amusing to think about how different your life would be if you made a different choice, or made a different decision on something. I try to picture what I'd be doing right now if I told Mr. JONES that I wasn't interested, would I have finished school? Become an architect? A mechanic? A carpenter? Would I be married by now with kids? It's interesting to think about how one tiny decision may have had a colossal impact on how my life is being lived at this moment. I take one last sip of my coffee, glance one more time at Athena say to her "Have a good day beautiful" then walk out the door.

I am now heading to the hospital to see my older brother Nate. As I mentioned before, he is suffering from ALS. For those who don't know exactly what ALS is, let me break it down for you. It is simply a progressive neurodegenerative disease that affects nerve cells in the brain and the spinal cord. Motor neurons reach from the brain to the spinal cord, and from the spinal cord to the muscles throughout the body. The average survival from onset to death is three to four years. Only 4% survive longer than 10 years and a majority die from respiratory failure as their lungs just stop working. You may ultimately lose the ability to initiate and control all voluntary movement, although bladder and bowel function and the muscles responsible for eye movement are usually spared until the final stages of the disorder, then after that, you lose the ability to see, control your bowels, then eventually lose the ability to breath. As of today, there is no cure for my brother.

Nate first became aware of this over a year ago when he was around twenty eight years old which is extremely young for a person to get this disease. Nate started having trouble speaking, it was slurred and garbled almost like he was drunk; he was having trouble getting the words out and didn't know why. At the same time he had trouble chewing his food and swallowing. I had no idea what ALS was and certainly never thought anything would come out of these symptoms. Then, one rainy Tuesday morning, I got the call from my Dad saying that Nate was in the hospital and was diagnosed with ALS. My world was rocked, but I thought that with treatment and medical care he would be cured. Unfortunately, that wasn't the case. I couldn't imagine a more brutal way to die, everyday not knowing which motor function you may lose. Nate is confined to a hospital bed as his legs do not work anymore which is absolutely devastating. I visit him every week for a few hours. Each visit, I notice a little more of the brother that I knew, gently fading away.

I knew Nate could pass at any time and I will have to accept it and get use to the fact that my big brother is no longer with me. That's the thing, I don't think you ever got used to it, the idea of someone being gone. Just when you think it's reconciled or accepted, someone points it out to you, and it just hits you all over again and you are in shock all over again. I just hope he doesn't suffer, I mean, even death must have a heart. Every night I pray to the good Lord to watch over my brother, protect him, keep him safe, make sure he feels no pain, and if you choose to take him from this earth, please take him peacefully in your loving embrace.

I pull up to the hospital and walk up to the front. "Mr. Slaughter, he's been waiting for you all morning" the secretary says to me. They know me by name now on the account I come here every week, plus I'm always so courteous and charismatic.

I walk into Nate's room and look at the person who I remember to be my brother. He's so thin now because of the fact it's hard for him to eat. He looks so sick and so weak and it breaks my heart knowing he will never get better. Still, I can't show that to him, he may not be here for too long so I need to put on my happy face. "Hey hey Nate Dogg, how's my brother doing?' I say excited to see him.

I see a big smile draped across his face as he looks at me. I hug his frail body and he says "Hey Chris, how's my brother doing?"

"I'm doing well. I brought you the opening day baseball magazine you wanted" I say as I pull it out of my jacket and hand it to him." Nate is a lot taller than me, he's about six foot four or so, messy bushy auburn hair and a scruffy full beard. He's usually a very outspoken person and loves to hear himself talk but even that is gradually dwindling. He has always been a genuinely good human being that anybody could get along with.

He looks like a little kid when he gets it and says with excitement "Oh thanks bro" and starts to flip through it. "Wonder how the Dodgers are going to do this year after they disappointed me last year."

"They're looking good, they signed Gonzales and Crawford. That's huge" I say.

"Ya I saw. My hopes are high for these morons this year, it'd be nice if they can bring us a World Series" he says still flipping through the magazine. He stops, puts it down and asks me "So. What's new in your life man?"

I smile at him while I sit in a chair next to him "I'm done Nate. Today was my last day, I'm out of the business for good, and am happy about it too. We're moving to Mexico and I have already arranged a hospital for you to be at there, it's all set."

Nate says "Wow" and I can see he's computing this information in his head "I knew you were thinking of calling er quits, but I honestly never thought you would give up the money and go through with it."

"It's not about the money, it's about having a normal life with Trina and my brother and not worrying about who might find out about me or if the cops are going to be coming to my door in the middle of the night. No, I'm just done with it, new chapter is about to start, turn the page, don't look back all that crap."

"How'd Jimmy take the news?"

"Surprisingly well. Not sure if it was an act or if he was genuine. Either way, he's accepted it and I am happy" I say. Jimmy is like my second Dad, he would take a bullet for me if my life was ever in danger. He risks his life every time he takes a new client for me you know, just to keep me safe.

"Gee, last I saw Jimmy he was having money problems, but you didn't hear that from me."

"Money problems?" I asked a little concerned. "What kind of money problems?"

"Nothing. I'm sure it's all taken care of on this last job, no biggie" Nate says trying to change the subject. So be it, I'll drop it. "You talk to Dad lately?"

"Not for about three months or so." My Dad was a former member of one of the most notorious infamous gang in the world, the Hells Angels. He got out of the business when he had me and never looked back. My Dad is a good man and good Father, but the problem is, me and him are both stubborn and pig headed, so we butt heads a lot. Still, I know I can always count on him if I ever needed help. Our mother died when we were young, Dad says it was a car accident, I still think there may have been a hit on her to get at my Dad, but, I'll never know nor will Dad ever tell me.

"You should call him, he worries about you" he says in a big brother tone.

"Ya, I will" I change the subject now "You eating well? Or enough?"

"Ah man, my appetite has diminished. Besides, it's almost a chore to eat now. Although, I have a new nurse and let me tell you, she is a dime bro!"

It's amazing how in good spirit he's in knowing that any day he could pass, but I think he lives each day to the fullest because of that, blessed that the Lord has given him one more day on this earth every time he wakes up in the morning. Everyone on this planet should think that way, but we all take each day for granted, knowing that there will be more days ahead of us so if we squander one, we have plenty more. He has always had an astonishing outlook on life, he always faces the sunshine leaving the shadows behind him. Some people grumble that roses have thorns, he sees it as thorns that have exquisite roses on them, that's his outlook on life even in the state that he is in.

"Hey, you still have that nice Porsche? Man you have to let me drive that thing before I die" he says with a huge smile on his face.

I smile at him and jokingly say "Your legs don't work you crazy bastard, how are you going to drive my car?"

"Got it all planned out, you be the gas and brakes, I'll be the wheel. We could so do that" he says. I know he is just kidding, but I'll humor him.

"You'll complain the whole time saying I'm not going fast enough. How am I going to be the gas, brake and clutch anyway?"

"Minor details, we'll figure it out" he says now chuckling. "Hey can you get me some new movies, I forgot to ask you last time. I think I've watched Ironman and Fast and Furious about a billion times now" he complains.

"Ya no problem, I'll get a few for you. You ain't gonna be here much longer anyway. We are going to be packing up for Mexico within a few days here, but I'm sure they have Blue Ray players and televisions in Mexican hospital, and if not, I'll buy you one."

"Make it at least a fifty incher. This TV is so small my eyes hurt from squinting at it" he says making a squint with his eyes.

"Will do your majesty" I say sarcastically. "So, where is this new nurse that is your new dime?"

"Hey now, you keep your eyes off her, you'll wear her out. Besides, I'll let Trina know your eyes were wondering" he says.

"Ha, ok she's all yours. You going to take her out on a date?" I ask again humoring him.

"Ya, soon as you give me the keys to that car" he says putting out his hand.

I laugh and say "Let me think about that. Uh, no. And not only no, hell no" I say laughing.

He now turns serious and says "I know I don't have much time on this earth bro. Each day I look at the stars wondering what heaven is like up there. Perhaps they aren't stars, but rather openings in heaven where the love of our lost ones pours through and shines down upon us to let us know they are happy and soon I will join them and look down on you brother." He then looks up to the sky and grins "I'll be the brightest one up there and sparkle brighter than them all. Life is a brief intermission between birth and death and I have lived a good life with a wonderful brother and had a beautiful loving wife."

Nate's wife died just before he came down with ALS, she was killed in a horrible gruesome work related accident. She was a great lady who loved Nate very much and Nate took her passing extremely hard. I often wonder why the Lord was so merciless to such a good person like my brother. Why take his loving wife from him so soon, and why take his life away at such a young age. Perhaps these are questions that I am not privileged to know the answer to yet. How can I complain about death when I am responsible so many others death?

"The LORD bless you and keep you; the LORD make his face to shine upon you and be gracious to you; the LORD lift up his countenance upon you and give you peace. When it's your time Nate, I'll we see you up there in the night sky. Until then, you are still my pain in the ass big brother" I say with a grin and hold his hand.

"Thanks. Besides, I'm not ready to die yet. I know it's inevitable but so is the death of everyone. Some die sooner, some die later, but death is a part of life. Maybe the dam Dodgers can give me a World Series first" he says.

You see what I mean, even talking and knowing he will die soon, he still has such an incredible attitude. "I'll get you a decent radio so you can listen to the games that aren't televised okay?"

"Great, then I can hear them loose rather than see them loose" he says "Oh, I have to have a positive outlook;

they will do good this year" he corrects himself. "You really giving up this hitman gig for good then?" he says more serious.

"Ya dude. I've thought this over long and hard, racked my brain and weighed the pros and cons. If I want to start a life and a family, I can't be doing this, this isn't the life for a husband or Dad. I mean, just say somebody finds out who I am and knows that I am the one who is responsible for killing their brother, fellow gang member, husband, father, whatever, I'd be putting everyone I love in danger. That's the way they work, they wouldn't come after me, they'd come after Trina, Jimmy, Dad, and even you to make me suffer by watching them kill everyone I love before they do me. I can't live like that Nate, I just can't" I lean back in my chair "I love you guys way too much and I could never live with the fact that I may be responsible for getting one of my loved ones hurt or killed."

"You go see Father WHISTLER yet?" Nate asks changing the subject on me. Father WHISTLER is someone I consider a close friend, not just the guy I go confess all my sins to. He was there for me in my most trying times like when my mother died, and when I found out Nate was diagnosed with ALS. He has always been there for me when I need him always comforting me like a father figure. I know he's a Priest and that's what he is supposed to do, but I know that he is genuine when he tells me how much he cares for me.

"Right after this, that'll be my next stop" I say.

"You should go see Dad too. Not telling you what to do, just a suggestion" he tells me now taking a sip from his juice box.

I look down almost trying to avoid giving him an answer "Ya, maybe I will" which I really never had any plans to do so, just wanted to appease Nate.

"You know one thing I want to do one last time before I leave this world? It's something that we easily take for granted. I want to see the ocean one more time." Nate sits up and smiles at me "There is a magic about the sea, people are just drawn to it. People want to live by it, swim in it, play in it, look at it. You know, it's a living thing that is as unpredictable as a great mystery novel that keeps you intrigued, it could be calm and welcoming opening its arms to embrace it's audience one moment, but then could explode with its stormy tempers, flinging people around, wanting them out, attacking coastlines, breaking down islands. It has a playful side too, as it is enjoyed by the crowd, tossing the children about, knocking them over, tipping over surfers, and giving people an amusement type ride on their boat, and occasionally giving sailors a helping hand. It's majestic and just awe inspiring, makes you realize just how small you really are. The smell, the sounds of the waves, and the hypnotic movement of the water, I use to just sit and watch for hours. That's all I want before I go" he says softly.

I look at him with promising eyes and say "I'll make it happen, I promise you. I guess we do take small things like that for granted, Lord knows we all are guilty of that. You just hold on a while longer you hear me?"

He smiles and nods "Will do."

"Good" I say.

"Good. Alright brother, come give me a hug and get the hell out of here, I'm exhausted" Nate says with a smile extending his arms to me.

I hug him while I say "You hang in there brother, I still need you around."

"I ain't going anywhere just yet" he says in a whisper still hugging me. We let go of our embrace and I slowly walk away.

"See ya soon. We got a new life ahead of us" I say to him walking towards the door.

"Looking forward to it, although I'd prefer Canada, just an FYI" he says with a chuckle.

"Too cold. Later brother" I say walking out the door with a final wave. It's never gets easier seeing him in that fragile state. When I hugged him, I could feel his bones, he seems to be just fading away every day. Time to go see Father WHISTLER to confess my sins, I need to save my soul from going to hell.

"So when the devil throws your sins in your face and declares that you deserve death and hell, tell him this: "I admit that I deserve death and hell, what of it? For I know One who suffered and made satisfaction on my behalf. His name is Jesus Christ, Son of God, and where He is there I shall be also" MARTIN LUTHER

CHAPTER IV

KUSHINADA

(Goddess of sacrifice)

I pull up to the church, saunter up the stairs and enter. The church is empty, I look at the Virgin Mary and she almost seems to be judging my soul and seems mortified by the sins I have committed. I sit down and look up with my hands together in a prayer manner. I think of all that I have wronged, all the lives I have taken and hope for forgiveness and that the good Lord can cleanse my polluted soul and make it clean again like it once was.

"He can hear your prayers from all the way up there Chris, even if you do not voice them" a male voice says.

I look over and see Father WHISTLER approach. He was dressed in a nice suit and tie, salt and pepper hair and glasses resting on the bridge of his nose. "Father, sorry to intrude, I know it's not time for open confessions, I just felt that this is where I needed to be right now."

WHISTLER sits beside me, takes off his glasses and gazes up at the ceiling. "Chris, I know you have a good soul and I know that you are not evil" he looks at me now "You have a heart that is noble, but your soul is stained my son" he says as he cups his hands on mine.

I look down as those words hit my heart. "I know Father, I know my soul is stained, and I may not even deserve forgiveness from the Lord, but that doesn't mean that I will stop trying." I now look at him with a serious look "I'm done with it Father. Today was my last, never again shall I take the life of another. I want to start my own life free from sin, a new heart a new soul." I put my hands together in prayer, look down and say to the Lord *"Create in me a clean heart, O God; and renew a right spirit within me."*

"Psalms 51:10. You still know your passages" he says getting up "come, let's go into my quarters and talk."

As we enter his impressive office and I say to him "Like what you've done here Vincent." I say in a playful way.

"Re-did it all in oak, see this desk" he says as he leans over and takes a smell "mmm, pure oak. Sit down my son" he says as he sits. "I know you are genuine when you come to confession and tell me all of your sins but it's hard to hear sometimes you know? Sometimes I wish I could just tell you to cut it out and stop doing it, but I know that you are pure of heart and I don't want to sound like an overbearing Father."

"You really believe that Father, that I have a pure heart?"

"I remember that little boy who came to me and asked me why God took his mother away from him, and I told you..."

"...because God needed the help of a beautiful Angel and needed to borrow her, but wanted to let me know she sees me every day, and one day, you promised me that I will see her again" I interrupt him, now trying to fight back the tears "I remember, it didn't take away my pain, but it helped me understand. I miss her so much Vince it hurts."

"You loved your mother, you love your beautiful girlfriend, you love your brother and therefore, you have a good heart Chris. Evil shows love to no one, and you are not evil for your heart does love. Tell me, why did you come and confess your sins to me the first time? Guilt? Remorse? Fear?"

I look bewildered, not really knowing what to say. Why do I confess? "I don't want to hide my sins from anyone, not even the good Lord. Whoever conceals their sins doesn't prosper, but the one who confesses and renounces them finds mercy. Confession of errors is like a broom which sweeps away the dirt and leaves the surface brighter and clearer. I feel stronger for confession I guess, I feel clean."

He smiles and me and says "You know, there are three conditions are necessary for Penance: contrition, which is sorrow for sin, together with a purpose of amendment; confession of sins without any omission; and satisfaction by means of good works. I truly believe you have met all three."

"Do you think that I will ever be forgiven of what I have done?" I ask not wanting to look him in the eyes.

"You need to forgive yourself first. You need to tell yourself you are a good person and allow yourself to forgive. The truth is, unless you let go, unless you forgive yourself, unless you forgive the situation, unless you comprehend that the situation is over, you cannot move forward. Do you truly forgive yourself for what you have done?" he asks eagerly anticipating my answer.

A tear now cascades down my face as I still am looking down "No" I say almost crying "How can I possibly forgive myself and say what I have done is okay?"

He gets up, strolls towards me and tenderly puts his hand on my head "Repent then, and turn to God so that your sins may be wiped out, that times of refreshing may come from the Lord" he says "you are forgiven Christopher" he looks as me and asks "Do you still have the nightmares you keep telling me about?"

I never told him exactly why I have the nightmares or even what they are about, not sure if I can even confess that to him. I nod and say "Ya, all the time. Sadistic, disturbing images that I can rid myself of or run from. Seems like every morning I wake up in a cold sweat from the night terrors and demonic visions of my subconscious. Sometimes I don't even realize that I had a nightmare, but waking up and feeling the sweat run down my chest reminds me that my subconscious won't forgive me. No guilt is forgotten so long as the conscience still knows of it. When you are guilty of committing something as horrendous as I did in Russia that day, it is not your sins you hate, but yourself. How do I stop this?"

"You learned to run from what you feel, and that's why you have nightmares. To deny it is to invite madness in, to accept it is to control it. You may not be able to truly rid yourself of that guilt, but it can make you stronger. Guilt turns mistakes into poison and fills your veins with insecurities, self-doubt and despair. Find elation in the choices and life that you have made so far, reminisce about that mistake and then turn what you have labelled an error into your most trusted teachers and watch your soul awaken with wisdom, forgiveness and joy. There is no magic potion I can give you that will rectify the error or sin that happened that day, true forgiveness comes from within. Can you try to forgive yourself and try to tell your soul that you forgive yourself?" he says.

I look up and say "I just want this life of sin to be over Father."

"It is. You have a brother to take care of, and a lovely girlfriend who" he pauses and smiles "I take it will soon be your wife?"

I smile and nod "Yes. She means the world to me, she will make me a better person. I don't even think I deserve her you know. She is such a good person and I am such a bad person, it's like positive and negative ions clashing and shouldn't be together. But I love her so dam much."

"She loves you more than you know. I saw it in her eyes when I saw you two together for the first time. She is a great girl, treat her like a princess you hear me?" he says.

I look down and say "Will do Father. Can you do one last thing before I take off?" I ask

"Of course" he says

"Actually it's more for Nate. Can you say a little prayer for him and ask the Lord to watch over him. I ask him all the time, just wondering if you could in case he doesn't hear me".

"Of course" he says

I walk out, look back and say "thanks" then walk towards the door.

"Chris?" he says as I stop in my tracks but don't look back. "Are you truly finished with this?"

"Yes, I am." I say and continue on out the door.

Chapter V

KARMA'S WATCHING

6:00p.m

I pull up to my meeting and walk into the door, take my seat and listen quietly as a man walks up to the podium. His name is Richard and he is the speaker and guide so to speak. "Good evening everyone" he says in a very soft comforting voice. "We have a new member with us tonight. Please come and introduce yourself to the group."

Everyone all at once puts eyes on the female approaching the podium and waiting with anticipation on what she is about to say. She looks pretty run down, almost like a homeless person, raggedy clothes, hair not done and no makeup on her sad almost defeated looking face. "Hello my name is Maggie" she quietly says into the microphone.

In unison the entire group including myself welcomes her with a "Hi Maggie."

Maggie looks around almost overwhelmed to speak "My name is Maggie and I am an alcoholic. I've been battling this for almost five years now and I cannot get sober. Um, I have been arrested twice in the last year for DUI, I've recently got divorced from my husband and last week I was fired from my job." She tears up and says "I just really need the help, I feel helpless, like I can't beat this demonic being that has consumed me and taken over my life."

I heed her words and sympathize with her. I have been coming to these AA meeting for over seven years now and I have heard all kind of demoralizing stories from seemingly good honest people who just got hooked on the Devil's cough medicine and lost so much to this malevolent liquid. I became an alcoholic in my late teens but always denied that I ever had an addiction let alone a problem. They always say that the first step to recovery is to admit that you have a problem, but those same people who say that maybe don't realize that it's the hardest step of all. Nate and Tony would constantly tell me that I had a drinking problem but I always shrugged them off and had a good chuckle. I justified to myself that I could quit anytime I wanted to, or I was just a social drinker, or alcohol isn't the boss of me and so on. Addiction is a word that a lot of people may associate with people being weak or weak minded, or weak-willed or even cowards, basically thinking that "*if it's an issue, just quit*". Addictive behaviors such as drinking have always had quick fix maneuvers aimed at rapidly and dramatically changing one's emotional and hedonic state, and are natural and common targets for resolutions of reform, whether at New Year's or any other time, to "do better," to "turn over a new leaf" or to "quit once and for all." And even more than in the case of the typical New Year's resolution, the solemn promise of is well known by just about everyone familiar with such issues to be, more often than not, written in water referring to all of your enemies and their maliciousness and have caused one much grief and sadness due to the alcohol. A beautiful spirit being drowned in an alcoholic poisonous thunder shower, that is what happens to you once the demon of alcohol clutches you in its diabolic vice.

My wake-up call came on my eighteenth birthday while I was celebrating with a bunch of my friends at a local pub. Unfortunately Tony was not there as he was on vacation with his new bride or else this story may have ended differently. I had driven my car to the pub with plans to get inebriated beyond belief and take a cab home. Well the inebriated part was right as we all closed the bar and stumbled out. Two of my friends walked off saying they are going to walk home as they only live a few blocks away. My other friend with me told me he was going to walk to the corner and grab a cab and asked if I wanted to share one with him. I told him I'd catch my own cab a block over as I lived in the other direction that he was going, so, he staggered away and I was alone, gazing up into the majestic night sky without a care in the world. I reached into my pocket and realized I had my car keys on me. I was so intoxicated that I forgot I even drove to the pub and then decided to try to hunt down my car to see if it was there or not. Sure enough I stumbled to my car. It took me almost five minutes to put the right key in the lock and unlock my car door as my motor skills and eye sight were as hazy as a hobo's next meal. I stumbled into my car fighting back the puking sensation and just wanting to get home to bed. To this day I was not sure what was going through my brain when I had the notion of driving a vehicle in the state that I was in. I started my car, looked around and drove off towards home, I struggled to stay on the road, my hearing was blocked and muffled almost like being underwater, my body was tepid like hot cider coursing through my veins, and my vision was out of focus like looking through a block of ice. Still, I kept murmuring to myself the whole way "I'm fine, I'm fine." Then I swayed onto the sidewalk and heard the most sickening sound I've ever heard in my life, the "thud" of me hitting a human being as I saw a person fly off the hood of my car. I instantly panicked and was more petrified than I have ever been in my life at that moment. I stopped the car, then slammed my head into the steering wheel with anger and frustration realizing the magnitude of the situation that I had just got myself into. I slowly opened my car door and looked back and I was horrified to see a person lying motionless on the ground. My throat tightened, my head got light, and I was almost paralyzed with terror as I begged for the person to show some kind of life. I knew I had to do the right thing and go help this person, so I darted out of my car and rushed to the person's side and to my gut-wrenching horrific realization, the person was not moving. I screamed and looked around "Somebody call 911, this person isn't moving, we need help!" I saw people looking at me and just ignored me as they walked right by. "Please! For the love of God, this person isn't breathing!" I cried. Again, people ignored me and walked by me, this time I caught a glance of people actually snickering and laughing at me. "What the fuck is wrong with you people! This person needs help! Call 911 for fuck sake!" I said almost in rage and dismay. Finally I stopped someone walking by who was laughing at me "What in God's name is so fucking funny about calling 911 for someone who has been hit by a car?" I screamed.

The person laughed at me and says "Because I think that person is already dead."

I looked confused and say "What are you talking about?"

The person was laughing hysterically and said "That's a manikin dude. Holy shit man have another drink you fucking booze bag" and walked away.

I knelt beside the person and realize that it was in fact that it was a store manikin that I had just hit with my car. Still, to this day I will never forget the horror that I felt, the stomach churning feeling I had when I thought I had just hit another human being. That was the day that I admitted to myself that I had a problem. I realized the countless mornings that I have slept through and the nights that I could never remember. I tried to look for excuses for my drinking problem like my mother's death, my Dad never being around or why Nate and Tony didn't force me into rehab or AA meetings. Why did everyone just watch me kill myself for the past three years and let me drown and not say anything? Well, turns out everyone was telling me but I refused to listen or get help and told them to mind your own dam business, I guess if I needed help, it had to be help I was willing to get rather than someone forcing me to do it. This was probably the lowest part of my life, this was as low as I had ever got in my life and I was desperate to climb out of it. I couldn't see how far I was sinking because denial seemed to always give me the illusion that everything was okay and I was just fine. I had to admit to myself that not only did I have a problem, but was willing to seek help for it and rectify my life by whatever means possible.

I remembered walking into my first AA meeting and feeling almost like a little kid attending his first day of school. I thought all eyes were judging and evaluating me, looking at me like a drunk, a slob, a good for nothing derelict, but that wasn't the case at all. Everyone was sympathetic, understanding and most of all could relate to what I was going through. At AA meetings there is nobody really in charge, which is one of the traditions of Alcoholics Anonymous, members are all but trusted servants; no one governs anyone. I listened to others stories and the progress that people were making and how full their life was, how clear the world now seemed, how food tastes better, how their mind were opened, and how opportunities that they have never seen before are now starring at them in the face, and I wanted to feel that way too. I continued my meetings, had the support of Tony and Nate and I began to start getting that feeling that everyone was describing. I remember one night sitting outside gazing at the sky with a sense of freedom as I starred at the magical twilight, and looked at the world as an endless container of possibilities and opportunities. One should always be drunk, but what you choose to be drunk on is completely up to you, whether it be with joy, with virtue, with love, or with life. I loved the feeling I had and the accomplishment that I felt when I announced to the group that I was sober for a year and I remember going home that night and crying tears of joy, tears of pride, tears of self-worth.

I still attend the meetings on a semi regular basis as I feel it gives me stability or rather keeps me in check. I take the podium now and say with pride "Hi my name is Chris. Some of you may know me and for those who don't, I am proud to say that last month was my seventh year anniversary of being sober." Everyone in the room gives me a genuine applause. "I can't tell you how much this has changed my life and I just want to let you all know that there is a pot of gold at the end of the rainbow, a light at the end of the tunnel and with the support of one another and family and friends, you can reach it. Thank you" I end and walk off in a sea of applause.

I walk to my car and then feel someone reaching for my wallet in my back pocket. I swiftly turn around and snatch their arm in my steel vice grip, and to my astonishment it was a small boy, no older than fifteen. He had grubby clothes on, messy hair, mud caked face, and no shoes, clearly homeless. I look at him with awe as I say "Need to be quicker than that sport" and let go of his arm. "You know, if you wanted to get money for something to eat, all you had to do is ask."

He looks at me as if I was laying judgement upon him and says almost offended "I don't need your charity mister, I'll get the money from some other fool."

I look up and say "Gee that's too bad, I was on my way to have a late dinner and wanted some company. It's a shame that you don't accept charity" I now look at him with a smile.

He looks at me with a street tough look and says "I don't need anyone to feel sorry for me okay?" "I don't feel sorry for you" I said "I just thought it'd be nice to have some company. Too bad because the diner that I am going to has the biggest burgers I have ever seen. I'm talking the size of your head, but you probably don't like burgers anyway" I say.

"You trying to trick me into having you buy me a dam hamburger?" he says again offended.

I smile at him and say "Ya, is it working?"

He stalls and I can see him debating in his mind what to say. He puts his hands on his hips and with his grubby face looking up at me says "Fine, but only because I ain't never had a burger as big as my head before."

I laugh and say "Understood."

We enter the diner and he has a burger with fries in front of him as I have a piece of pie and coffee in front of me.

I drink my coffee and watch him scarf down his burger and fries and ask "When was the last time you ate?"

With a mouthful he says, "I dunno, few days ago, Tuesday I think."

"What's your name or should I just call you hey you."

He looks at me with his burger in his hand and says "Tyson, my friends call me T" and then bites into his burger.

"Pleased to meet you T, I'm Chris." I sip my coffee and ask "so how old are you anyway?"

"Thirteen" he simply says.

"Mind if I ask what you are doing living on the streets at thirteen? Where are your parents?" I ask.

He chomps on his fries and says "Never met my Dad and my Mom don't want me. I'm okay on my own ya know, that's how I've lived and it's worked out pretty good for me."

"I don't think your Mom doesn't want you? What makes you say that anyway?"

He puts down his food and looks me in the eyes "My Mom was fourteen when she had me and didn't know what to do. So, one day we were at the Mall when I was about seven or so, she told me to stay put and she'd be right back" he pauses.

I look at him and ask "And?"

"I waited for almost six hours and she never returned. Cops drove me to my house and discovered it was abandoned, just like I was. They put me in all kinds of Foster homes but I hated every one of them and ran away a lot. So last year I decided I'd be more happy living by my own rules on the street ya know. This way I make up my own rules and I will never get hurt by someone who just doesn't want me" then picks up his burger and continues to eat.

I was speechless as I stared at him in astonishment "I'm sorry T."

"I told you not to feel sorry for me. What's your deal anyway? Fancy suit, nice car, what are you a drug dealer or something?"

I chuckle and say "No not quite." I look at him and try to explain so I just reply "Let's just say I do favors for people" and sip my coffee.

T smirks and says "Shit, you like a gangster or something?"

I laugh and say "No, nothing like that. More like a garbage man."

"You do a lot of shooting I see" T says biting his burger.

I look at him confused and ask "What makes you say that?"

"Your one pointy finger is a little crooked, usually from carpel tunnel from pulling a trigger a lot. Also you keep reaching into your jacket with reflexes of having shoulder holsters for your pieces. And you have some redness on the top of your hand reminiscent of gunshot residue build-up" he says then takes a drink of his pop.

"Jesus" I say bewildered. "Pretty perceptive aren't you?" I ask as he just shrugs. I glance over at the back pack that he has been carrying "What do you carry in your backpack if you don't mind me asking?"

He looks at it and says "Stuff like a water bottle, knife, clothes, matches, and some cigarettes."

"You smoke?"

"Nah I ain't smoke, I use them to trade for stuff ya know" as he finishes his meal. "What's with the necklace?" he asks looking at my cross hanging from my neck.

I touch it and explain "A friend gave this to me when my Mom passed away, told me as long as I wear it, God will always protect me and my Mother will always be with me. It's a small token but it makes me feel that she is always with me as long as this is around my neck."

"Lost your Mom too huh?" he asks.

"Ya, I think about her all the time, I miss her alot." I look at him and ask "Want my pie? I'm not that hungry after all." He looks at me as I shove the pie over to him and say "go on, I haven't touched it."

He grabs a fork and begins to chow down on the pie. "My Mom told me something just before she left me. She told me, "*T, you only have one life. Do whatever you want because in a thousand years from now, nobody will remember the mistakes you made, so have fun, don't be afraid because if you spend your life trying to impress other people, you will never be happy with yourself.* Guess I should have taken that as a hint of her saying goodbye but I really like that philosophy."

"That's a good last lesson your Mom gave to you, more people should understand what that really means before it's too late in life to truly appreciate it."

"I try to live like that, but I just don't know where one day is going to lead me. I tell myself that eventually I'll get through this and eventually life will be okay, but then I snap back to reality and ask myself 'how the heck do you plan to do that?' Kind of feel hopeless, but not defeated, not by a long shot."

"Good for you T. I had that feeling once a long time ago, I felt my life was on a downward spiral and I wasn't going anywhere and had no idea of what my life may turn out to be like. But you know what, I needed help, I needed the help of other people to help me get back on my feet and give me a push in the right direction." I glance at T with a serious look "Don't ever be too proud to accept help if someone offers it to you, that's what people do to one another, they help each other."

"Tough to ask or get help from people, most people just see me as either a little thief or another bum on the street begging for money."

I look at T and can't help but feel sorry for this poor little kid that never had a chance in life. He finishes his pie and just then, a black male wearing a wool toque and scarf over his face enters the virtually empty diner. The male had on a heavy dirty trench coat and marched directly to the counter. "Stay here" I say to T while my eyes stay locked on this mysterious male as I slowly get up.

"What's up?" T asks.

"Little too hot outside to be wearing a wool toque and scarf don't ya think?"

Just then the male brandishes a butcher knife and says to the terrified cashier "Open the fucking cash register and give me all the money bitch! Don't make me ask again!"

I stand up and approach the male, he sees me and immediately turns the knife my way. "What the fuck are you doing!" he demands.

I raise my hands in the air and say "Nothing man, you don't need to do this tonight okay? Don't do something stupid that you'll end up regretting."

"What are you a fucking cop or something? Don't give me no after school bullshit speech, I need to pay my rent white boy and I am dam sure that I'm going to be getting some money! I ain't having my wife and kid get kicked out of their home man, so I'm getting some rent money and if I were you I'd sit the hell down and mind your dam business before you get sliced" he screams pointing the knife at me.

"Ok man" I say as calm as can be "I'm going to give you a choice here and I really want you to think about your next move" I say still with my hands up. "Option one is you put down the knife, turn around and leave this place in peace, and we all forget this ever happened. Option two is I snatch that knife from your hands before you can blink then deliver a brutal elbow strike directly to your nose. Thing is with a broken nose, it'll hurt like hell and you will bleed profusely as you stumble out of here in pain and embarrassment. You'll leave with no money and have a crooked nose for the rest of your life all because you were too dumb to take option one. Don't be too proud to just do the right thing."

He glares at me and now looks almost afraid rather than angry. "What about my rent huh? I got no money to pay my rent and I ain't living on the street with my baby man! So I need this money and I ain't leaving without it! And if I have to stick you with a blade to get that done, then so be it I'll do it" he yells waving the knife at me.

"How much you owe for rent if you don't mind me asking?" I inquire still with my hands up.

"What the fuck do you care?" he asks confused.

"Because, maybe I can help you help yourself."

"One hundred, that's all I need" he cries. Seems almost like the Wild West, me and this guy in a stand-off, neither one wanting or willing to back down.

"If you scored one hundred from here you'd be pretty happy then huh?" I reach into my pocket and pull out two hundred dollar bills "so two hundred would be a really nice score then am I right?" I ask.

"I guess" he simply says almost perplexed. He has the knife still pointed at me, he may be unpredictable so I better stay on my toes here.

"Make you a deal. I'll trade you two hundred bucks for that knife and you make a promise to me. That promise is you take a hundred and pay your rent, and use fifty of it to take your wife and kid out for a nice meal. Deal?" I say and extend the money.

I can see it in his eyes that he was deliberating in his mind what to do. I then say "Take the deal man, don't let your pride get in the way of good judgement." I look at the frightened cashier "Look, there ain't no surveillance in here is there?" I ask her and she simply shakes her head. I then look back at the male "Okay then, nobody will know what you did here except for us, you get the money, you walk out of here unharmed and get to pay your rent. Look, I can see you're afraid, your hands are quivering, you try to put on this tough guy act, and I can tell you're an amateur at this. I have no doubt that I will be able to disarm you with little effort and you will get hurt as a result. People do desperate things when they are desperate themselves. You don't take this deal, you'll regret it for your life, I promise you that."

He points the knife at me and says with fury "What makes you think you can snatch this knife from me before I stick you with it huh?"

I respond still with calmness to my voice "Because I'm not the one who is afraid here, you are. Your judgement is clouded, your reflexes are hindered, and I have a strong feeling your knife skills are rather poor. Nobody robs a place with a kitchen butcher knife man so I'm guessing this is probably your first try at doing something like this."

The male looks at me and just stares. I could tell that his mind was telling him to give up, but his body was fighting him trying to tell him to not to.

"Call my bluff if you want" I say "but you won't like the outcome brother, I promise you that. Don't listen to your gut, listen to your head which I know is telling you to put that knife down. Take the deal man, walk out of here with a victory."

The man tears up with emotion, puts down the knife and covers his face as he sobs. I walk up to the man who says "I ain't never want to hurt anyone man."

I put my hand on his shoulder, grab the knife and say "I knew that, I could see that in your eyes." I put the money gently in his hands "here, take the money and go pay your rent and don't forget about your wife either."

He removes his hands from his face and looks at me bewildered still sobbing "Why are you doing this man?"

I respond "I have my reasons, call it karma I guess. Now, get out of here" I smile at him.

He looks around and says to T and the cashier "I'm sorry ya'll" and leaves.

"You okay ma'am?" I ask the cashier.

"Yes" she simply says still visibly shaken.

I look at T who looked like he just finished watching an action movie in the theaters "You good T?"

He looks at me in amazement and says "Ya man. Shit, that was dope!"

I leave some money on the table for the bill and ask T "You got somewhere to stay for the night?"

"Ya, the shelter opens at nine, I always stay there most nights" he replies.

I reach into my wallet and pull out a wad of money and hand it to T. "What's this for?" he asks.

"It ain't charity ok? Just some cash to help you out a bit, get some new clothes, some good food and all that. Remember what I said, don't be too proud to accept help" and give him the money. "I have a friend who runs a cool youth sort of facility, gives somewhere for kids to hang out, eat hot meals and go to school, and best of all, a bed at night, how's that sound?"

T looks at me confused and asks "Why are you doing this? What's your deal?"

I smile and say "No deal, just figured I owe Karma a lot, this is a good step in the right direction" and hand him the money.

He takes the money and asks "Dude! How much is here? Like a million dollars?"

I chuckle and say "Not quite, I think it's just over $2500. That'll last you a bit until I get you set up in that facility. It's a pretty sweet setup T, you get to go to school, hang out with kids around your age and best of all you have a place to hang your hat every night. Sound good?" I ask.

He smiles and extends his fist to me. I pound his fist and he says "You're a cool dude man, I ain't never had anyone be so nice to me in my life. Thanks man."

I smile back and say. "My pleasure man, everyone needs help once in a while. I'll come find you in a week or so and get you set up in that facility cool?"

"Cool" he responds.

"Keep that money hidden in your backpack somewhere and don't let anyone know that you have that."

He nods and says "Will do Chris. Later" then walks out of the door.

CHAPTER VI

A FRIEND IN NEED

Next morning, 10:30 a.m.

I wake up and look at my phone and see a new text from Jimmy saying "CALL ME ASAP PLEASE". I stroll to the mirror and once again give myself a look up and down as I stare blankly without any thoughts.

I saunter down the stairs with my phone in hand ready to call Jimmy.

"Morning sleepy head" Trina says dressed like a million bucks, nice skirt and a pretty looking white dress shirt.

"Hey babe" I say giving her a peck on the cheek. "Wow, you look good, you going to see your other boyfriend today or something?" I smile.

"That's only on Friday's" she smiles back. "No I have that meeting downtown about that new sponsor for my business I told you about remember?"

I scratch my head and say "Oh ya right, I remember."

Trina smiles and says "You're a terrible liar sweetie. What are you up to today?"

"I dunno, debating on whether to see my Dad or not. Guess I probably should before we pack up for Mexico huh?"

Trina takes a sip of her juice and says "Yes babe that's a good idea, go see him, he's a good person and he's your Father." She looks at her watch and says "Shit, gotta go" kisses me and says "call ya later, love you."

I smile and say "Love you too babe."

I then pour a glass of milk and call Jimmy "Jimmy, got your text, what's up?"

"Chris. I just got a phone call. Before you say no, please hear me out okay" he says almost in a panic. "I just got a call, one last job" he says.

I immediately say "Jimmy come on man, I'm done, over. Why would you even ask me this?"

He pauses, "He's offering one million."

My heart races now hearing that number and I am intrigued a bit but say "Jimmy, I just can't do it, I don't have it in me, MYERS was the last one the final curtain dropping on a great show. Come on man, we had a great run, we are both set for the rest of our lives, we got everything we want. No Jimmy I'm sorry. How do we know this guy is legit anyway, a million? Come on."

"He's already deposited $500,000 in our bank he's serious."

"Jesus Christ Jimmy!" I say knowing that I took the Lord's name in vein. "What the fuck did you accept that for?" I think of what to say "give it back, tell him we aren't interested."

"Chris" there is a long pause. "Chris, I need this. I don't have two pennies to rub together. I'm..." he pauses again "I'm flat broke. The bank is going to take my house and I owe some really bad guys a lot of money."

"You gambling again?" Jimmy had a horrible gambling problem, he used to do large bets with highly respected, highly formidable bookies, the kind that will break your legs if you are late in paying them, and bash your skull in if you don't pay at all. I thought he was done with all of that. "Fuck sake Jimmy, how'd you get yourself into such a hole?"

"I thought we'd be doing this for a long time and I'd get myself out of this mess after a few more contracts. I am so sorry, I fucked up, I fucked up bad" he says. I can tell he's genuinely sorry too.

I deliberate in my mind what to do. Let's face it, Jimmy takes all the risk in this partnership so to speak. He's the one dealing with these low lifes and gangsters who put out the contracts. I guarantee Jimmy has taken a few punches to the face, had threats galore on his life, and was willing to sacrifice his own life and safety to keep my identity protected. He has been like a second father to me, he has loaned me money, connected me with the right people, and has kept me safe for all these years. Now, he needs my help, how do I say no. "You sure this is legit?" I ask Jimmy not knowing if I should be doing this.

"Yes, I checked him out, the client is clean and legit."

"Who is he?" I ask.

"Pierre Q BOUCHER, former gang leader of the Tueurs Cartel."

One million though, that's unheard of. I mean my biggest payday ever was $700,00, and that was on a former Mafia Don, who the fuck is this, the President? "Who the hell is the target for that price?"

"Some low level former thug names Henry WINCHESTER, rolled with 1A1 French Connection. He apparently killed this guy's only son drunk driving a few years ago. He was driving hammered to the gills and plowed into a small child who was playing on the sidewalk, turned out to be BOUCHER's kid. Court pled it all the way down to a simple careless driving charge due to some technicalities and a paid off Judge courtesy of the 1A1 gang. BOUCHER being a former gang leader did pretty good for himself so a million bucks is like pocket change to him. Here's the catch, it needs to be done by the end of the day because the target apparently may be leaving for France tomorrow for good on the account that he knows he has pissed off some people in high places and figures BOUCHER will be coming after him" Jimmy says.

"Jimmy, that's insane, I've never done a hit with that little of time, it's suicide. No time to prep, to learn who this WINCHESTER is, nothing." I say with extreme apprehension.

"Here's the beauty, this guy has done all the homework for us. The target wears the same green ball hat every day so he'll stick out like a sore thumb, and always visits the hospital everyday like clockwork at 2 p.m. to visit his son. The hospital on the east side as you know is a little on the remote side and there is a perfect little bushel area about six hundred meters away that will give you a perfect view of the hospital rear parking lot where he always parks his dark blue Chevy truck. I'm telling you, this will be easy. He got the number through Simon *tueur furtif* PELLITIER."

Simon PELLITIER better known as Tueur Furtif aka Stealth Assassin in French, is a connected French Mafia leader that has been our client on three occasions, one to take out a snitch, one to take out a rival gang member, and one to take out a fellow gang member who was stealing drugs from the gang and selling it on the side.

"Sounds too easy Jimmy" I take my phone from my ear, think for a moment and continue "I will do it on two conditions." I say. My head is not sure of this decision, but my heart has spoken for me.

"Name it, I'll do it" he says almost begging.

"One, you get some help for your gambling. I'm not talking about some focus group or shit like that, I mean a fucking top of the line shrink head doctor you hear me?" I say in an uncompromising voice.

"Done."

"Next, how much in total do you owe, I'm talking about everything, grand total? Your house, your gambling debts everything?"

"About $350,00" he says.

"Fine. Next condition is that you keep the entire million, pay your debts and live the life that you should be living and the life you and I deserve to live after all these contracts. We've put our necks out on the line every job, we deserve to reap the rewards of our work" I tell him.

"I can't do that Chris. Shit, you're taking all the risk here man I mean..."

"Jimmy Goddamit! You risk your life and safety on every dam contract we do. You are the one that deals with these customers, and let's face it, they aren't saints. Accept this deal or there is no deal."

"Thanks Christopher. I'll send you the photo of the target on your phone. You know the hospital?"

"Ya I know the hospital and I know the bushel you're talking about. I'm doing this one last one for you Jimmy. I owe you that much for your loyalty." It's true, I'm sure Jimmy has been offered loads of cash to give up my identity, and as tempting as it probably was, he always stayed loyal. Money will only get you so far in life, but it's hard to keep it all the time. Money is like friendship in a way, it's easy to make, but harder to keep and mine and Jimmy's friendship is genuine despite money. I love money don't get me wrong, but after a certain point, money is meaningless. It ceases to be the goal, friendship, love, and living well is the goal that counts, and I'd much rather count the good things I have in my life rather than a stack of green paper, and I truly believe Jimmy feels that way too.

"I just want to say again, I am sorry. I know you wanted out of this, and I dragged you back in" Jimmy says in sorrow.

"I'm happy to do this pal, a small gratitude that I can do to help out a friend in need" I say now a little more confident. I know Jimmy has done all the homework and if he says this is as easy as it sounds, then I trust him.

"Thanks. Call me if you need anything. I wish I could do this last one with you" he says.

"No you don't" I say as I hang up the phone. I'm not going to tell Trina about this, she wouldn't understand the reason I'm doing it and wouldn't approve either. I ponder in my mind and still wonder if I am doing the right thing. I know morally it's the right thing to do, but the movies always taught us that anytime you end up doing that one last job, it always seems to go sideways, never fails.

I search my text messages and see the one Jimmy sent just a few seconds ago. I open it up and see this guy's photo. Ha, there's the green hat he's talking about too. Grainy picture, hard to see the face good, but if he always wears that hat like Jimmy says, it won't be an issue. I look at the caption under his photo. William Henry WINCHESTER, date of birth 1961 October 21st, five foot nine, one hundred ninety pounds, married to Anna Gabrielle WINCHESTER for 15 years, owns his own small business and has one son Gregory Fredrick WINCHESTER and one daughter Alicia Dian PERRY. Drives a 2005 Chevrolet Silverado truck. Visits his son every day at the Holy Mary Eastern Medical Facility who is in a comma from a car accident. Wow, doesn't really fit the profile of a drunken killer, seems like an honest family man. Oh well, who really fits the profile of a criminal anymore. Crime runs ramped in L.A causing good people to turn bad which in turn causes people to get out of LA as fast as they came in. Los Angeles is the kind of place where everybody was from somewhere else and nobody really drops anchor. It's somewhat of a transient place, people drawn in by a dream, while other people are running from a nightmare. Twelve million people and all of them ready to make a break for it if necessary. Figuratively, literally, metaphorically any way you want to look at it, everybody in L.A. keeps a bag packed just in case. Just in case they need to do something desperate and leave fast or if a crime of opportunity rears its head and they get sucked into temptation. Maybe WICHESTER had a bad day, sucked back a few cold ones at a bar, drove home drunk and killed a small innocent little boy who was just minding his own business. Or who knows, maybe he was driving down the street and saw BOUCHER's kid on the sidewalk and had some drunken malevolent thought to get the ultimate revenge on a rival gang member. Then after words he returns to the normal life that he was already living, paid off the Judge and lawyer to reduce the charge to a simple traffic ticket and presto, it's gone. He has a bag packed just in case he needs to leave in a hurry because of what he has just done. Just a blip on the radar, the one speed bump in life that he regrets driving over literally and figuratively speaking. Who knows why he did it or even if he did it on purpose, but he did and now that it's over, his bags are packed and yet another soul will be leaving L.A.

I will let you know the kind of man Jimmy DENT is. Jimmy way back in the day knew some people who knew some people who knew some people with a lot of power. Jimmy was a former contract killer for 18 street Grim Reapers, a small time Miami gang known for putting hits out on local law enforcement. In 1999, police forces in Miami Dade County arrested 67 alleged Reaper members after ascertaining an extensive "hit list" that included five police officers and three gang prosecutors. Those arrested in the raid were charged with conspiracy to commit murder, possession of illegal weapons and identity theft and were facing a range of fifteen to life in prison. Jimmy however was arrested, but somehow got off without charges due to lack of any evidence connecting him in the hits even though it was his list and he was going to be the one spear heading the hits. The other gang members thought Jimmy was a snitch thinking that the reason he got let go by the cops is because he flipped on his fellow members to escape any prison time. This was entirely not true, only reason he didn't get charged was because he was smart and covered his paper trail leading to him. The other members who got arrested had either the photos of the potential hits on them, didn't delete their text messages with crucial information about the hits, or forgot to take down the big board with the words TARGETED VICTIMS on it and all the hits photos underneath with big red X's on them. The rest of the Reapers went after Jimmy and thought the best plan of action was to rig Jimmy's house with explosives and blow him along with his wife and kids sky high. So, when they saw Jimmy walk into his house one night, they set off the explosives and blew the house to smithereens with an explosion that illuminated the night sky. Only problem was, it wasn't Jimmy walking into the house, it was Jimmy's brother in law coming over for a visit, luckily, Jimmy and his son weren't at home at the time, but his new born baby girl and wife were. Cops arrested the rest of the Reapers for the brutal deaths of Jimmy's brother in law, Jimmy's wife, and Jimmy's daughter. As of today, the

18 street Grim Reapers no longer exist because all the members are serving heavy sentences for their crimes. Jimmy had nothing to live for and started to accept money to do contracts for local gangs. Only problem was, they all knew who he was so any time a gang member was smoked, Jimmy was the most likely suspect. Jimmy was only responsible for killing two gang members, but local gangs suspected him to doing more than twenty four hits. One gang seeked out Jimmy for a hit that he allegedly did on one of their members. They beat Jimmy with chains and bullwhips and it was only by the grace of God that the police showed up as a result of someone witnessing this poor man being beat severely by six people with chains and whips. Jimmy spent three months in the hospital with a police officer outside his door every night in case the gang wanted to come and finish him off. When Jimmy was released from the hospital, he split to L.A to look for work. He wanted to continue in the contract killing business because it was all he knew and had local gang connections in LA as well. Unfortunately, the beating he received extensive damaged to his hand that was so bad he couldn't properly squeeze the trigger of a gun. His fingers bent every which way and the muscles and joint were so brutally damaged, and he only had limited movement in his fingers and hands. Then Jimmy found me, and well, that's a whole different story.

I get into my car, give Charlotte a kiss and tell her "Be good to me baby." I pull out my cell phone and open my contacts and go to Tony. I suppose I should call him and give him the heads up about this hit. I am about to push the dial button, but something stopped me, that little voice in my head for some reason was telling me *"this is one he doesn't have to know about".* I am unclear on why this small voice is telling me to not call Tony. Going with my gut feeling is usually the best route. One's intuition already knows all the other aspects of our life and will communicate the right answer in the form of a gut feeling or a small voice in one's head. My Dad always taught me that your subconscious already knows what you should do before your mind even realizes, rationalizes or produces an answer. I will listen to my gut and not call Tony. I look at WINCHESTER's picture one more time and study it. He looked familiar for some reason, don't know why; maybe he just has one of those faces.

I have to say, this was the most uneasy I have ever felt about doing a hit in my life. I am starting to feel apprehensive about the whole thing but I know I can't feel this way, I have to shake it. Worrying is like a rocking chair, it gives you something to do, but it gets you nowhere, I need to be confident in order to see this one through. I try my hardest to instill self-assurance in myself and flush out the uneasiness and nerves. You need to be confident in this, one hundred percent confident if you want to make the hit a success because any self-doubt will result in critical errors. I've made this decision to do this contract and I need to be sure that I'm doing the right thing. When you're confident about a decision, you have to be courageous enough to see it through and be self-assured that the outcome will be exactly as you envision. I think back to when I was on that range a few years ago facing a target that was 2125 meters away and people watching me including my Dad. I wasn't nervous at all, I was so sure that I would hit that target because I knew how good I was and visualized the bullet striking where I wanted it to go. Had I been nervous and unsure that day, I would have never succeeded. Besides, my motivation for this hit is to help my friend out and set his life up for him. I will be focused, I will be strong, I will be confident, I will prosper.

I take a quick look at the weather, temperature, wind, pressure etc. on my cell phone. Distance Jimmy says was about six hundred metres or so. I will get there early and calculate my elevation, and the exact distance and all that other stuff. So many different factors will come into play that are unforeseen, like where exactly will he park, is he coming with anyone, is there anyone else in the parking lot, will he for sure park in the back, what if he isn't wearing the green hat? The photo is really grainy so it's hard to get a proper look at his face. I'm going purely on the fact that he is wearing the hat, meets the physical description, and is driving up in his blue truck. If I can't tell it's him, I will not take the shot, period.

I make it to my destination, not much of a place to park my car out of sight, but it'll have to do. I check my watch 1:44 pm., lots of time. I get out with Charlotte and walk to the bushel overlooking the hospital. It's a slight elevation, just enough so I have a clear shot over the fence into the parking lot which is relatively empty. I assemble Charlotte, and get ready for show time. I am still nervous, this has got to stop or I won't be able to do this. My hands are getting clammy and I feel my forehead building perspiration, "No, not now, please don't get nervous now" I say to myself as I feel the nervousness in the pit of my stomach. Shit, too late to calm down because a blue truck is now pulling up. "Calm down, control your breathing, relax, stay focused" I say to myself.

I verify that it is a Chevrolet, and is it. Once he pops out, he's mine. This drunk will be meeting the Grim Reaper soon and retribution will come for Mr. BOUCHER. The truck stops and the door opens as I wait anxiously to see a green hat on his head. A figure slowly emerges from the truck and there it is, the green hat, this is my target, this is WINCHESTER. I verify quickly his height weight and approximate age which all looks good. My heart is still beating fast, I have to make this shot quick, I set my aim, calculate for elevation and distance then pause for a moment before I slowly retract the trigger. I wait, and I feel the jolt as the gun goes off.

I now am frozen like an ice cube with panic, this has never happened before. I MISSED! I see WINCHESTER curiously looking around as I'm sure he either heard the small pop of Charlotte or the bullet whistling past his ear. I try my best not to panic as I quickly load another round into Charlotte. WINCHESTER now ignores his curiosity and now walks towards the hospital entrance.

"Fuck sake, fuck sake" I now say as I try to recalculate everything as quick as I can. If he makes in to the door, it's over. WINCHESTER is only a few feet from the door and I still don't have him locked in my crosshairs. I try my best to stay composed, try to focus, don't panic, ignore your sweaty hands, ignore your heart beating out of your chest. I see WINCHESTER sticking his arm out ready to open the door, then all of a sudden BANG! I get a shot off and see WINCHESTER fall face first just before the hospital entrance as his blood sprays over the door. I got him. Not ideal, but it was a clean shot right to the back of the temple. He's at a hospital yes, but he is dead and they won't be able to save him from that fatal shot.

"Your time is up murderer." In the midst of all this chaos, I forgot to one important thing, to pray for his soul before I took it. I summon up a bible verse in my head quickly before I depart.

Then shall the dust return to the earth as it was: and the spirit shall return unto God who gave it. **Ecclesiastes 12:7**

Chapter VII

PRODITIONE

As I slowly drive away, I can hear police sirens really close. "Wow, that was fast" I thought as my heart starts to beat a bit faster. I don't want to drive away too fast and raise suspicion, but at the same time, I don't want the cops to see my car either. I'm not worried about them finding Charlotte as I have a special compartment cut out in the rear floorboard of the car, they'd never find her, but, I didn't wear my gloves on this one so there is a possibility of gunshot residue on my hands.

This whole contract seemed sloppy on my part. I didn't have time to think or prepare and I never, I mean never miss my shot. I forgot to wear my gloves, didn't have time to mentally prepare, barely had enough time to factor in all of the elements, and forgot to say my prayer for WINCHESTER before I took his life. This was the only time in five years where I felt like an amateur. I am so flustered right now I actually turn on the radio to try to sway my mind somewhere else. I look in my rear view mirror and see the red and blue lights arriving at the hospital. This whole contract gave me bad vibes, that uneasy feeling of not knowing what may come next. Who exactly was this BOUCHER? Who exactly was WINCHESTER? I am hoping Jimmy did his research thoroughly on these two guys, because it just seems too fucked up of a hit for me to feel at ease right now. I feel my forehead damp with sweat as I wipe it from my head.

I need to pull over and calm down a bit. "The job is done. It was sloppy and ugly, but it's done" I say to myself. "That was it, the last one. I am finished forever", as I close my eyes, I lean my head back and begin to snooze for a few minutes.

All of a sudden my cell phone rings. I look at it, it's Jimmy. Dam, forgot to call him.

I lean my head back to where it was before, close my eyes and say "It's done. For the love of all that's Holy, it's done" I say with a big sigh.

"Chris" Jimmy says sounding distressed then takes a big pause. "Chris, we have a major problem."

I open my eyes at this news and sit up "What?"

"The man you just shot was" another long pause.

"What Jimmy? What's going on?" I say now concerned even more.

I can hear Jimmy trying to get the words out "The man you shot and killed was Grant BOULDERDASH. Senator BOULDERBASH, not Henry WINCHESTER."

I now sit up straight as I feel a huge lump in my throat and my head go light "What! Jimmy what the fuck are you talking about?"

"I am watching the TV right now. They are saying that Senator BOULDERDASH was killed twenty minutes ago outside of H.M.E hospital with a bullet hole in the back of his head. Said he was visiting his son who was battling his long battle with cancer. My God, what have we done?" Jimmy says softly.

I am lost for words right now and can't speak. What is this? What is happening right now? "How is that possibly?

I saw the photo of WINCHESTER, green hat, blue truck, two o'clock, how the fuck is a US Senator lying dead instead of him? Jimmy, what's going on?" I say getting infuriated now.

"I don't know. The photo I got from BOUCHER stated that it was WINCHESTER. All his date of births were good, his whole story, it all matched up. I don't understand" Jimmy says almost in a panic.

"Dam! Did you verify that the photo was in fact WINCHESTER? Did you look in depth on who BOCUHER was exactly?" I say now in my angry tone. I am hoping Jimmy did his job properly and not just take the money and forget all logics.

"I didn't have time. I am so sorry, I just honestly didn't have that kind of time. I got caught up in the fact that we were getting this money, I didn't verify the photo or anything. Maybe there was a part of me subconsciously not wanting to look at verifying it in case there was a miniscule chance that the photo didn't check out, and the money would not be there. I fucked up, God forgive me, I fucked up huge."

I lean over my steering wheel now thinking that I may have been set up. Did BOUCHER actually want Senator BOULDERDASH dead and just used me to do his dirty work? Or is he trying to sewer me and either make me look like a stone cold killer or a ruthless gunman for something I may have done to him in the past? "Dammit Jimmy" I say trying to keep calm. I realize the damage is done, there ain't no changing what I just did. "What about BOUCHER?"

"He checked out too. My Lord, he dropped PELLITIER's name, new all the right things to say, shit, it sounded like the same ole routine, I didn't pick up anything suspicious at all." I could tell Jimmy knew he screwed up and was trying to apologize. This was beyond a screw up, this made me a murderer. I don't kill people that I don't have a contract for, no politicians, and nobody significant to the community or country. Strike three on every single last one of those points.

I didn't feel like talking right now "We should get off the phone Jimmy, no telling how deep this is or who's listening, besides, I need to wrap my head around what is happening." I said in my most disappointing voice.

"Ok. We'll talk later. We'll get this figured out my boy" Jimmy said in a sad voice, then just hung up.

Thoughts were now racing through my mind. Did Jimmy set me up along with BOUCHER? He never goes into a contract without tying up every last detail. But why? What would he have to gain by screwing me over and setting me up? Something stinks, and it smells rotten. Could this man who is like a father to me really try to set me up? I have to do something, I can't just sit here.

I drive off and think to myself, who can I trust. Tony! I hurry up and dial Tony's number. It keeps ringing and ringing "Come on Tony pick up your dam phone" I shout.

Finally he answers in a whisper "Goddamit Chris, tell me this wasn't your work!"

"Tony, you have to believe me. Yes it is my work, but somebody is setting me up, they gave me the wrong guy, they told me it was some former gang banger, I had no idea it was a U.S Senator" I say talking a mile a minute.

Tony murmurs "I'm at the scene right now wondering why a fucking sniper took out a US Senator who was going to the hospital to visit his dam sick kid! If you were gonna do a job, you bloody well tell me, that was the deal. You didn't tell me about this and look at the shit pool you are swimming in now" I could tell Tony was annoyed.

"I know, you're right ok. It was a last minute contract from another mob boss who shoveled a dump truck full of money my way to have this done ASAP. I swear on my life man, I had no idea it was BOULDERDASH, you have to believe me" I said.

"How'd you know it was BOULDERDASH?"

"Jimmy told me, it's on the news. Look, I have a feeling I was set up. The dam cops were there literally minutes after the shooting, and it was on the news minutes after that. It was like someone knew this was going to happen and called the police ahead of time. Tony, I'm telling you, I was set up. BOULDERDASH was not my target, please believe me, you know I'd never lie to you."

Tony takes a deep breath "Ok, let me deal with this here and I'll meet up with you in a bit okay. And Chris..."

"Ya"

"I do believe you. We'll figure this out brother" he says trying to re assure me.

"Thanks" I say as I hang up my phone. I'm still shaken up and perturbed about everything. The names of people that would want me out of the picture are endless, but why would this BOUCHER guy would agree to set me up? How would anyone know who I was in the first place? Jimmy is the only person who knows my true identity as this contract killer. Jimmy is the only path that this mystery leads to. "Oh please Jimmy, say it wasn't you, anybody but you." I say as I drive, not really sure where to go. My phone rings, it's Trina. I can't talk to her now, I'm still almost in a state of shock as I regretfully hit the IGNORE button. As I drive the radio catches my attention:

"Police have identified the man as Senator Grant Jeffery BOULDERDASH. BOULDERDASH was on his way to visit his son in the hospital who as you may know is battling

cancer. BOULDERDASH appears to have been shot once in the back of the head with what is believed to be a high powered rifle. Police do not have a suspect as of now, but will continue the investigation into this brutal senseless tragedy."

I bang my hand on the steering wheel in frustration "Fuck!" I scream. I feel like my world is just rocked. My phone rings, again it's Trina, no time to talk, I need to calm down somewhere. Somewhere safe, the only place I know, the Church. I turn off the radio and my cell phone and drive to the Church. Suddenly, I see red and blue lights coming up behind me and he's lighting me up. Now I start to panic beyond belief as I could literally feel my heart beating. I started to think to myself just how grave of a mistake I have truly made. It was like when you make a move in chess and just as you take your finger off the piece, you see the mistake you've made and there's this panic because you don't know yet the scale of disaster you've left yourself open to and can't do anything about it except watch it unfold in front of you. I contemplate on gunning the gas pedal of my Porsche to the floor and taking off, maybe take my chance in a high speed pursuit. I can't go down for this, my whole life, Trina, Mexico, everything will be over. What do I do? I look at my rear view mirror again hoping that the squad car just wants to pass me on the way to a call, but I could see he wanted me. I feel my temperature rise, my hands getting sweaty, my face going white, it's now or never, do I pull over or gun it and take a risk? Finally with my legs now shaking in fear, I calmly pull over to the curb and stop. "Come on Chris, pull yourself together, if they see you are panicking or becoming unnerving, they will know something is up for sure, stay calm be cool" I mutter to myself. I keep peering in my rear view waiting for the cop to approach. I know it's only been a few seconds, but it feels like an eternity for this cop to get out of the car. I quickly search for my driver's license, insurance and registration so I am ready for the officer when he approaches. As I grab my insurance papers from the glove compartment, I forget that I have two pistols in there. I think to myself, "In desperate times, we resort to desperate measures." If I need to, I may have to do something desperate, there is no way I'm going to jail for the rest of my life. I will call this my last resort plan, it's there if I need it. I can see the cop talking on his radio in his car, maybe calling for back up since they know I have a gun and just shot and killed a US Senator in cold blood. I keep my eyes peeled on the cop in my rear view trying to read his lips "What are you saying, who are you calling for?" I ask myself.

Finally, his door opens and he slowly approaches the vehicle. I am in such fear my body is almost numb, I can't go to jail. I take one last deep breath as the cop approaches my window as I role it down.

"Afternoon sir" the officer says in an austere sounding voice. He peeks inside my car, then looks at me with concern. "Sir, do you have some identification on you?" he asks.

"Yes sir" I say as respectful as I can and hand him my license and paperwork. I swallow and ask "Did I do something wrong?"

The cop now examines my paperwork and license and slowly says "I saw you bang your hand on the steering wheel then swerve out of your lane. Is everything all right with you today sir?" he asks now looking me right in the eye.

"Oh that" I start to laugh and quickly think of something. "Just listening to the game, gets me frustrated."

I look at the cop and see if he's buying my story. He looks at me almost scrutinizing me with judgement in his eyes as I could see my nervous reflection in his sunglasses. He then grins and hands me back my driver's license and paperwork "I know how you feel, dam Dodgers piss me off too."

He stands up and looks like he is going to walk away as I start to breathe again. He then leans in and asks, "Sir, do you have anything illegal in your vehicle? Drugs, weapons, anything like that? I ask because you seem extremely nervous. Is there anything that I need to know about that you want to tell me?"

Now I start to panic again. Literally within arms-length is two loaded handguns. If he finds them then he is authorized to search my entire vehicle which means he may find Charlotte and link me to the shooting. "No sir nothing."

"Mind if I check?" he asks. "Just have that feeling you know, it'll put my mind at ease."

My heart beats fast again, I have this insane deliberation now that as I put my papers back in the glove compartment and feel the cold steel of one of the guns. "No, I don't mind" I say as I slowly lean towards the glove compartment. I grip the gun and think to myself "This is judgement time right here right now, I can't go down for this, I just can't." As I feel the steel in my hand, my mind is tugged back and forth but then, I see the cop reach for his radio. I gradually start to take the gun out. "Make a decision Chris" I think. I slowly feel the gun with my hand while keeping an eye on him. He quickly looks at me and says in a panic "Sir! I have to get going, we have an emergency. I'll let you off with a warning, drive safe" as he darts back to his car, gets in and drives away with lights and sirens on.

I remain frozen still. I can't believe my luck, or is it the cops' luck? Now I ask myself, would I have really done something so horrific as what I was thinking? I stop myself from thinking because really, I don't even want to know the answer. I was going for the gun, but would I have stopped myself before I actually went through with it? I don't know, I honestly think I was desperate enough to the point where I may have done something unspeakable. I'm not sure what life had in store for me, testing me? Taking a shot at me? Why did it give me this second chance? Sometimes giving someone like a second chance is like giving them another bullet because they missed the first time. I feel that I have been dodging life's bullets for the past five years and if I keep this up, I will get one right in the head.

I sit up now, slowly calming down and trying to focus on the epic totalitarian circumstances here that have lead me to put a bullet into the back of the head of a US Senator. But first, I need God right now and a good friend.

I pull up to the Church and park around back, just so nobody sees my car that sticks out like a sore thumb. I enter the Church and hope that Father Whistler is here. I look around and don't see anyone. I walk forward slowly and look around, then I'm startled by "Chris."

I look over and see Father Whistler standing there looking at me confused.

"Father" I say.

"What are you doing here?" he asks.

"Father, I need someone to talk to" I say almost begging him.

Father Whistler looks at me puzzled and says "Confession isn't for another two hours."

"Father, Vincent, please" I say almost in desperation.

He bows his head and says, "Let's talk, you know my door is always open for you."

I walk into his quarters and sit down with my elbows on my knees and my face in my hands.

"What in the heck is going on? Please tell me that it wasn't you that took out a US Senator" Vincent says concerned.

How does the whole fucking city know about this already? I look up and say "It was, but, I think someone set me up. Senator BOULDERDASH was never my target, it was supposed to be some former gang banger of the French mafia or something. I was given the wrong name and wrong photo for the contract. How the hell was I supposed to know what Senator BOULDERDASH looks like? I trusted Jimmy, and for that I got screwed over."

"My word Chris" he says in a soft almost comforting tone. "You said you were done and over with this yesterday. You told me that this life style was done. What happened?"

I lean back in my chair and put my hands to my face "Jimmy. He needed the money and needed me to do one last job to help him out. I couldn't say no to him Vince, my head was screaming at me not to do it, but my heart was telling me that I owed Jimmy and I needed to do this to help him out so he could keep his house. Now I just think what a Goddam sucker I am. Forgive me." I say lowering my voice.

"I've known you since you were a small boy and I know there is a good soul inside that body of yours. You have a good heart, you were trying to help out a friend and ignored the other protocols for your job putting his needs first. *let your light shine before others, so that they may see your good works and give glory to your Father who is in heaven.*"

"Matthew 5:19" I say.

"Very good" he smiles. "Do not neglect to do good and to share what you have, for such sacrifices are pleasing to God. I believe you when you say that you were doing this for a friend and you had no intentions of killing a US Senator." He leans forward and asks "who do you think did this to you?"

I look to the side and say with sorrow "Only person I can think of is Jimmy." I now turn my head and say to Vincent "but why would he do this to me? What could he gain from this?"

"Did he receive the payment yet?"

I look dumbfounded now and say "I'm not sure. He did say he got half of it already deposited in his bank for, you know, good faith on the client's part, but that doesn't make any sense either, I told him he can have it all. Why? I'm not sure if it is him and I almost feel bad for thinking it, but I don't know who could have done this. I'm lost. What do I do?"

"You need to seek the truth my boy. It won't undo what you have done, but it will help you find out what exactly the reason for this and who is responsible. Someone either wanted Senator BOULDERDASH dead or they wanted to frame you for doing something as heinous as take out a public figure. I think more than anything you want to find the truth behind all of this and who is benefiting the most as a result."

"How? Whoever did this set me up good and I'm sure has covered their tracks. I don't know who this BOUCHER is or where to find him. I don't even know where to even begin to find out the truth, and I'm not sure if I can" I say.

"Chris, there are three things that can't be hidden in this world, the moon, the sun and the truth. Now I know you aren't an evil person, but someone out there wants to make it look like you are by having you gun down in cold blood a US Senator who was visiting his sick son in the hospital. The Chris I know wouldn't stop until he finds out the truth. Now from hearing the news, they have not released any names of any suspects, so for right now, there is no path leading to you. You have time to figure this out, then leave the country and start your new life" he says stern like a father.

"I know. I won't be able to rest until I figure this out" I say letting out a big breath. "I need the Lord's help to keep me resilient and sane through this Vince. I need to stay strong and the Lord needs to be with me every step of the way."

"those who hope in the LORD will renew their strength. They will soar on wings like eagles; they will run and not grow weary, they will walk and not be faint. The Lord will be with you Chris, he will help you find the truth. But be aware, the truth may be ugly. It's like wanting to know what day you will die. Curiosity about finding out something like that is overwhelming, but once you find it out, you may not like what you see and maybe wish you hadn't revealed it. You see Chris, you need to be prepared that the person who set you up is probably somebody who is very close to you and knows you very well. Might be hard to accept once you reveal the truth."

I look down "I just can't think of anyone who is close to me that would want to do this to me. Why sacrifice an innocent man who is just trying to visit his son, to get back at me?" I ponder.

"Perhaps that person is the true evil. Are you sure it isn't one of your former, uh, clients?" he asks.

"Anything is possible Father. Who knows, I'm just hoping one clue leads me to another then eventually leads me to the door with the truth on the other side."

"And you sure you want to open that door and see what's on the other side?"

"I have to" I say "I can't live a sane life without knowing why this BOUCHER wants to make me look like a monster. Maybe he just used me to do his dirty work and take out a US Senator that has wronged him, maybe someone out there wants to make me look like a heartless assassin, who knows. I don't even know who BOUCHER is or what he has against me." I shake my head "Heck, can you believe that I actually missed my first shot? Should have backed out right there and taken the hint."

"Chris" Vincent says as he stands up and sits in front of me on his desk "I know this may be an ugly road and you may face some evil along the way, and you think that you have had a lot of bad luck in your life. Remember this, there's always the same amount of good luck and bad luck in the world. If one person doesn't get the bad luck, somebody else will have to get it in their place. There's always the same amount of good and evil, too. We can't eradicate evil, we can only evict it, force it to move across town. And when evil moves, some good always goes with it" Vince looks me right in the eyes "But we can never alter the ratio of good to evil, all we can do is keep things stirred up so neither good nor evil solidifies. That's when things get scary. Life is like a stew, you have to stir it frequently, or all the scum rises to the top. Expose this wickedness and clear your name, not for them, but for you and your soul."

"You know what, from the moment I got the call from Jimmy, everything felt wrong. Seemed too easy, too straightforward, the job was a rush, it reeked of uncertainty, and you know what else? For the first time, I actually missed my shot. Took me two shots to hit my target. I mean, this was doomed from the beginning, cursed even" I say to Vincent.

"Maybe you overlooked all of the signs that the good Lord was trying to give you not to do this. The perturbed feeling you got when Jimmy told you about it, was God telling you it was wrong. When you missed your shot, maybe it was the Lord redirecting the bullet giving you one more chance to not go through with it. Sorry Chris, I'm not trying to beat you down."

"No, you're right" I say looking at the floor. "First rule I always have, if it doesn't feel right, don't pull the trigger. Why Vince? Why the fuck didn't I listen to my gut!" I say now bellowing.

"Because. The will to help out your friend took over the rationale of the job. Chris, what's done is done, you can't take it back or go back in time and stop this. You have to move forward, figure this out and get on with your life" Vincent says.

"Gee Father, are you telling me to run from the law and be a fugitive?" I say in a chuckle.

"I'm not speaking as a Priest, I'm speaking to you as a friend. Your time will come with the Lord to be judged and be forgiven. Luke 6:37..."

I interrupt the verse as I already know it "*Judge not, and you will not be judged; condemn not, and you will not be condemned; forgive, and you will be forgive.* Of course, one of the most famous quotes of all time. You know Father..." I say reaching into my shirt and pulling out my small cross necklace. "...I still wear this to this day. You remember when you gave this to me when my Mom died? You told me that as long as I wear this cross, my mother will protect me until it's my time to visit her. I never forgot that day, it never made me stop missing my Mom, but you made the pain of missing her go away."

"You remember that poem I taught you and Nate when you were little?"

"If Roses grow in Heaven Lord, please pick a bunch for me. Place them in my Mother's arms and tell her they're from me. Tell her that I love her and miss her and when she turns to smile, place a kiss upon her cheek and hold her for a while. Because remembering her is easy, I do it every day, but there's an ache within my heart that will never go away." I say trying to hold back the tears. "Me and Nate say it all the time when we went to Mom's grave." I look up at Vincent, "You've always been good to me Vince, and I will never forget what you have done for me" as I get up hinting that I have to go.

Vince stands up too and gives me a hug. "Take care of yourself out there Chris. Don't do anything foolish or unnecessary you hear me? You know you are always welcome here whenever you need sanctuary."

"Thanks Vince, you are one of the few people in this world I can trust" I say as I leave, not looking back. Now my sorrow turns to rage. It's time to burn this motherfucker responsible for this to the ground!

Chapter VIII

YEARS TO EARN, SECONDS TO BREAK

I was desperate, I knew one man who man who still may have a lot more connections in the gang world than me. MY DAD. As I drove to my father's place, I tried with all my might not to turn on the radio and hear what is being said about my killing of BOULDERDASH. "Don't do it, it'll just drive you crazy" I said to myself. I figure I should at least speak to Trina in case she was worried about me not answering. So, I swiftly snatch my phone and give her a short text message: BABY I AM OK. I JUST NEED TO TAKE CARE OF SOME THINGS FIRST. I WILL CALL YOU IN A BIT AND EXPLAIN EVERYTHING. LOVE YOU. TTYL.

I must say I was getting anxious about seeing my Dad. We left of bad terms last we spoke, but he was, I should say is, a really a good father but as stubborn as a mule. He rolled years ago with the notorious Hells Angels of L.A, and I know he still keeps in touch with some of the underground scene. My Dad is a complicated man, he is not a lazy man by any means, but at the same time he feels he does not need to work, so he spends his days living on welfare in some broken down house in north east L.A. As I pulled up to my Dad's place, I actually had butterflies in my stomach, just hope he doesn't tell me to turn around and get back in my car. I walk up to the door and knock. The door opens and there was my Dad wearing a blue raggedy bath robe in utter surprise to see me.

"Chris" he says surprised.

"Hi Dad." My Dad looks so run down these days, mange shoulder length grey hair, grey messy beard, beer belly and bloodshot eyes with heavy crows-feet. One would almost mistake him for a homeless person who'd been aged from years of living on the streets.

"Come on in please" he says moving out of the way to let me in.

"Thanks" and I walk in. He has a small little quaint bungalow run down house with ratty furniture and a dense piquant odor to it. I've tried several times to buy him a place or at least new furniture, but he was too proud to accept any charity from his youngest son. Where do I even start this story about the last few hours that have unfolded?

"What are you doing here Christopher?" he inquires.

"Dad, I told you not to call me Christopher, makes me sound like a little kid" I say.

"Sorry. So, what brings you by?" he says pointing to the couch wanting me to sit down.

I sit and take a deep breath trying to gather my thoughts. I look up at my father and say "I'm in a lot of trouble, or at least I think I may be, I'm not sure." My Dad leans into me anticipating what I have to say. "You hear about that US Senator that was killed earlier today?"

"Ya, I heard it on the news. Why?" My Dad now looks at me with the realization that I may have had something to do with it "You didn't kill a US Senator did you?" he says as his eyes widen.

"Well, not on purpose. Somebody is setting me up Dad. They provided Jimmy with BOULDERDASH's photo and told me it was this former French gang banger named WINCHESTER. The hit was from another former French gang member named BOUCHER and the payout was a million. After I shot which I thought was WINCHESTER, I now know it was BOULDERDASH. I was set up to kill a US Senator that was visiting his sick son in the hospital. I mean, I feel so bloody angry and sick to my stomach all at the same time, makes me wanna vomit."

"Jesus Christ. What the fuck did you get yourself mixed up in? A US Senator assassination, really? Holy shit, they'll fucking hang you for this one." My Dad says. He pauses and collects himself. "I'm sorry, I know what you must be going through, but my God Chris I thought you were smarter than that. I told you being a hitman would catch up to you eventually."

"Dad, I'm not here to get a lecture, I came for your help. Dammit, I know I screwed up, I screwed up huge, but I need to find out who set me up and why and who this BOUCHER dude is okay" I say now annoyed at the lecture my father just gave me.

"Of course. You're still my son and I am still your Father. Now look, first thing you have to do is try to find either BOUCHER or WINCHESTER and see if they know anything about this. I have heard of both their names, French gang members but that's about all I can remember about those names. Next, you have to find out who will prosper from this guy being dead and who has the capability and insight to pull something like this off. Don't trust anybody from here on in, because I guarantee, this was planned by someone who knows you very well. Someone has betrayed you and the rage and furry will have a powerful grip on your mind soon. It's almost like a python, it can squeeze out all other thoughts, suffocate your emotions until everything is dead except your rage. You need to suppress that rage and keep your eyes on the prize which is the truth. This may be from someone that you know and trust, someone who is a good person and you may never suspect, people can do these acts of betrayal which may be completely out of character. That's what funny about the human race, on the one hand they are able to perform noble acts of charity and kindness, on the other hand, they are capable of the most underhanded forms of betrayal and evil. Son, I know I haven't been the best Father to you, but you are my son and I want you to be safe."

"I know Dad. I know" I say.

"Now. First things first, you need to find both BOUCHER or WINCHESTER to get this ball rolling and who may benefit from WINCHESTER's death. You need to figure out why these two names are involved in this and how they tie in with you."

I look up at my Dad and ask "And how am I supposed to find these guys? For all I know, it was one of these guys who was trying to screw me over here."

"True, but they wouldn't be working alone, they wouldn't have the knowledge of how you operate or who you even are for that matter. The person who did this knows you very well and knows your vulnerability. Finding out and talking to WINCHESTER or BOUCHER may get you some answers, or, get you killed."

"You know where I can find either of them?" I ask.

"No. But I know who will." My father reaches for his cigarettes, picks one up lights it and puts it in his mouth. "My name is still known and respected in the old neighbourhood. You want to find some answers, start on the street, talk to Python, he may be able to help you out, he knows the streets well and has connections everywhere. You need to look for a connection to the French gang scene. Not sure who's running the game now, but let me tell you son, you better ask for the right name because the wrong one may get your guts split open. These French gangbangers ain't no joke. There are ones you can get good information from and the ones that will cut your throat because they don't like the way you asked a question. Python may be able to at least point you in the right direction."

"Thanks. You know I just want to say I'm…"

My Dad cut me off before I could finish "…no need. Why don't you go upstairs and take a shower, wind down a little. You wanna stay for supper? It ain't much but you're more that welcome."

I deliberated on whether or not I wanted to stay. "Sure, that'd be great" I say as I get up and walk towards the stairs "I'm gonna take a shower and be right down."

As the warm water hits my naked body, all I can do is reflect on everything that is unfolding now. My Dad said not to trust anyone and I may have to stick to that. It hurts my heart to know that that means I can't trust Jimmy or Trina, or even Tony for that matter. Somebody out there wants to sewer me and I have to find out who and why. There seems to be no loyalty in this world anymore, we are stuck in a generation where loyalty is just a tattoo, love is just a quote and lying is the new truth. What does friendship mean now days anyway, are enemies more of our friends now? I'd rather my enemy's sword pierce my heart and die quickly, then my friend's dagger stab me in the back and die a slow agonizing death. My bitterness is slowly starting to stew inside me as I just think of someone close to me doing this and wanting me to go down hard. But I can't let the anger get the best of me, anger clouds the mind, turned inward it is an unconquerable enemy that can leave you with tunnel vision and not seeing the big picture. I get out of the shower and look at my phone, I need to call her but, I can't tell her too much.

The phone rings "Chris, where are you baby, are you okay?" Trina says sounding alarmed.

"Ya I'm fine Trina, just at my Dad's, gonna stay for dinner. You okay?" I ask.

"Me? I'm fine, what about you?" she asked.

I smirk and say "Been better."

There is a hesitation "Chris" her voice goes soft and disturbed "I saw on the news that a Senator was gunned down at the H.M.E hospital" another pause "said he has one bullet in the back of his head from a high powered rifle. Please tell me this wasn't you" she said weeping.

I lower the phone to my side and hang my head. I don't want to lie to her, but I can't say too much. I raise the phone up and say "Baby, you have to just trust me on this, I need to take care of some things before we leave town ok. I'm gonna get this thing figured out and then get hell out of this city. Please baby, if you love me, you'll trust me."

Trina is now crying "My God Chris, did you kill the Senator?"

"Trina, please, I will explain everything to you, but not now. Please baby, trust me. Know that I love you and want to be with you, but I need to take care of something first or I'm going to be looking over my shoulder for the rest of my life. You trust me?" I ask.

Hesitation, "Yes of course I do."

"Ok, know that I'll be all right and I will see you soon. I'll keep you update." Now I pause, "love you babe."

"I love you. Please whatever you are going to do, please be careful."

"I will" I say and push END without saying goodbye. I gaze in the mirror and tell myself "I'm gonna find you. Whoever you are BOUCHER and whoever you are working with, I will find you."

I get dressed and walk downstairs then into the kitchen where the table has been set. I sit down and my Father looks me up and down "See you helped yourself to some of my clothes" he says with a chuckle.

I look at the plain white shirt and ratty old jeans "Ya, hope you don't mind?"

"No no I don't mind, what's mine is yours." He is a very caring man, and one would think after years of being part of one of the most ruthless biker gangs in the world, that side of him may have vanished, but on the contrary, I think he is more compassionate than ever. He now places two large bowls down and sits, one with chicken, one with mashed potatoes, simple. "You visit Nate recently?" he asks.

"Saw him yesterday. He said he hasn't seen you in a while. He really needs us, don't know why you don't see him as often as you could."

"It's not that I don't love Nate, of course I do, he's my son. But it tears my heart out seeing him in that bed, so helpless, frail, malnourished, and exhausted. I know it's no excuse but it's troublesome to see my son that way. I mean I remember watching him play football, riding his bike, playing outside, now, he can't even stand on his own two feet and it just burrs a whole in my heart."

I bite a piece of chicken and say "I manage to visit him. I know what you mean, but avoiding it won't make it go away or make him any better. He needs us now more than ever, he needs his family."

My Dad looks at me almost stern "Don't Chris. Don't give me a lecture, I'll go visit him, just have to work up the nerve."

"Sounds like a cop out, he misses you. You two were close, closer than me and you, don't make him feel like he's got some infectious disease and you can't be near him."

My Dad takes a deep breath, looks at me and says "Nate is a fighter, he always has been, but this is a fight he can't win, I know that, you know that. It hurts knowing that any day I will get the call from the hospital telling me that my first born has passed. I lost your mother now I'm losing my first born, that ain't easy for any person to bear."

"I understand that, I really do, but it just sounds like you're just avoiding it and if you don't see it, it can't hurt you. I saw Nate yesterday and ya, it's brutal to see my big brother bound to a hospital bed and clinging to life, but it makes him feel better seeing us. I'm not going to tell you to visit him if you don't want to, but think about if you were Nate, lying in a hospital bed waiting to die all alone. He needs us now more than ever."

My Dad lowers his head "You're right, you're absolutely right, I'm a bad father."

"Fuck sake Dad, don't do this. If you were a bad father Nate wouldn't care if you came to see him or not. I don't know if I've ever said this to you, but you are a great father. We both have made some pretty dam stupid career choices, and I for one am glad that Mom isn't around to see what I have done with my life. But you never judged me or disowned me. You are a good father, I mean that."

"Thank you" he says. He then perks up and says, "Before I forget, I have to give you something" he says and gets up.

I smile and say "Now? I'm eating." He doesn't listen and keeps walking, so I get up and follow him. We walk into his make shift office consisting of an old beat up desk with a chair behind it and he reaches into his drawer and pulls out an exquisite old pine box. He opens it and I see a magnificent thin pocket retractable knife. I examine the knife and it says on the handle "1% 81 for life". The one percent is a patch most outlaw biker gangs have sown on their jackets, this is claimed to be a reference to a comment made by the American Motorcyclist Association (AMA) in which they stated that 99% of motorcyclists were law-abiding citizens, implying that the last one percent were outlaws. The 81 is simply the "H" being the eighth letter in the alphabet, and "A" the one being the first. My Dad picks up the knife and opens the blade, a stunning gold polished refined blade. "They gave me this as a gift, won't go into the details of why, but I was going to pass it down to Nate, I want you to have it Chris" he says as he passes me the knife.

I examine its elegance "It's absolutely stunning Dad."

"That's a 14 carat blade and sterling silver handle, thin as a piece of paper so nobody will know you have a blade on you" he says with pride.

"I can't take this Dad, this means a lot to you."

"Ah, I'm finished with that life style my boy. It's a great monument sure, but I ain't going be around forever so, thought it'd be a good time to officially pass this down to you. Has a special little clip here so you can tuck it under your sleeve without anyone knowing you have it" he says showing me the clip. "Now this button activates the record, the knife is also a voice recorder. We all use to carry these around on the basis of recording any interaction we have with the law. Hopefully you'll never need it, but, if you are going to go down this path Chris, it may get ugly. You know that right?"

I nod and say "ya, I know" My phone alerts me to a text message. I open it, it's from Tony. It reads HEY BRO, MEET ME AT THE END OF 21ST AND 119TH AT MIDNIGHT-ISH. WE'LL FIGURE THIS OUT MAN, WE'LL GET TO THE BOTTOM OF THIS. DON'T WANNA TALK, NEVER KNOW WHO'S LISTENING. SEE YA THERE. B4L.

B4L was brothers for life, something we stared saying when we were in High School. I text him back THANKS TONY. SEE YOU THERE.

My Dad asks "Who was that?"

I smile and say "Oh it's just Tony. Hoping he can help me out, maybe give me some answers, or at least buy me time so I can get my answers."

"Just be careful, remember what I said, don't trust anyone. That includes your girlfriend, Jimmy and even Tony. Who knows if this BOUCHER guy was working by himself or with someone that is close to you. DTA Chris, letters to live by" my Dad says almost as a lecture.

"I hope I can trust Tony, but yes I hear you Pops, I'll keep my guard up." I then turn my attention to the knife in my hand. "I'll cherish this Dad, and I'll be proud to give it to my kids, let them know who their Grandpa is" I retract the knife and say "I have to get going, I'm gonna head out and talk to Python.

"Ok" he says and hugs me "Take care of yourself boy, keep a level head and be safe." He lets me go and says "call me if you need help, I still have connections out there."

I smile and say "Will do Pops. Thanks, for everything"

"Go get'em and good luck" he says as I walk away.

I get into my car and start making my way to the old neighborhood, I have a few hours before I meet up with Tony. As I continue to drive, I notice a car that appears to have been following me for a while, a black tinted out car, not one I recognize. I test it out and make the first turn I see, I glance in the rear view, sure enough, it turned with me. I try to get a look at the driver but I'm not able to see. I make the next turn and look in my rear view, sure enough, he makes the turn as well. I don't think I'm being paranoid, I can't take any chances now more than ever, who knows if this is a conspiracy, set up, or what. One last test, I'll take this next turn and see if I'm being paranoid or not. I look in my rear and sure enough the car follows almost like a shadow mimicking every move I make. I then stop the car in a nearby alley, put the car in park as the black car pulls in behind me and stops. At this point I am not nervous or scarred, just ticked off, if this person wants a war, then today is a great day for my rage to be unleashed. I'm already having the worst day of my life, I don't need whoever this joker is to make it worse or try to do something he may regret. I get out of my vehicle ready for a possible confrontation with eager anticipation. I try to see who is in the car behind me but only see the silhouette of two figures. Finally, at the same time, both the passenger and driver door open, the driver is a colossal black man, shaggy beard and a tight black t-shirt. Nobody that I recognize, but he sure seems to mean business and looks ready for war. I look at the passenger and my heart almost stops, Alonzo VALENTINE aka Lil Alonzo. He's dressed in a typical black wife beater tank top with a gold necklace dangling around his neck. "Zo?" I ask. "What the heck are you doing here?" I figured me and him are cool, but this seems very unusual, why is he tailing me? What could he possibly want so bad, he has my number, why didn't he just call me? "DTA Chris" I whisper to myself.

"Chris Chris Chris. Good to see you" Alonzo says almost in a cynical way.

They both advance towards me almost like a lion moving in for a kill and I think to myself "this doesn't look friendly" I critically evaluate a possible threat, kind of like when Spider Man senses danger and he says *"my spidey sense is tingling".* I have to stay cool and calm as I left my pistol in the glove box. Luckily, I am a third degree black belt and I know these two chumps will have a death wish coming to them if they try anything stupid. Alonzo is a low life and he is definitely someone I wouldn't trust to babysit my dog.

"Chris, I heard something through the grape vine and I ain't too dam impressed" Alonzo says.

The big guy approaches me and stands in front of me with a look like he is ready to rip my head off and kick a field goal with it. I still remain composed and say "The grape vine eh? What exactly did you hear through the grape vine? And by the way, can you get your pet monkey here to stop looking at me like I'm a banana."

The big guy grins and stands his ground. Alonzo says "The other day, I got busted for some drugs in my car. Same place I operate every single Goddam day, never had any problem with the pigs coming around. Funny thing though, the other day I get busted selling my rock right after I spoke to you. Now how the fuck do you think that pig knew who I was, where I was, and what I was doing there? You think that is some dam coincidence?" he asks bellowing in my ear.

"How the fuck should I know Zo? What the heck does that have to do with me?" I ask. Now I kind of get what's going on, Zo must have figured out that I dimed him out to Tony. But how?

"Cause motherfucker!" he yells in my ear, then pulls out a switch blade and holds it under my chin "you dimed me out you no good rat snitch motherfucking sell out! Thing is about a rat, they are vial critters filled with disease and a plague on society, we don't need em, don't want em, so what do we do with em? We exterminate them, you hear me cuz? You need to be eradicated Chris, and I'm the exterminator."

I calmly say "Zo, I have no idea what you're talking about, but get that bloody knife out of my face!"

"Lucky for you white boy, the cop made a nice deal and I didn't go down for it. Seemed he liked my charming smile and unthreatening like demeanour. Now I'm gonna cut yo ass up into a million fucking pieces and feed you to my dogs!" he says and he seems like he is about to jab the knife through my jaw.

I swiftly grab his arm with the knife, make a closed fist with my other hand and drive it as violently as possible into Alonzo's face knocking the knife loose and sending Alonzo to the pavement with a thud. The big guy looks at Alonzo then looks at me and scowls like he was about to feed on me. He lunges at me and I fearlessly don't back down and stand my ground. He takes a mighty swing which I duck then counter it with a booming punch to his kidney, elbow to the stomach, then deliver an explosive upper cut elbow connecting right under his chin knocking him back as he tumbles to the ground like a ton of bricks. I see Alonzo trying to get up with blood all around his mouth, so I quickly deliver a swift kick right to his chest jolting him back down again. I look over at the big guy who gets up and pulls a pair of brass knuckles from his back pocket. I see him quickly trying to put them on with bad intentions in his eyes, so as he's getting up I deliver a thundering punch directly into his face knocking him out cold as blood flies through the air. I see Alonzo moving towards his car in pain and he's now sitting against his tire bleeding from his mouth. I look and see the knife on the ground, pick it up then march towards him with it.

"Look dipshit" I say to Alonzo as I kneel in front of him "I don't know who the fuck is feeding you this shit about me diming you out or being a snitch, but it ain't true. You call me that again or come near me, I'll drive this fucking knife through your dam heart so hard it'll pop out the other side of you" I say with rage. I calm down a bit and collect my thought "Just out of curiosity, who's been feeding you this crap about me?" I ask looking into his eyes.

Alonzo doesn't look at me and says "Fuck you, I ain't telling you, cause I ain't a motherfucking snitch like you. Think I'm just going to roll over on someone, think again. Snitches always get what's coming to them, one way or another, a rat will always get killed by the strict nine, and I will make you drink that poison one way or another you can guarantee that snitch!"

I get infuriated now "I told you" I say as I raise the knife up like a scene in Psycho ready to stab his victim. I bring the knife down in a stabbing thrust past his head and right into the tire as I hear the air leak from it. "Don't call me a snitch again." I get up and see Alonzo had turned his head in fear of me actually stabbing him. I look at him, leave the knife in the tire and walk away.

I get into my car and hastily drive away not looking back as I have no need to. "What the hell was that all about" I ask myself. Something is really starting to stink now, who would rat me out to Alonzo and why? Sounds weird but I really don't like hurting people, but sometimes you have to be a ruthless person to save yourself, and it takes a little chunk out of your soul but you do it anyway, my soul can heal, my life can't. I have been double crossed by somebody, and this somebody wants me out of the picture. Is this a coincident that Alonzo finds out I'm a snitch the same day I have been set up in killing a US Senator? I really think not. I can't trust anybody, anyone could have done this and my trust is wearing thin on people. Trust is kind of like and eraser, it always seems to fade away and get smaller over time. No matter who this person is, whether it is a friend, and family member, or a loved one, there is four things in this world you cannot recover from, a stone after it has been thrown, a word after it is said, time after it is gone, and trust after it is lost. I have trusted somebody with my life, and they have now used it against me, and for that, there will be no forgiveness.

Put no trust in a neighbor; have no confidence in a friend; guard the doors of your mouth from her who lies in your arms; for the son treats the father with contempt, the daughter rises up against her mother, the daughter-in-law against her mother-in-law; a man's enemies are the men of his own house. Micha 7:5-6.

CHAPTER IX

STREETS WITH ANSWERS

I drive into the industrial sort of area on the South East side, that's where a gang known as the LA Justice hang. They are relatively small time mostly sticking to things like drug dealing, laundering, extortion, and petty armed robbery. Back in the early 90's, LA Justice used to be a sister club to the Hells Angels, which basically means they worked and operated under them. It was a good deal for both gangs, the small time LA Justice gang got to do some big time work for the H.A, grunt work like collecting debts, checking in on the clubs the H.A owned, and sometimes even laying a licking on someone who needed it avoiding any H.A getting blood on their hands. It wasn't the glamorous gang stuff by no means but it gained them notoriety and power. For the H.A, well they got cheap labor from them and best of all, they never got their hands dirty or full of blood. LA Justice though became greedy and gluttonous, demanding a bigger piece of the pie, more of the profits and more of the power so their reputation could grow as well. Lucky for them they didn't try to take all that from the H.A by force or else, or well let's face it, they'd all be swimming with the fishes with their heads cut off. Instead the H.A told the LA Justice to hit the bricks and get out of North LA and the West coast, and as a parting gift they put a bullet in the head of the LA Justice's leader. They weren't stupid enough to dare to fight back so they high tailed it out of there and gained control a very small part of the South East district. Their new leader is now a guy named Ty "PYTHON" McDowell. He got that name because he is notorious for killing people with his bare hands, putting his hands around their neck and literally squeezing the life out of them, sort of like a python hence the name. I met Ty a while back and we have become good acquaintances, little does he know I have used a lot of the information he tells me against him by feeding it to Tony. Tony made over a dozen arrests on the LA Justice gang from my information, mainly small busts like a money laundering charge, two armed robbery charges, a few possession of hand gun charges and a whole lot of drug related charges. Not only that, one of my very first contracts was on an LA Justice striker named Bale "PUPPY" JHINOWSKY which was put out by the Hells Angels. Apparently Bale was pushing his weight around all over the place, intimidation, beatings, and even killed a dude. He was trying to make a name for not only the LA Justice gang, but for himself as well. Bale crossed the line a few times when he beat the shit out of some bouncers at a night club owned by the H.A, so in response, the H.A sent two of their own strikers to go and mess him up a bit and teach him a lesson. Unfortunately, that back fired as Bale put both of the H.A strikers in the hospital, one with a shattered orbital bone and crushed larynx, and the other with server brain trauma. Neither of the badly hurt H.A strikers wanted to say anything to the cops, that was kind of an unwritten rule and they knew that eventually Bale would have pain and death coming to him anyway, just a matter of time. The H.A knew if they were to take Bale out themselves, the cops would be all over them as the obvious suspects, plus the cops would now tightened up the surveillance on the H.A anticipating a retaliation. So, Jimmy gets the call from one of the H.A's top dogs to take Bale out and paid us $375,000 for it. It was one of the very few times in my career that I ever did a close kill, meaning I didn't snipe the guy from a distance. Close kills are always precarious for numerous reasons, the obvious one is that there is a huge potential of someone seeing you either interact with the target, or notice you walking away from the target which you don't want. The other thing is that without realizing it, you may leave something near the crime scene of vital importance, a footprint, a hair, piece of clothing who knows. If you are at a distance, none of those factors come into play, the risk is dramatically lower and the chance of anything leading back to you as the shooter is zero. But after following Bale for over a week, he never had any real patterns so I had no idea where to take him out at. He did have one small ritual which I never understood. Late at night he'd always go to the beach and just gaze at the ocean, not sure if there was some significance behind that or if it was simply a way for him to unwind and be alone. That being said, there was absolutely no place near a beach for me to set up a decent sniper shot so I had no choice but to do a close kill. The night that the hit was going to take place or D-Day, I packed two pistols up and equipped them with a silencer each. Ironic thing was, I bought the silencers from Ty just a few weeks before the hit. I arrived at the beach that night, it was almost pitch black except for the glow of the moon that hit the ocean and produced an almost hypnotic reflection with the air being so peaceful and warm. The beach was completely empty except for a beast named Bale who was just sitting near the shore line like a kindergarten child in awe of the magnificent specimen before him known as the ocean. It was a perfect setting, dark, quiet, isolated, and the sand combined with the splashes of the waves onto the shore made it very easy to sneak up on him. As I silently crept up on this monster, I drew my guns out and was ready, if he turned around, I'd be poised to unload a few rounds in him. This was only my third contract and was my first close kill so to say the least, I was a bit nervous and my heart was racing. I came within a few feet of Bale anticipating that at any second he could turn around and I'd have to react quickly. I should have just stopped, drew my pistols right there and put two in the back of his skull before he even had the chance to turn around. I'm not sure why, but I kept inching closer and I got so close to him I could reach out and touch him, and being that close is tremendously risky, my reaction time at that distance is diminished dramatically. All he'd have to do was stand up quickly and knock me over and the fight would be on. Surely he must have heard me though, why was he not turning around? Did he know I was there? I looked closer and saw my answer, he had a pair of earphones in his ears and seemed to be grooving to some tunes. I put my guns both to the back of his head without touching him and just glare, surely it can't be this easy right? Well I had spoken to soon, he quickly turned around and stood up. I was almost frozen in a panic as he glanced at me with first with perplexity, then after seeing two pistols in my hand, his expression turned to rage. I stepped back and swiftly drew both pistols at his chest and began pulling the triggers. Round after round pierced his chest with small explosions of blood as he sluggishly moved backwards in agony. As he moved back I advanced forward continuing to pepper him with bullets not being able to stop myself due to the adrenaline rush. Finally he plummeted to the ground and both pistols were empty as the guns went into lock back. Bale's bloody body hit the shallow water while his legs remained on the shore. The moonlight illuminated the water where Bale laid as his bloodied corpse turned the water an instant crimson colour. I gawked at Bale and it was the most eerie sight I had ever seen, his face covered by the wine colored water was looking up at me with his eyes still wide open. I knew the brain could function ten minutes after the heart stops beating and I couldn't help but wonder if he could comprehend what had just happened to him and if he could see me staring down at his lifeless bloody body. I took one last look at my work and left in hurried back to my car. Lucky for me the beach would soon be filled with people so my footprints will be vanished and the tide will wash out anything including my footprints that potentially were left near the body.

As I now drive deeper and deeper into the area I scan around looking for Ty. I haven't spoken to him in a few months and I am just hoping that I am still welcome in his hood. One thing about any gang, they are extremely territorial, if you step into their part unannounced or uninvited, they'll take you for a potential threat and may just shoot first and ask questions later. That being said, I put my pistols into my inside jacket pocket to be sure of my safety and I realize the risk that I'm taking right now. I stop the car for a moment and roll down my window and think, I wasn't exactly sure where to go, usually Ty hangs out around here and I usually always tell him when I'm on my way to see him. Ty of course has no clue that I'm a contract killer, he just figures I'm some rich delivery boy for the Hells Angels. As I sit, I reach for my phone as I figured I should call Ty and let him know I'm here, but just as I'm dialing I feel cold steel to my head.

"Out of the fucking car. Now!" A demanding voice says.

I put my hands up and observe the gun pointed at my head held by some white guy wearing a green bandana over his mouth. I say nothing, just put my phone down and calmly step out of the car keeping my hands raised. As I creep out of the car I see another guy on the other side of my car with a gun pointed at me also sporting a green bandana over his mouth.

The guy with the gun to my head says "You gotta be lost fool, driving your fancy car up in here, this is LA Justice turf asshole, why are you fucking here!"

I coolly say "I ain't lost, I am a friend of Ty's."

"Bullshit" the thug says shoving the pistol into my head.

"Smoke his ass!" the other guy barks.

"Look..." I begin to say, and as quick as lightning I snatch the guys' gun from his hands and spin around back of him and now have the gun to his head confronting the other guy. I use the thug as a shield as I position myself behind him holding the gun to his head. "Chill out man or I'll put one in his head!" I say to the other guy pointing the gun at me. Just then I hear footsteps approaching from the right of me and out pops another guy with a green bandana over his mouth and he appears to be unarmed. I quickly take my other arm and draw a gun from my jacket and instantly point it at this other guy "Not one step closer home boy!" I yell. I have the one gun pointed a buddy's head in front of me and the other pointed at this thug to my right all while having a gun pointed at me by some thug in front of me. I quickly scan back and forth to my right and in front again not knowing exactly what my next move will be. My hands were starting to perspire, my heart was pumping faster, seconds felt like minutes as were all locked in a game of deadly chicken wondering who will make the first move. My trigger finger is itching just waiting for one of these guys to try something cute.

I was so fixated on all three guys that I never heard the person behind slink up on me. Next thing I feel is the cold metal of a gun barrel jammed right into the back of my skull with a voice saying "Drop the fucking guns now or you won't have a head!"

I close my eyes knowing I have no choice and drop each gun. The guy I was holding quickly moves away from me picks up my guns and points them at me. Now I have four guns pointed at me by these masked thugs, I'm pretty much fucked as I gradually raise my hands up.

The voice behind me angrily says "You have a lot of balls coming into my turf and pointing a gun at my guys. Give me one reason why I shouldn't pull this trigger and watch your brains splatter all over the pavement!"

Just then I clued in, I recognized the voice and say "Ty?"

He spins me around and looks at me, then smiles and says "Jesus Christ Chris" and gives me a hug. "Drop your guns guys, he's with me" he orders as all the thugs lower their weapons. "What the hell are you doing here man?" he asks.

"Need your help bro" I say in an alleviated voice.

"Sure man, come on in" he says, puts his arm around me then walks me into a building. He turns to one of the thugs and says "Don't let anyone breath on that black Porsche outside you hear me?"

I walk in and see a few guys all sitting around on a couch sporting green bandanas around their necks. I wasn't fully sure if I could trust Ty or not so I kept on guard.

Ty has been in the LA Justice gang for over ten years and became the main guy or leader over five years ago on account of his many connections with bigger more powerful gangs, mafia leaders, and some wealthy businessmen. Ty has a very violent and sometimes uncontrollable temper and can snap on a dime. When I first met Ty around five years ago, he had just been released from prison after doing four years for a man slaughter charge. Story was that some wanna be thug was going around sporting a green bandana claiming to be part of the LA Justice gang to try to get respect from people. Well, they sent Bale out looking for this dude to teach him a very painful lesson, but it so happens, Ty spotted the guy one night exiting a nightclub wearing the green bandana. Ty apparently took off his own green bandana and approached the dude casually in the alley. Ty confronted this guy and apparently beat him half to death leaving his face in a mangled battered bloody mess with facial fractures and lacerations all over. He wrapped his hands around the guys' neck, squeezed the life out of him and left him for dead.

Unbeknown to Ty, the guy actually lived and was eventually found a few hours later clinging to life practically suffocating on his own blood and suffering from a shattered trachea as a result of Ty trying to choke the last breath out of him. His face was almost beyond repair and he later died from massive brain trauma a few hours after being transported to the hospital. After hearing the news, Ty then took a knife and slashed himself once on the arm knowing the police would be knocking at his door at any moment. Police located Ty a few days later and arrested him as the prime suspect in the guys' death. The dead guy had Ty's DNA all over him and they discovered Ty's clothes with blood covered all over it in an alley trash bin nearby. LA Justice paid two random people ten large each to act as independent witnesses at the trial claiming that they saw the entire thing and the guy pulled out a knife threatening to kill Ty, so Ty was acting strictly in self defense and was lucky to be alive as the guy had already slashed Ty once in the arm with the blade and Ty had the scar to prove it. Well the judge bought the story and convicted Ty of aggravated man slaughter rather than murder and was sentenced to eight years in jail, but was released in half that time. Ty had respect from every LA Justice gang member when he got out, he made huge connections while in jail and since the Hells Angels put a bullet in their previous leader a few months before, Ty was the obvious next chosen leader.

I saunter past a few of the LA Justice members, they all look at me with judgemental eyes like a stranger who had just invaded their turf. "Boys, this is Chris, some ya'll may remember him, for those who don't, he is cool ok?" Ty announces to the group.

I recognize one of the guys as Tats. He got that name on account he pretty much has ink covering every inch of his body including his face. He stands up and shakes my hand "Hey Chris I remember you" he says in a welcoming voice holding an intimidating looking knife in his hand.

"Hey Tats, how are you? Did you get some ink work done or something?" I ask in a joking way.

He smiles and says "Got no more real estate for anymore ink man, I have to move on to piercings now."

Tats is a knife guy and is really good with his blades. As far I as know, he didn't believe in guns, he thought that was the coward way to kill a man. He was notorious for mutilating his enemies by carving messages onto them, kind of a way to remind them of the encounter. He carved JUSTICE SERVED across a rival gang member's stomach, TRAITOR across a snitches forehead and the letters LAJ on the cheek of dead beat customer who owed them money. These scars reminded those guys that they fucked with the wrong gang and the wrong person. Tats sported small throwing daggers all around his belt, two bigger blades in shoulder sheaths, and one Rambo size knife in his hand he called Wilma and knew how to use them all quite well.

Ty reaches into the fridge and grabs a beer "You gotta forgive my boys out there, they don't know you and hey let's face it, nice ride like that coming through here at this time of night, chances are he ain't coming to say hello."

"Sorry man, I was just about to call you when Clint Eastwood out there jammed some steal in my face" I say in good spirit.

Ty was an intimidating looking dude, he was at least six foot six and had a tattoo of a python wrapped around his entire neck and throat. He wore his green bandana on his head so that he wouldn't cover up his infamous python tattoo, was built like a football player and spoke rather intellectually. The green bandanas were simply a way for the fellow LA Justice members to recognize one another, so if a non-LA Justice person decides to be cute and wear a green bandana, let's just say he will meet an agonizing violent gory death or a severe beating.

I look around and say sarcastically, "Like what you've done to the place."

It was an old abandon factory with just a few couches in it, a television, a fridge, pool table, and a few tables and chairs. It had a pungent dank dusty stench to it with a rustic look to the walls, no carpet or hardwood floors, just cold cement.

"Shoot some stick?" Ty asks as he hands me a pool cue.

I grab the stick and say "Sure why not."

"Rack'em up, I'll break" Ty mutters. I rack up the balls and Ty cracks the beer open then slumps over and breaks. He watches the pool balls scatter and asks "So what brings you by? Hey do you want a beer?"

I put my hand up and say "No, thanks I'm fine. Just need some answers, hopefully you can help." Ty takes a sip of beer and nods. I scan the table and make a shot "I'm trying to find a guy named Pierre Q Boucher, former or current French gang member."

Ty starts to think and Tats jumps in "I've heard that name before. I think he rolled with the Tueurs Cartel."

I look at Tats with relief and say "Yes that's him, do you know him?"

Tats shakes his head as he walks over "Don't know him, just have heard the name somewhere before that's all."

"Where can I find the Tueurs Cartel?" I ask Tats.

"Pretty sure they don't exist anymore. Heck, half the French gangs in LA don't exist anymore man. Hells Angels, Bloods, Crips, and Black Dragons drove them all out on the account that they were trying to get greedy and run the entire State" Tats explains.

"You looking for a French gang member?" Ty states "Shit, there is only one dude you need to speak to, Tiger St. PIERRE" then takes another shot.

I look at Ty now and say "Ya, I've heard of him before."

Ty continues lining up another shot "Tiger is pretty much the main dude in the French gangs around LA what little of them there is. I mean the French gang scene has died off significantly and isn't what it used to be, but there is a few still around and Tiger runs them all. You looking for this BOUCHER guy? Tiger will know where he is."

"Where do I find Tiger anyway?" I inquire.

"He owns the French Kiss strip club on 104th, but be careful, he is a sadistic malicious dude and will bleed you if he doesn't like you. Tiger may be small time right now, but he is still well respected, well –armed and plenty violent" Tats says grabbing a beer from the fridge.

"You hear about that Senator being wacked today?" I asked looking at Tats and Ty while I make a shot.

"Been all over the news man, he got his brains blown out" Tats says.

"Fucked up dude" Ty says while he takes a shot and misses "Shit!"

I look at both Tats and Ty and ask "Who would have done that?" hoping they may have some kind of an idea.

"No clue man, but that is seriously messed up man" Ty says sipping his beer. "Never understood why people kill the President or politicians you know? I mean sure we've all thought about it, but really, what benefit does anyone get out of it? Makes no sense. You ask me, that dude died over something personal. You see, people need a reason to take out a public figure like that. Take the dude who shot JFK, Oswald, he wanted to make a name for himself and had an urge to find a place in history, and despair at times over failures in his various undertakings. Also he had an avowed commitment to Marxism and communism so he was some Commie or something. Or how bout what's his name, Hinckley who tried to shoot Reagan. I mean he was a whacko, and was so influenced by Robert De Niro's character in that movie... uh"

"Taxi Driver!" Tats shouts.

"Taxi Driver ya. Anyway, Hinckley said that that was his motivation to try to kill Reagan. De Niro's character attempts to assassinate a United States Senator who is running for president in that movie, so Hinckley felt such a strong connection with De Niro's character he decided to follow suit. And of course Ray who killed Martin Luther King confessed he was forced to do it because of a huge government conspiracy. There's always going to be some reason" Ty says scanning the table looking for his next move.

I looked at Ty with amazement and a smirk and asked him "How the hell did you know all of that stuff man? Half that shit I didn't even know."

He smiles and says "I read books man" and fires off a thunderous cue strike.

I laugh thinking he's joking "Fuck off really?"

"It's true" Tats says "It's creepy in a way."

"Why you so interested in this dead Senator anyway? You think this Boucher did it?" Ty asks looking at me now leaning on his cue stick.

"No, that's not why I need to find this Boucher dude, and no I could give two shits about that dead Senator, just making small talk" I said trying to avoid them asking any more questions about this.

"Let me tell you one thing, if you are going to kill a person like BOULDERDASH it's for a purpose. Someone either wanted to make a serious statement or could have framed someone to shoot a target that they weren't intending to kill" Ty says leaning on his cue stick. "I remember way back in the day, someone paid one of our hitmen to take out what was supposed to be some low life snitching thug. Well, after our hitmen took this so-called nobody out, we later found out it was actually a brother of a Mexican mafia Don. See, one of our rival gangs set up the hit posing as some former thug who stated that this guy snitched on him a few years ago and ended up costing him a dime in the slammer and now wanted him taken out which we gladly accepted. Once we found out who exactly it was we killed, well, LA justice became public enemy number one to the Mexican mafia and they publically slaughtered the hitman along with two other random Justice members. Let me tell ya man, taking out a big time player or public figure is a good way to frame someone and get them into a lot of hot water."

I thought for a moment and pondered that logic which made a lot of sense. "That's really interesting, something to think about, maybe this BOUCHER had a vendetta or something and used someone to do his dirty work."

"No idea man, why do you need to find this Boucher dude so bad anyway? Your Pops gonna whack him or something?" Ty asked. He still thinks my Dad rolls with the Hells Angels which is fine with me, keeps me safe and protected.

I shoot my shot and unfortunately sink the 8-ball. "Ya something like that" I put the cue stick on the table "Look I have to get out of here, I have to go talk to this Tiger guy, hopefully he can help me out and point me in the direction that I'm looking to go."

Ty walks up to me and looks at me in the eyes "You got bad intentions in those eyes homey. You know what they say, hell is paved with bad intentions."

I correct him "Paved with good intentions."

Ty chuckles and says "Well, I ain't never heard of anyone going to hell because they had good intentions."

I look at him with intensity and say "The intentions aren't what's important, the outcome is the only thing that matters."

"True that" Ty responds with a nod. "I can see that you are going to be heading out of here on a mission and hey, that's your business cuz, but be careful out there man, you get in too deep you may end up drowning. People get tunnel vision and forget that there in a whole nother world around them filled with danger and malevolence."

"Ya I know that all too well bro. I just got some things to figure out, it ain't gonna be easy."

"You have to solve a puzzle ya? Thing is man, you need to start off with the tiny pieces, see where they fit first. One piece will lead to another piece and eventually you're puzzle will slowly start to reveal itself. Problem is with most people is they try to get the big pieces first and ignore the little pieces thinking that they are insignificant and want the puzzle solved quickly instead of methodically. Take it from me and my experience, you try to dive right in to a puzzle head first, you may crack your skull on the bottom. Key is to gently ease into the water and slowly figure out how deep you need to go."

"Thick headed people usually end up with a bullet hole between their eyes because they don't pay attention to everything around them. Keep that in mind bro" Tats says.

"Thanks guys, maybe I was going after this a little bit too much like Rambo, maybe I need to go after this like Matlock instead. Or a combination of both" I say.

"Later Chris, you gonna need any heat or what? If you have bad intentions on your mind, you best be arming yourself accordingly. Got some nice armory in the back" Tats asks.

"No guys, I'm good. Stay out of trouble huh" I say as I leave the building. I see a guy with a green bandana next to my car as I walk up to it, he has a gun in either hand by his side. "What the hell is this?" I mutter to myself. I slowly walk up to my car and he moves out of my way and hands me the gun.

"Don't forget your guns" he says.

I smile in relief and take the guns from him "Thanks" I say. He nods and I get into my car and drive away.

Well I have got a little closer now, I'm hoping this Tiger guy can give me some answers or else I am back to square one. Hopefully Tony will have some answers for me too and I can put this puzzle together and figure this out.

CHAPTER X

TIGER ST. PIERRE

On my way now to look for Tiger St. PIERRE, hopefully he has some answers for me because I sure do need some. I don't know Tiger personally of course, but I do know of him. Here is how he became into power in the LA East side; The CAVALIER brothers in the early 90's controlled the prostitution and drug trades in the lower east side of LA and were considered to be Godfathers of French gang members before their assassinations in the mid-90s. After the CAVALIER's fell, prostitution and drugs had been gradually deserted by the major criminal areas of the lower east side of LA and then became poor suburbs with drug trafficking, robberies and homicides. Since the 1990s, many gangsters from the poor neighbourhoods were prominent in the French gang underworld. St. PIERRE on the other hand came from a very wealthy background and slowly became the leader of a new French gang revolution and began recruiting all local and even foreign French gang members to his side with the promise of wealth and prosperity. With PIERRE being the money man, he also had total control of all the gang members, they all followed him with loyalty and eventually adopted the name of The Impitoyables or *the ruthless gang*, and thus their rise began. PIERRE then brought in weapons and with that came intimidation and violence leading them to power in the Eastern Los Angeles area and with their ever growing army of armed gangsters. The Impitoyables became the main gang in the eastern part of LA., even the Bloods and Crips knew enough to stay out of East LA as it later adopted the name Tiger Town. In the early 2000's, PIERRE began importing cocaine and weapons to the west coast LA and the entire State for that matter. The Impitoyables began owning Casinos, strip clubs and bars in the lower East side and became so powerful even the cops wouldn't touch them. PIERRE also had a lot of the LAPD on his payroll which is why PIERRE was able to operate his drug sales, import and sell weapons, as well as launder money in the back rooms of all of his businesses. All of the other French gangs or French connected gangs basically worked under PIERRE and were in a way, satellite gangs of the Impitoyables. Then came the infamous battle with Simone PELETIER's French Devil Zombies, a south central French gang which were heavily armed and decided to challenge St. PIERRE for his power in hopes to overthrow him and become the main power gang of LA. The French Devil Zombies were a small French gang operating in the southern part of LA but they decided to try to make a stand and attempt to take over the East side from the Impitoyables and gain the power and the respect from St. PIERRE. It was a battle that was fought in an old abandon junk yard for nearly two straight days leaving over seventy gang members from each side dead on the grounds and over one hundred members severely injured and bloody. Cops later discovered the gruesome aftermath of the battle which left the junk yard blood soaked with slaughtered decaying corpses everywhere. Both PELETIER and PIERRE survived the brutal gang war and decided to shake hands so to speak and part ways as respectful enemies. Both gangs suffered catastrophic loses and the Impitoyable gang were never the same. In 2005 the LAPD arrested over twenty Impitoyables who were caught trying to smuggle a boat load of semi-automatic guns from Nigeria and tried to get those members to flip on PIERRE so that they could finally bring him down, but none of the Impitoyables took the bait and all kept their mouths closed and served a range of twenty five to life in prison. PIERRE lost several of his businesses and mafia gang ties as well as the LAPD members that he had on his payroll. He still operates in East LA and is still a well-respected gang leader, but he has given way to the larger LA gangs like, the Bloods, Crips, Hells Angels, Sinaloa Cartel and others. If anyone had information about BOUCHER and WINCHESTER, The Tiger would.

I approach the east side neighbourhood where PIERRE and his crew hang. It is definitely a poor low income area that's for sure. For those who don't understand the poor part of LA or how they role, let me break it down for you. In the lower income area or "the projects", have their own rules that everyone knows, follows, and respects. Police don't normally ever come around here unless shit is really hitting the fan, basically these people police their own. Aspects of how people behave in the neighbourhood is termed functional characteristics, example of that would be the extent to which neighbourhood residents behave in an uncivil threatening manner and tolerate or engage in unlawful behaviour, this is the social disorder. Not everyone here engages in a specific disordered behaviour so to speak, but everyone here knows the pecking order and who is above them, and who is below them. People here survive and are some of the most resilient people on earth. I say the word survive because sometimes it is just that, you need to sometimes just survive this place, not just live in it. Shootings, robberies, assaults, and thefts are just a part of this neighbourhood, you live with that and hope that you aren't a victim in the crossfire or a target. Kids out on the street till all hours of the night, they either don't have a home to go back to, have no reason to go home, or are trying to make money by being some drug dealers middle man. The kids grow up fast here, they have to or this place will eat them up, spit them out and flush them away. Twelve year old kids robbing liquor stores, eight year olds bringing drugs to buyers on behalf of their suppliers, prostitutes as young as thirteen on the street making their money to support themselves or even their baby boy or girl. PIERRE still runs most of this area and is still the kingpin. Even though his area is quite smaller than before, he is still a player who is well respected. I drive through and people stop a stare at the white boy driving a fancy car through their hood. The population breaks down as 60% blacks, 25% Mexicans, 10% white, and 5% other, but even though the French is only a small percentage of the population, they are all well respected and still feared, they have the weapons and can bring the violence.

I leisurely pull up to the French Kiss strip club and hope that Tiger is inside. Not sure how safe my car will be parked in this neighbourhood, but that is the least of my worries. I grab my two pistols and tuck one in the back of my pants, and the other inside my jacket. Never know, I just may not be welcome here either. I walk up to the bouncer outside, big huge massive white dude with a Mohawk looking like he's coming right off the set of a Mad Max. "Ten dollar cover man" he says to me almost trying to intimidate me.

I reach in my jacket pocket and pull out a $100 bill and hand it to him "Keep it, just tell me if Tiger is here and where I can find him."

The bouncer takes the bill and looks at me. "Ya he's here. You have business with him or something?"

"Ya, something like that" I answer. "Another 100 dollar bill if my car is still here when I come back out."

"Ask the bartender, he'll know where Tiger is at."

"Thanks" I say as I walk in. I look around, not too many people, but to my surprise, it was a really elegant tasteful looking place, neon everywhere and had a sort of classy vibe to it. The music was pumping and those who were in the club seemed to be having a good time. I walk up to the bar and see two bigger guys in suits at either end which were possibly bouncers or Tiger's thugs. They were wearing black suits, buzz cuts and looked like they don't mess around.

The bartender leans in and asks me "What can I get for you?"

I lean forward and respond "Information. I'm looking for Tiger."

The bartender leans back, looks at the two guys on either side of the bar and nods to them. They both approach me from either side in a confrontational manner. One of them says to me in a French accent "You wish to speak to Tiger huh?"

I look at him and respectfully say "Yes I do, you know where he is?"

"What's your business here man?" the other guy asks in a challenging French voice.

"Just looking for some answers that's all. Thinking Tiger may help me out, I got no beef with him or anything like that."

I could feel them both eyeballing and scrutinizing me trying to figure me out. "Does he know you?"

I put my head down almost in vexation "No, he doesn't know me alright. I just want to throw a dart at him and see if it'll stick okay, that's it" I look at both of them and they are looking at me with blank cold glares.

One guy looks at the other guys and says in a deep daunting voice "Follow me."

I follow behind him as the one follows behind me. We walk into the back of the club and into a magnificent looking office with a massive fish tank covering the back wall and a man in a chair sitting behind his huge oak desk. The one gentleman says to me "Stay here" and walks up to the man sitting down who I assume is Tiger. Tiger was dressed in an all-white suit, buzz cut hair and a pair of tinted glasses on his face. The one man leans and whispers in Tigers' ear as Tiger looks at me then says in a thick French accent "You looking for me ya?"

I look at him and say "If you're Tiger then yes." I couldn't help looking at a very nasty looking scar on the left side of his face near his left eye. Looks like a bullet wound or maybe a knife wound.

He scans me up and down trying to determine what to make of me. "Check him" he says to the man behind me.

I start to worry a bit, if he pats me down and finds the guns, this could get ugly and bloody real quick. These are the type of people who shoot first and ask questions later. The man starts to pat me down starting at my leg then working up. He then feels my gun from my back and roars "Fucker has a gun!"

Just then the other man beside Tiger pulls out a gun and aims it at me as I pull out my gun from my jacket and aim it at him. The other man behind me steps back and points his gun at my head. "Hold on!" I scream. "I'm not here for trouble" as I now glance at Tiger who didn't move a muscle throughout and seemed as tranquil as a rock. I was nervous now as I was out numbered and out gunned with no way out of this. I then drop the clip from my gun and cock the slide back disarming it then putting it gently on his desk. I raise my hands up slowly and calmly say to Tiger "My Dad is Big Daddy SLAUGHTER, former Hells Angels of LA, you may know him. I was also given your name by Python who said you were a well-respected man which is why I of course did not come here to start any trouble with you" I say hoping that he may recognize the name.

Tiger gives me a serious look, and then smiles "Big Daddy, yes. Former striker for the Hells Angels ya? I've heard of him before. I really hope you know what you are doing by dropping his name my friend. How do you know him?"

I say "Because I'm his son Chris. Look sir, I'm just here to hopefully get some information from you. I'm in a lot of shit right now and hoping you can provide me with answers to help me figure this out." I pause and look at him. "Please Tiger, I ain't here for any trouble you gotta trust me."

He stares at me for what seemed to be an eternity. I know that any moment he can instruct his two goons to blow my head off, wrap me up in plastic, and then toss me into the east river. He finally says "Lower your weapons." Both of the thugs lower their weapons as I assume Tiger now does not see me as a threat. "You're father, I have heard of him, never had any beef with the Hells Angels, they are well respected in LA. And Python, he's a good guy, runs his gang well and keeps to his own little section."

He then looks me up and down "So, Chris is it?" he asks. I simply nod my head to him and he says "What kind of information do you require from me, son of Big Daddy?"

"You hear about the shooting of the US Senator earlier?" I ask.

"Don't really keep up on the news so enlighten me."

"Someone set me up to do a hit on him saying that he was a former gang member named Henry WINCHESTER who rolled with the 1A1 French Connection back in the 90's. The contract was ordered by a man named Pierre Q BOUCHER another former French gang member. Story was that WINCHESTER killed BOUCHER's son back in the day and got off virtually scott free in court due to lack of evidence, charter issues and some bribes. So, BOUCHER put the hit on WINCHESTER, got my name from a guy named PELLITIER and gave me the contract to do it. But, this BOUCHER fed me the wrong information for some reason, instead of it being WINCHESTER that I shot, it was a US Senator named BOULDERDASH." I look at Tiger who seems to be listening to every word I'm saying so I continue "I'm just trying to determine why this BOUCHER guy would do this? If he wanted BOULDERDASH executed, why not just ask it rather than make up some story about his dam son being killed by this WINCHESTER guy?" I realize that I'm putting my neck and my life on the line by telling him that I did a hit, but I'm desperate for some quick answers.

Tiger leans back and taps on the glass to his fish tank and says "Piranhas. Aren't they beautiful? If I was to submerge your body in this tank, after ten minutes the only thing that would be left would be your skeleton and the hair on your head, they don't eat the hair. I find that absolutely fascinating."

I wasn't sure if he was threatening me with that statement or just giving me a biology lesson, I remained silent.

"So" he says as he spins around and looks at me with a blank cold look on his face "you want me to figure out how all the pieces fit and solve your little puzzle huh?"

"No" I said. "I mean, I just want to talk to this BOUCHER guy and ask him why the fuck he set me up like that, and who was behind it and maybe figure out this mess that I'm in. I think he was working somebody that I know and trust but I can't put the pieces together. Why would someone do this to me? What do they gain from this? This dam mystery makes no sense to me at all, there is no logical explanation to this."

Tiger then grabs a cigar, clips it, puts it in his mouth and lights it. He then says "There's always an explanation to everything in this world, and it's usually a pretty straightforward one." He takes a puff of his cigar and leans in his chair "You ever hear the story of the Flying Dutchman ship?"

I shake my head.

Tiger continues the story "The legend of the Flying Dutchman started back in the 17th century. It's about a ghost ship that sails the deep oceans, full of lost souls who can never make port. According to the story, the Flying Dutchman sank in a terrible storm some centuries ago, and since that day it has drifted aimlessly because apparently when ships are destroyed they become ghosts. Legend says if you see the ghost of the Flying Dutchman, it's a sign that an abysmal storm is coming to make ghosts of you and your ship. As implied by the name it actually flies or floats over the seas, that's how you know it's a ghost ship and not just some regular ship you've mistaken it for which, it'll be the one that's hovering above the water. No non-ghost boat can do that as far as I know. Sailors who report seeing the Flying Dutchman have kept this legend alive for centuries because it's a flying boat that forecasts storms, how many of them can possibly be out there? And of course when the floating ship is spotted, a ferocious unforgiving storm always seems to follow, never fails." Tiger takes a puff of his cigar and looks at me and shrugs his shoulders "Well how can this possibly be? Were all the sailors delusional, there can be no explanation to this mystery right? Turns out all this is in fact an optical illusion called fata morgana. It's a form of mirage that plays with light and moisture in a way that can and often will cause faraway ships to appear as all sorts of terrifying apparitions that float well above sea level. It's the reflection of the sun on to the water reflecting it back into the sky. The Flying Dutchman is heavily associated with the areas that have conditions ideal for fata morgana mirages, such as the North Sea the phenomenon is most likely to occur in colder water temperatures. Ah, but what about the storms you ask? How many optical illusions do you know that can control the weather? Actually, it's the other way around. Guess what kind of atmospheric conditions are perfect for creating the fata morgana mirage? The onset of storms, mystery solved. For centuries, people had no explanation or vindication for the flying Dutchmen and were baffled by a ghost ship that appears just before a violent storm is about to take place. All this was, was really a very common reflection on the ocean water." He then leans over at me "you see Chris, no matter how fucked up you think something is and think there is absolutely no explanation on earth, just know that is not true, there is ALWAYS an explanation to everything, you my friend just gotta find it."

I think to myself, wow, this guy actually seems to be well educated and well spoken. Just kind of unexpected that's all. "How do I do that?" I ask in confusion.

Tiger takes another puff and says "Find BOUCHER and that may answer a lot of questions."

I look at him and say "Ok, well where can I find BOUCHER?"

Tiger starts to laugh and says "Try the Holy Mary's cemetery up on 29th street."

I look at him bewildered "He's dead?"

Tiger is still laughing and says "Ya, he's been dead for a long time, he was killed in the French bloodbath of 2003. He was with the East Side French Cartel who fought with us. I didn't see BOUCHER die, but saw his body in the bloody aftermath, his skull had been beaten severely and had several bullet wounds riddling his body. He was a virtuous guy and let me tell you something, if he wanted someone dead, he'd do it himself. That's the truth" he says pointing at me.

"What the fuck!" I think as I say it out loud to myself "so someone pretended to be BOUCHER, made up some fake story about his son being killed by WINCHESTER..."

"...whoa whoa" Tiger interrupts me. "That part is true. WINCHESTER did kill BOUCHER's little boy, drunken idiot, and yes he did get off of the charge in court, but of course BOUCHER was already dead."

"I guess that makes sense. This person pretending to be BOUCHER would know I'd check up on the story and see if it is legit. Well, what about this WINCHESTER guy? Maybe he'll know what this is all about. You know him?"

Tiger grins and says "Ya, ya I know him too."

"And where is he?"

"Ha ha. Same place BOUCHER is."

"What!?" I say.

"Ha ha, WINCHESTER blew his brains out the day after the trial. WINCHESTER knew there would be payback and retribution for what he did and everyone knew he paid off the Judge along with half the jury. He knew that if he got off he may not go to jail, but he knew that BOUCHER's people would come looking for him and torture him before they eventually put a bullet in his head. So he became so overwhelmed with paranoia, he took out his gun, held it under his chin and pulled the trigger."

"But BOUCHER was already dead, who would have offed him anyway, wasn't he in the clear?"

"Hey!" he says abruptly. "Even thugs have rules and laws man. You don't fucking kill a little boy homey and think that you're gonna get away with that shit, especially one that is a son of a well-respected gang member like BOUCHER. You see, there are two sets of rules up in here. One is the government rules and laws, those are the rules and laws that protect the majority law abiding citizens with a wife and kids, a beautiful house, nice neighbourhood and a great job. The second is for the other small population of people, the people that never had a chance in life, that live in the projects or hoods, or those who chose not to be one of the majority. Those laws are determined by the people and justice isn't served by someone with a badge, it's served by the people in whatever form they deem appropriate. WINCHESTER knew that and knew that the people would not stand for him breathing the same air as everyone else after killing a rival gang member's son in a drunk driving incident then paying his way out of any justice that needed to be served. So he knew his time was coming and just sped up his death and died by his own hands rather than theirs. In a way WINCHESTER did the right thing and made the situation right with everyone."

"So this may not have anything at all to do with the French gangs, it was just a front? So that means this was definitely orchestrated by someone that I probably know very well " I ask.

"I can guarantee it was homey. We don't role like that man. What are you anyway? You a gangster? Hitman? What?" he asked.

I look at him and smile "I'm nobody, just a person that got screwed over by someone who I obviously trusted. Just trying to find out who."

"Fair enough. Look man" Tiger stands up from his chair "since this so called person pretending to be one of my boys and using the good name of BOUCHER as his own, that ain't cool and he just took his plane into a no fly zone you feel me?"

"Ya, I feel ya." I say.

"BOUCHER was a good dude, I don't appreciate this fool dragging his name through the mud like that. You need some backup, you holla at me you hear? We got your back, you seem like a good dude, and the son of an H.A member and friend of Python is cool with me" Tiger says giving me a piece of paper with his cell number on it.

I take the paper and ask Tiger "Why you being so cool with me? You could have easily just put two bullets in my head and thrown me in the dumpster out back."

Tiger grabs my magazine from the floor then my gun. He slams the magazine in the butt of the gun, and locks it into place. He hands me my piece and says "Cause, I trust you. Don't know why, but you seem legit and genuine and seem like you need some help right now figuring some shit out. I don't have much anymore, but I still have mad respect for my dead home boys. You gonna go at this person that set you up, you have to start trying to think like them and try to get to know your enemy and gain respect of those around you. Knowledge will give you power, but character will give you the respect. That's how I gained my power back and now I got the 411 on anybody in LA. You wanna start a legacy, you need to start with those two things, once you got them, it becomes a lot easier to solve any puzzle that you encounter."

I take the gun and say "Thanks Tiger" and shake his hand. Again I can't help noticing the scar now that I see it up close. Is it impolite to ask him about it as I am curious now?

Tiger I think caught me looking at it and says "You wondering about the scar huh?"

Not sure what to say. If I say yes will that offend him, or if I say no he'll know I'm lying? "Ya, I noticed that" I say.

"Got this two years ago, almost to the day. Not sure who done it, but we were in the mist of getting questioned by the cops, next thing I know guns start thundering in the air, boom boom boom. I had no idea what was going on, heck I didn't even have a gun in my hand as I was trying to figure out what erupted this gun battle. Next thing I know" he makes his fingers into a gun and points it to his scar "boom! Somebody done shot me right in my fucking face, blind-sided me like a coward, then just left me for dead. Lucky for me, the bullet missed every vital part and exited through the back of my head. Not sure how I got so lucky, doc said it was a one in a million shot and 99% of the time, the person who received a gunshot like that to the face would be either dead, be a vegetable, or suffer severe brain damage. All I did was suffer minor injury to my left eye which left me legally blind in it, and had a nice ugly scar as a parting gift. My left eye waters all the time and is extremely sensitive to light, that's why I wear these specs and have my office so dim. Heck, with me out of commission for the time I was in the hospital, my crew The Impitoyables nearly ended again. But we recovered and here I am today, never figured out who that gutless son a bitch was who shot me, but he haunts me to this day and he's gonna get his mark my word."

"I'm sorry, I didn't mean to look" I say not sure if he was mad or not.

He smiles and says "No worries my friend, I don't mind. Heck if you had a hideous scar on your face, I'd stare too."

I smirk "Thanks again for the information, it kind of cleared up a bit I suppose and got me a little further ahead."

"Chris, you know that some mysteries are just like onions. The more layers you peel away, the more it stinks. Whoever is doing this is probably one step ahead of you already. Whatever you think of doing, this person has probably thought about it and has planned for it. Trust me man, I've been in your position before, take it from experience."

"Thanks, I'll keep my head up" I turn and walk to the door and the one thug hands me my guns back. Just as I'm about to leave I turn and ask "so, how do you get the name Tiger anyway?"

Tiger smiles and says "Wrestled a Tiger when I was sixteen, you pretty much become a legend after that."

I smile, pause, and then continue out the door. I walk past the outside bouncer and see my car intact. I reach in, pull out another 100 dollar bill and give it to him "My car looks in one piece, thanks."

The bouncer takes the money and quietly says "thanks."

I get in my car and look at my watch, 10:12 p.m., time to meet up with Tony, maybe he can make some sense out of this, I can only hope.

CHAPTER XI

JUDGEMENT NIGHT

As I drive, my mind wonders and these abysmal images from Russia were getting worse and more violent. Haunting phantasmagorias causing my dreams to turn into nightmares, the horrific subconscious gruesome visions remind of that horrendous day that just won't leave me alone. Bloody corpses, demonic hallucinations, blood curdling shrieks of terror, all metaphors of the unspeakable thing that occurred on that day.

My stomach turns as I anxiously wait to see if Tony can get some answers for me. I hate to think of the fact that this may be Jimmy's doing, he faked the whole thing to screw me over and save his own skin, but something still doesn't make sense, what did he have to gain from doing this? These pieces just don't fit, the puzzle isn't clear at all. I'm not even sure if I have all the pieces needed to solve this puzzle, heck, I can't even figure out what the big picture even looks like. But I can't be narrow minded and put all my eggs in one basket thinking this is all Jimmy's doing, maybe it was someone else, Tony? Trina? My Dad? I don't know anymore. I hate the thought that it could be any of those people and then again, you never know. Maybe I'm way off and this was not set up by anybody that is close to me, maybe somehow someway, somebody figured out who I was, but again, what would they have to gain from me killing a US Senator? "Stop thinking Chris or you'll give yourself a migraine" I tell myself. My phone beeps and quickly look at the text, it's from Tony: ON MY WAY PAL, SEE YOU IN ABOUT 10. TELL NO ONE, YOU DON'T KNOW WHO YOU CAN TRUST RIGHT NOW."

He's right, I can't trust anyone, maybe not even Tony, but I'm desperate for help to figure this out. I text him back: "I'M ABOUT 10 MINS OUT TOO, THANKS TONY"

He text me back: "B4L"

I smile. Tony and have known each other since we were kids and he is like my second brother, we are inseparable. Tony grew up poverty-stricken, his Dad died in the line of duty as a proud police officer when he was very young in a shootout with a couple of ruthless petty robbers and was given the top award for police officer bravery and courage. His Mom was disabled from a horrific car crash that left her legs completely smashed and didn't work much. You'd never know that Tony was poor though, he seemed to be the happiest kid I knew with a carefree attitude and always talked about his Dad. I guess I always thought that if you were poor and didn't have the newest video game or newest bike, you'd be a very unhappy kid, but not Tony. Heck, he was the only kid I knew that didn't own a bike, but still, he always had a smile on his face and was content with what he had. I always envied that about him, here was a kid who had three shirts to his name, one jacket, and three pairs of pants but he was always a blissful kid. He never owned a bike and only had basic cable, and then there was me with a new bike every year, plenty of food, drawers full of clothes, and I'd get outraged and say life wasn't fair because my Dad wouldn't get me the newest video game. Tony always told me that one day he would be a millionaire and be a police officer who was as famous as Elliot Ness and his Dad. He loved the idea of being a police officer, not just anyone, a legendary one and admired his Dad so much and wanted to make him proud. Tony was always fascinated with my Dad too being an Outlaw Biker, and would always ask him to tell stories about how he beat up this guy, and whooped that guy's ass. Tony never really knew his Father so my Dad really took to him and would entertain us kids with stories of his past. Not gruesome stories by no means, but stories about how the H.A was the baddest dudes on earth. Tony, as happy as he was, would never take shit from anyone, and he was tough, I mean tough. I once saw Tony fight three kids at once when he was thirteen. He took a beating, but in the end, the three kids were laying on the ground while Tony walked home sporting some new battle scars of pride. He always stood up for me, even though I took martial arts as a kid and could defend myself quite well, it gave him elation and pride to stick up for me, I guess that's why he became such a good cop. I remember when my Mom died, Tony was the first person that I wanted to see when my Dad told me the news that day. Tony always knew the right things to say and usually always solved things for me, and that's what I'm hoping for now.

I pull up leisurely to an old run down building that hasn't been occupied for as long as I can remember. Probably better, nobody can see me talking with Tony, who knows who's eyes are watching me. As I get out of my car I see headlights approaching hoping that it's Tony. Sure enough, it's him.

"Chris man, let's go inside" he says and I follow him into the building. He turns around and says "Ok Chris, what in God's name is going down man?"

I run both my hands through my hair in utter despair and say "I have no idea man. I mean, I got this contract to do a guy named WINCHESTER who was some former gangster who apparently killed another dudes little boy named BOUCHER and BOUCHER is the one that ordered the hit" I pause as I feel myself talking way too fast and starting to get flustered "and all of it was bullshit. I had no idea that the person I shot was BOULDERDASH, you gotta believe me Tony."

Tony looks at me in astonishment and says "So you killed Senator BOULDERDASH?"

"Yes Tony, but not on purpose, I mean, I did but I didn't know it was him man."

Tony rubs his chin and says "Geese Chris, how many does that make that you've killed? MYER's yesterday morning was what, twenty three, now BOULDERDASH makes twenty four. Is that right?"

I look at him curiously and say "Ya, so what, what does that have to do with anything? Fuck Tony you have to help me out here!" I say now getting impatient. "I don't know what to do, I don't know where to turn..." I pause as my ears perk up. I hear the door behind open and my heart almost stopped. A man walked in wearing a trench coat. Who the heck is this dude I speculated.

"Ah, Mr. DILLINGER come on in" Tony says looking behind me at this person.

I look back at Tony and whisper "Who the fuck is this dude? Did you bring another fucking cop here, what the hell is wrong with you?"

Just then I feel DILINGER quickly clutch my hands pull them behind me and wrap them with duct tape. I tried to resist but he was too quick in wrapping the duct tape around my wrists. "What the fuck is this Tony!" I scream.

Just then DILINGER pulls up a chair and sits me down on it with a forceful push. My eyes are stilled peeled on Tony in utter shock. I was now scared, almost panic-stricken, what the heck was going on?

"Ah Chris Chris Chris" he says in almost a jaunty sinister voice. "Chris, your reign of terror on this city has now come to an end, you're done Chris, finished, fineto, your rapture has come. I got you now and you are a very valuable item to me."

"Tony, what the hell are you talking about, why do you have my hands wrapped in duct tape?" I ask as I feel DILINGER now duct taping my ankles and arms to the chair legs.

"Well Chris, it's like this." He says now pacing back and forth with an evil grin on his face. "I've watched you for what, five years or so? Taking out your little gangster contracts and living in your beautiful mansion with your elegant girlfriend and millions in the bank. Now, I have always been the one investigating a majority of these shootings of yours and, well I've done a pretty good job of swaying the investigation away from you. Scratching up bullet casings found inside the victim, leading the investigation to a rival gang hit, swaying other detectives away from it being a professional hit and so forth. Basically, giving you the life of luxury and me in a two bedroom apartment with a wife that hates me, and the idiot cop who is unable to solve any of these shootings. See how that really doesn't work out Chris? Not once, did you ever offer me a cut of those contracts, even though I'm the one that keeps you safe, I'm the one that leads the investigation away from you and who do you give a percentage to? Jimmy. How the fuck is that fair man, answer me that" he now glares at me with a grim stare.

"Money? This is about money? Why the hell didn't you just ask? You know I'd cut you in man, I just never thought you take it on the account that you're a cop, thought you'd consider it dirty money."

Tony laughs sarcastically "Money is money Chris. Dirty, clean, all looks the same to me and spends the same too. Well doesn't matter anyway I guess, you ain't gonna be here much longer."

"So I take it that it was you who pretended to be a dead man named BOUCHER on the phone with Jimmy huh?" I ask.

"Oui Oui. That was me. I've been working on my French accent for a while." Tony smiles. "How'd you find out that BOUCHER is dead anyway out of curiosity?"

"Guy named Tiger told me" I said.

Tony says "Tiger?" and begins to think. "You mean Tiger St. PIERRE?"

I nod and Tony bursts out snickering.

"Holy shit are you kidding? Wow, I thought I killed that French fuck a few years ago."

I slowly look up at Tony as he seemed to be a stranger now to me "You mean you shot Tiger in the face?"

"Ha ha. Ya, fuck, I blasted him point blank in the head, boom! Thought it'd be one less piece of trash in this world if I put a bullet in his head. How the hell did he survive that? Dam Frenchman are tough to kill." He now looks at me and smiles "Shit man, he must be all fucked up in the brain and have half a head or something eh?"

"Ya, you messed him up good, congratulations." I say sarcastically. I lower my head and say "Why Tony? What do you gain out of doing this anyway?"

"Ah, very good question Christopher" he says as he takes off his jacket. "You see, over the last five years, you've taken out some pretty heavy hitters in the underground world. Heck you've taken out strikers, enforcers, middle men, money men, you name it. I'll tell you one thing man, you take out the main players in the game that's for sure. Well I'm sure that any of these gangs would love to get their hands on the person responsible for the murders and slaying of their boys, their home boys, and probably would pay pretty handsomely for that information. Now, one hit you did comes to mind and this dude pretty much outbid everyone out there for a piece of your ass. You remember last year you took out a dude named Pedro TORRES? Well, bet you had no idea who TORRES was exactly did you? Probably thought he was just another thug targeted by another gang huh? Well in retrospect he was, but you never seen the big picture. TORRES was a major guy in the 88 Mexican Cartel gang. TORRES was their accountant so to speak, he was the guy who kept the money in order for them, kept everything legal, and kept the cops away as he made it look like the 88's were earning money legit so the Feds wouldn't come snooping around. Not only that, TORRES was the new step son of the 88's main leader, Don ALVEREZ. He was so proud of that kid, smitten almost, he was going to marry his daughter in a few months and treated him like a son. Well, when you took out TORRES the 88's were in all kinds of trouble with the Feds now and ALVEREZ was heartbroken and plenty pissed. They had nobody to manage the books, nobody to keep the cops away from looking suspicious about all the money they were earning, and the Feds came after them with full force. The 88's almost went into the tank but somehow ALVEREZ by the skin of his teeth was able to hang on and grow his empire again after that substantial hit. Turns out just a while ago, I told ALVEREZ that I may have the person responsible for killing poor little TORRES and nearly bringing his empire down." Tony then reaches into his pocket and puts a stick of gum in his mouth and continues "I told ALVEREZ that there were other gangs willing to pay big bucks to get their hands on you so he asked what the highest offer was and whatever that number is, double it. Well, he is the winner in the auction to get you as the prize, he's giving me ten million cash for your ass and will be by in, oh about twenty four hours or so with my money and to collect you. Heck the Mexican mafia stepped in a financed almost all that money for ALVEREZ" Tony said with a sneer.

I lower my head and shake my head not knowing what to say. How could he do this, he was my best friend, like a brother to me, I'd risk my life for this guy, and he betrays a friend for greed? Just goes to show, sometimes the person you'd take a bullet for ends up being the one behind the gun. "So why have me kill BOULDERDASH? What did that prove?" I say still looking down as I can't even look at him.

"Ah, very good question. Why kill the Senator you ask? Well I'll tell ya why. BOULDERDASH was a guy that was loved by all people in LA, he was a kind hearted giving man who has helped out a ton of people in the area, progression in the economy, industrialised new jobs, was the voice of the people and genuinely cared about how to restore and enrich communities. He was like the GIULIANI you might say. I kind of counted on the fact that you didn't follow politics and would have no clue who BOULDERDASH was or what he looked like. Anyway, BOULDERDASH was very loved by the people and they were crushed when they heard of his son being stricken with cancer." Tony looked at me with a sinister disproving stare "Everyday that beloved man would visit the hospital to be with his son, and that green hat he always wore, that was his son's baseball teams' hat and he always wears it when he visits him. Now, figuring you had no inkling of who the Senator was, I posed as Mr. BOUCHER and sent Jimmy a photo of good ole BOULDERDASH sporting his boys green hat and ordered the hit on him. I told Jimmy that the man was Herny WINCHESTER, an old scum of the earth former gang member. When he was gunned down in cold blood visiting his sick boy at the hospital, well, people immediately started to demand that justice be served. I needed a guy that people all knew, loved and cared about, BOULDERDASH fit the bill perfectly. I mean killing some thug off the street, that ain't gonna get anyone's attention, but killing a well-known, well liked US Senator, well now that will get everyone's attention."

"Why now? Why'd you do this now?" I asked.

"Well, cause when you told me earlier that you were getting out of the business, I needed to act fast. I knew Jimmy was in some grave financial trouble and knew he couldn't resist a million dollar payday and I figured he'd persuade you to do the job. Heck, Jimmy owes some big money to some ruthless people."

I look at Tony "How'd you know that?"

He smiles "Oh, Chris, I have lots of connections, as Garth Brooks said *I got friends in low places.* I know how desperate Jimmy would be to get some money and pay off these thugs before they bash his skull in. I knew I could convince Jimmy to convince you to do the job so he can get out of his mess".

"What do you gain from BOULDERDASH being dead" I ask.

"Good question. Well, now I can be the one to solve the case. I can tell everyone that the shooter has been identified and the people can rest easy now and I'm the hero cop just like my Dad was" he says.

"How you gonna prove to everyone that it was me dipshit" I say.

"Ah, yet another good question" he says and reaches into his pocket and pulls out a recorder and holds it up to me "Take a listen:

Tony: "SO YOU KILLED SENATOR BOULDERDASH?"

Me: "YES TONY, BUT NOT ON PURPOSE, I MEAN, I DID BUT I DIDN'T KNOW IT WAS HIM MAN".

Tony: "GEEZE CHRIS, HOW MANY DOES THAT MAKE THAT YOU'VE KILLED? MYERS YESTERDAY MORNING WAS WHAT, TWENTY THREE, NOW BOULDERDASH MAKES TWENTY FOUR RIGHT?"

Me: "YA SO WHAT, WHAT DOES THAT HAVE TO DO WITH ANYTHING

He stops the recorder and says "Your confession will be all the proof I need."

"Bastard!" I say to him.

"Oh, and added bonus, I can say that I also have solved twenty three other unsolved murders over the last five years. I can see the headline: HERO COP SOLVES SENSELESS DEATH OF BELOVED SENATOR. DETECTIVE BECHERELLI ALSO SOLVED TWENTY THREE OTHER UNSOLVED MURDERS AROUND THE CITY. UNFORTUNATELY THE MAN RESPONSIBLE WAS FOUND DEAD, BEATEN BEYOND RECOGNITION, BUT BECHERELLI WAS ABLE TO IDENTIFY THE GUNMAN AS ONE CHRISTOPHER SLAUGHTER. Heck Chris, I'd be like the modern day, uh…"

"Elliot Ness" I said.

He looks at me with a big grin and says "Yes, Elliot Ness. Ha, you remembered huh? Wow. I said I wanted to become and millionaire and be a cop like Elliot Ness and my Dad when we were young. Ha, guess mission accomplished, yeah me!" He looks at me in an intense manner "You know the one single thing in my pathetic life that will make this all worth it will be getting that Top Cop award and make my Dad proud of me as he looks down from heaven. They hold this elaborate ceremony in Washington and present the award and congratulations to that cop who has shown excellence and he is enshrined into, well basically the police Hall of Fame sort of speak." Tony looks at me with intensity and pounds his fist on his hand "I have been striving for that ever since I joined the force and that would be the crowning jewel in my achievements in life and the ultimate tribute to my Dad. I tried getting that with all the little tips you gave me over the years, but that was small potatoes compared to this. I mean, my God, solving the shooting death of a US Senator as well as twenty three unsolved murders all in one week, that honor and dignity will be mine. Can't you be the least bit excited for me?" he asks me in a cynical voice.

"Congrats" I say back in an equally sarcastic tone.

"Oh come on now Chris, don't be resentful."

"The whole time Tony? We were friends, practically brothers, and your greed and jealousy lead you do this?" I ask with piercing eyes on Tony.

Tony now sits on a chair, crosses his arms and says "No, not the whole time, you see, you had your days in the sun, you've lived the high life, extravagant house, elaborate cars, the whole nine yards, now it's my turn, and if you have to go down in order for me to live that life, well so be it." Tony now peeks at his watch and says, "you see, twenty four hours from now, Mr. ALVEREZ will be coming to get you, I'll be ten million dollars richer, then when ALVEREZ is finished beating you to death, I'll find your body and make this miraculous discovery that this was the body of the man responsible for killing our beloved Senator as well as twenty three unsolved murders. I'm assuming your rifle is somewhere in your car, I'll match up the gun to the bullet in BOULDERDASH and viola, instant hero."

"Greed" I snap.

"Beg your pardon" he asks leaning in.

"Greed will always end up biting you in the ass. It's a living breathing thing greed is. Its flourishes the more you feed it, and consumes you before you know it." I snicker "Your mother never read you the Goose that laid the golden egg before."

Tony leans in with anticipation and says "No, how does that one go?"

I frown and say "A farmer had a Goose that laid a golden egg every day. He figured that the Goose must contain a great lump of gold in its inside, and in order to get the gold he'd killed it. Having done so, the Farmer found to his surprise that the Goose differed in no respect from their other hens. The foolish farmer, thus hoping to become rich all at once, deprived himself of the gain of a solid gold egg of which he was assured every day. You see Tony, greed will bury you in the end."

Tony smiles looking amused "I like that story" now starts to laugh and clap his hands together in joy. "Yes, I really like that story." He looks at DILINGER now and asks "Effron, you every hear that one before about the Golden Hen?"

"Goose" I say.

Tony corrects himself and says "Sorry, Goose?"

Effron smiles and says "Ya, Mom used to read me all kinds of nursery rhymes."

Tony still beaming says "Really? Huh. Never heard of it, but I like it, it's a good moral." He looks back at me with that sinister grin "You know what the definition of opportunity is Chris? A situation or condition favorable for attainment of a goal. Another definition of it is, a good position, chance, or prospect for advancement or success. That my friend is why I am doing this."

"Never took you as a dirty cop Tony" I say to him disappointed.

Tony scowls and was not impressed as he leans in close to me "You fucking have the nerve to say that to me? You kill people for a living my friend. Ya sure they are scum, but you have also killed two innocent people as well haven't you."

My heart stops and I look at him shocked and mortified with goose bumps running down my arms. How would he know?

Tony looks at me surprised and says "Oh, didn't think I knew about Russia did you?" He now bends down in front of me. "You did the ultimate no-no by killing an innocent person that was not on your list that day didn't you? A little girl, thirteen years old wasn't she?"

I stare at Tony lost for words. This was the incident that has plagued me for close to five years, how did he find out? I was in Russia doing a contract there. The Russian mob that operated out of North LA had used my services on one of the first hit ever did not including VOLKOV and liked my work so they employed me to take out a target in St. Petersburg. The guy that was my target was a repulsive low life of a human being named Victor Alexander BRESHNEKOV. Victor was a twice convicted pedophile but those were the only two times he was ever caught and convicted, locals figured he was responsible for over a dozen sexual assaults on under aged girls as young as nine years old. He was revolting to the extreme and local gangs didn't want their hands dirty with his blood so they hired me to take him out and wipe him from the face of the earth. Thing is with pedophile's, there ain't no cure except to take'em out back and put two in their head and leave them to the wolves. Victor lived in a small secluded shack in the woods on account that if he lived in the city he'd probably get lynched and beaten beyond all recognition by the townies. It was a relatively easy gig, a week in Russia, find out who this guy is, study his routine, smoke the pig, then back to LA. I remember it was a bitter cloudy rainy Monday evening around dinner when I crept up to this monster's little shithole, a small wooden shack in the middle of a dense forest. I found a perfect spot for the shot, about 100 yards out with a clear shot at him through his window. I loaded up with a higher than normal power rifle for the job to compensate for the fact that the shot had to pass through a pane of glass. I lined up my shot as I saw Victor sitting down at his table eating his supper, mange beard, grubby fingernails, tattered clothes, and decaying skin, heck he fit the definition of a pathetic human if I ever saw one. The rain didn't even bother me, I felt each water drop pelting my shoulders but my focus remained on Victor in my cross hairs. I needed to wait for the perfect shot as I watched with eager anticipation. Everything was calculated and planned, it was really an easy gig to pull off and the people would be better off without this revolting scum breathing again. I saw Victor lift his head up from a bite of food off his plate and begin to chew, this was the moment, this was the shot. I pulled the trigger and heard a small glass shatter as the bullet passed through with ease and found its mark right into the side of Victor's head just above his ear confirmed by the splash of blood. Victor instantaneously froze with his eyes wide open with horror and disbelief as blood began gushing out of his head. His head fell against gently the wall he was leaning on as his body lets him know that he was dead. I waited to make sure there was no movement from Victor as I stared at his lifeless body with his eyes still wide open as if in amazement of what had just happened, then he plummeted to the floor in a thud. I loaded up the gun and drove off, mission accomplished easy contract and I was actually glad to have taken a human being like Victor out, now he can't harm another innocent little girl. When I got back to LA the next night, I almost collapsed when the client informed Jimmy that not only was Victor confirmed dead, but a little girl by the name of Arina FINAGOV, age of thirteen was also discovered dead in the house killed by the same bullet that ended Victor. Arina was apparently abducted by Victor a few weeks ago and was tied up in the next room. The bullet being such a high velocity passed through Victor's head and came out through the wall striking Arina in the back of the neck and out threw her throat. Arina was sitting against the same wall Victor was, and she died a lingering death suffocating on her own blood from the bullet hole in her neck. She probably gasped for air trying to take a breath but all she could do is swallow the river of blood from her wound that was slowing drowning her. There was no indication from the client that Victor had anybody with him, and when I followed him for over a week, there was no indication what so ever that Arina was in the next room. Usually I never use that powerful of a rifle, but I was young and new to the game not realizing that a bullet will pass through glass like a hot stick of butter and really wouldn't significantly slow a bullet down that much at all. Besides, I had no idea that there was someone else sitting on the other side of the wall. Police cleaned it all to the public by pinning Arina's death on Victor saying he was the one who shot Arina then took his own life, not wanting to glorify a possible vigilante. When I heard the news that Victor was shot along with Arina, I was rocked to the core with repulsion. That feeling of daggers in your chest, needles in your throat, your body numb, your hands shake, and your eyes wide open, that feeling hit me harder than a freight train. I felt paralyzed and was riddled with extreme panic, remorse, and dreadfulness as I remember dropping to my knees and just remaining tranquil with my mouth open unable to even speak. The only sentence that I kept replaying in my mind was **what have I done**? I felt like a monster, a murderer, a person that killed an innocent little girl who has not had the chance to live a full life, I took that from her and can't give it back. At that moment I wanted out of the contract killing business forever, the scar of that moment would never be reconciled. It was only my third real contract but I did the ultimate thing no contract killer should ever do, that is, kill someone who you are not paid to kill or kill a child. I took poor Arina's life that day and I have never forgiven myself for it. I spoke to Father WHISTLER almost on a daily basis trying to get him to rid the guilt and sin from me, but it didn't seem to work and I never told him all the details anyway. "*Repent, then, and turn to God, so that your sins may be wiped out, that times of refreshing may come from the Lord*" WHISTLER always told me and eventually I was able to move on with my life. I never forgave myself, but I tried to forget. The nightmares though still didn't let me forget, I had nightmares of seeing a little girls bloody decayed bodies, and apparitions of me shooting small children in the dark with the echoes of the gun blasts and their agonizing screams that felt so real. Sadistic disturbing images that haunted me and would make me fearful of going to sleep not knowing what my subconscious may brew up. The nightmares soon became less frequent and after about seven months, I was able to resume business with Jimmy. That was a secret only me and Jimmy shared, I never even told Trina about Arina as I was petrified of what she would think of me, and, who'd blame her? Now, my best friend turned Benedict Arnold knows this filthy secret.

Tony looks into my eyes and says "I know all about it Chris. So you see, you can call me what you want, dirty cop, trader, backstabber whatever, but one thing I am not, and that is a child killer."

My emotions erupted with rage and I tried to lung out of my chair at Tony wanting to rip his throat out, but the dam duct tape had my hands and legs bound to the chair.

Tony leapt up and back at me lunging at him then smirked at me then Effron. "Wow, guess we know the trigger word is don't we?" and laughed. He then became serious again looking at me. "Don't take this personal, you are a good guy and my friend. I'm doing this because I want my piece of the pie, and off the record, I was jealous of your life of luxury and wanted it to be me, but that's just between you and me. But now I will be rich living the life of luxury and to top it off I'll be the super cop of LA. You know what, I can now solve Victor's and that little Russian girl's murder too. Ha, I'll be an international crime solver. Wow."

"You're scum Tony" I say to him in disgust.

"Oh, hold that thought, never told you the best part that will make me even wealthier. You see, I told some of the gangs about you and stated that if they cannot have you, perhaps your business partner may be of some value. I mean if you can't have the main course, might as well have the desert right?" he says laughing. I didn't even want to hear what he was going to say next as I already know. "See, the Arian Brotherhood were very captivated by that offer. They are connected to the German mafia and you took out two of their key members in 2004 and 2005. They were some pissed at that boy let me tell you, they went out and killed six rival gang members in retaliation thinking it was a gang related killing. As a result, twelve of the Arian Brotherhood members were sentenced for life in prison for those killings, so in essence, you were directly and indirectly responsible for wiping out fourteen Arian Brotherhood gang members thus wiping them out of LA. Anyway, I said that the shooter's partner was the one who organizes the hits and supplies all the details to the shooter. So, the leader of the German mafia were licking their chops and offered to pay a cool million dollars for Jimmy's ass, and get redemption for putting an end to their gang in LA."

I once again became overwhelmed with wrath and screamed from the top of my lungs "Don't you fucking touch him you dirty pig, I'll kill you Tony, mark my word!"

Tony stood still and smiled at me and coolly said "Now now, no need for threats and bad words. Just accept the fact that you are going to be dying a horrible gruesome death and so will Jimmy. They will do some nasty horrendous things to you guys before they decide they will just end it by putting a gun to your skull and pulling the trigger. I mean, the things they do to people and to their enemies..."

he shivers "...terrifying. You know that they take...well, I won't tell you what they do, I'll let your imagination go wild about those thoughts. Just deal with it ok, it'll make it go a lot smoother for you."

"Go to hell Tony" I say in a composed voice realizing that screaming and insulting him won't get me anywhere.

"Ha ha. I probably will go to hell, just gotta live the good life first" he says walking away. "Keep an eye on him Effron, gonna have a cigarette and make a call to ALVERES. Don't mess him up too bad, we need him in mint condition" Tony then pulls out a pack of cigarettes and his cell phone and steps out back.

I look around then at this Effron guy. I feel something up my sleeve and realize what it was then had a bright idea "The Dodgers" I say.

"What?" Effron asks. He is a tall thin guy with balding blonde hair, bad teeth and sporting a brown leather jacket.

"I think they are gonna do well this year don't you?"

He just snickers at me and looks away.

"The Dodgers I mean. You don't watch baseball? I think that they are overpaid though don't you? I mean twenty million dollars a year to swing a bat at a ball, I mean wow huh?"

Again he ignores me and doesn't make eye contact with me just shakes his.

"Effron? What kind of a name is that anyway? Is that Dutch? Kind of a weird name" I say. I look at him and ask "So you're a dirty cop too or what? Or are you just a hired monkey?"

Effron snickers almost in amusement and tries to keep ignoring me.

"How much is he paying you for this? I'm sure you're wife and kids would be real proud of their Daddy wouldn't they?" I say trying to get infuriate him.

His expression gradually turns from a smile to a scowl as he raises his arm and cracks me with his back hand as hard as he could across my face "Talk about my family again you dirty filthy murderer and I'll make your face not so pretty anymore" he says incensed.

I tasted blood on the corner of my mouth, wow, he must have cuffed me hard if I'm bleeding. "Come on, he must be cutting you in on some of this, you ain't doing this for free are ya?"

He glances at me and I can tell he doesn't want to tell me the answer to that but seems like he reluctantly says "hundred grand okay. So no, I ain't doing it for free smartass."

"You and Tony a couple or something" I ask. He looks at me with a curious look on his face. "Gay. Are you guys, you know, queers?" I ask.

Effron gets really mad now and lunges at me clutching my throat with his strong vice grip like hand. Perfect. I now begin to cut the duct tape on my wrist with the knife my Father gave me and I hid it up my sleeve like he showed me and I can slowly feel my hands becoming free. "Listen you Goddam worthless piece of shit. How bout I tell Tony to keep his money and let me squeeze the fucking life outta you" he says with foam coming from his mouth as he screams at me in rage.

I feel my hands break free and bring them around to the front of my body. With my one hand I clutch Effron by the hair and move him closer to me, and with the other arm holding the knife, I come underneath his arm and inject the knife with a forceful thrust right into his throat.

He gives me that stupefied look and immediately grabs at his neck with both hands as I push him away from me. He continues to gawk at me unable to talk and struggling for air as I see the blood start oozing between his fingers now. He slumps to his knees still clutching his throat tight with both hands still bug-eyed and staring me in the face with his slowly fading lifeless eyes. The blood is now streaming down his neck onto the floor, at this point he probably realizes that his life is slowly coming to an end. I stay seated with the bloody knife in my hand and I glare back at him with my unforgiving eyes watching him struggle as he takes his final few breaths of life. He sluggishly starts going down as he places one arm on the ground bracing himself up as the other hand remains clenched to his bloody throat which is spraying like a fountain of blood everywhere. He then opens his mouth, tries to speak, closes his eyes and his body plunges to the cold floor in a thud. The blood begins to pool underneath him as he now lies in a river of crimson liquid.

I quickly cut myself free and scamper out the door. As much as I would love to take this knife and jam it into the heart of that turncoat, I realize my first priority is to get away and make sure Jimmy is okay. I have no idea how much help Tony is getting from these hired thugs, gangsters or even police officers. Heck, I don't even know if this dude lying in a pool of blood is a cop, gang banger, friend or partner, and frankly, I don't care. I gently open the door and see Tony in the distance talking on his cell phone with a cigarette in his hand. I look at my car and estimate that I can get to my car and start it before Tony can get to me. I'm unarmed and I'm sure Tony would have no thoughts about firing a few shots at me to prevent me from getting away, I mean, I'm worth a cool ten million to him. I focus on Tony and wait until his back is turned to me so I can make the dart towards my car and make my get away. Tony slowly turns and has a puff of his cigarette and my heart starts to race as I make the dash towards my car. As I sprint, I briefly glance at Tony who now spots me. He hangs up his phone and as I reach for the door to my car, I see Tony pull out his gun and point it at me. I get into my car and start it up as I look at Tony pointing the gun at me seemingly hesitant to pull the trigger. I glance at him one more time and jam my foot to the floor as I kick up gravel and dirt behind me in a shower of rocks and dust.

"Fuck!" I hear him bellow and I see him dash towards his car and frantically gets it. Time for a good ole fashion car chase as I see the headlights of his car turn on and hear the screech of tires as he peels out after me.

I wasn't really familiar with this area, so this may be an adventure. I take a sharp turn on the gravel road as I feel my back end fishtail but I maintain control and straighten up. I see the dust that I've kicked up from the turn then witness headlights bust through the cloud almost like a set of piercing eyes looking at me. I see a long stretch of road in front of me so I figured this was a good time to put my six hundred horse power to work and put some distance between me and Tony. I pop the clutch and slam it right into fifth gear as I then transition from the clutch to the accelerator and punch it. I get sucked back into my seat from the G-force as the headlights in my rear view mirror gradually get smaller. I knew that Tony would never give up so I know this wasn't over by any means.

As I drive I am scanning for a way onto a main road or any paved road for that matter. These gravel roads are unpredictable and I am nervous that a sharp turn may spin me out and this race would be over. I slow down a bit as I can't see the road ahead of me. I rapidly make a sharp left turn down a road and just hope there is no dead ends waiting for me.

I see the headlights now catching up and fishtailing making the same left turn as me. I grasp the wheel tighter and maneuver down a tricky road with a few dips and turns. I observe a right turn up ahead, maybe if I can take this turn at the last second, Tony may skid past me and I can get away. Risky, but I'm desperate. As I approach the turn I begin to calculate at what moment I'm going to try this extreme sharp turn, possibly risking me going off road or losing control of my car. As the turn approaches I grip the wheel with all my might and swing it clockwise. My front end goes right as my back end tries to catch up as I feel it slowly going off the road. I begin to recover from the turn and see Tony drive right past me missing the turn and continue driving straight on. I feel a sense of liberation as I see my dust kicking up and no headlights in pursuit. I slow down a bit and let my heart rate come back down to normal as I continue to scan my rear view. As I casually drive I see a paved road in the distance "Thank God" I whisper.

Just as I am cruising along for a bit, I feel a thunderous jolt from my back end as I see a pair of headlights ram me from the right coming out of nowhere. I fishtail and recover from the impact continuing to drive, it was Tony, must have taken a shortcut that intercepted this road. I again pop the clutch and let loose as I see the paved road and headlights of cars in the distance ahead. I stay focused on the road ahead not even glancing once at Tony in my rear view. I almost had a wrathful determination on my face as I become angrier now. The road is approaching fast and I see an oncoming vehicle to right of me. With my rough calculations, me and this car may be coming together at the same time. I can't slow down, I need to speed up and avoid this potential deadly T-bone. I stay fixated as the road is upon me and I see the headlights of the oncoming vehicle now as big as saucers gleaming into my car almost blinding me. I make a hard left right into the path of the oncoming vehicle nearly missing the potential catastrophic collision.

I now am on a highway which is still a little unfamiliar to me, but nevertheless I have to keep pushing on. I see Tony make the turn and continue the pursuit after me. I make a hard left at a set of lights hoping that I will run into a street that is familiar to me so I can have some kind of an advantage. As I make the left turn, I see a long stretch of road with no traffic on it at all and it gave me a crazy idea. I ram my foot to the floor and reach for my gun in the glove box as I see Tony making the left turn. I gain distance on him as I hear my engine's RPM accelerate as I am sucked back into my seat. Just then I grab the emergency brake and slam on my brakes while skidding sideways across the road. I am now perpendicular to Tony as I see him approaching my passenger side coming to T-bone me. I roll down my passenger window and I take aim with my pistol at Tony's car which is less that about fifty yards from me and closing fast. I fire three times as the echo of the gun blast fills the night air. My aim is at his tires as I hear the loud bang of a tire popping, direct hit. I see Tony slowly start to swerve as he was losing control of his car as a result of the tire being deflated. I quickly put my car in gear as I see Tony's car still creeping forward to my side door. My tires squeal as I rip out and peel away. I look in my rear view and see Tony's car come to a stop as I see his front tire completely flat and his pride probably as deflated as the tire.

As I drive on I and collect my thoughts, what the fuck has just happened, how could my best friend on earth do something like this to me? And for what, money? Does he love money that much as to turn evil? Love of money is the root of all kinds of evil, and some people craving wealth have wandered from the true faith and pierced themselves with many sorrows leading them down an ugly path of sin. Money is the true root of evil and vise verse, evil is the true root of money. Tony was willing to lift his foot up over me and squash I like a bug just for green pieces of paper. Money can make good people bad, truthful people lie, honest people cheat, and saints become sinners. All those years of friendship, gone. Take the dagger, and stab me in the place where our friendship use to be so that it can spill out of me and I can rid my body of the tainted bond we once had. "How could you do this to me Tony?" I say to myself envisioning his face as he looked at me with his devil eyes.

So when Abner returned to Hebron, Joab took him aside into the middle of the gate to speak with him privately, and there he struck him in the belly so that he died on account of the blood of Asahel his brother. 2 Samuel 3:27

I knew Tony was not going to quit on this and I knew my night was just getting started. I knew that this may get nasty, this may get ugly, this may get violent, blood will flow, but one is for sure, this will get bad before it gets good.

Chapter XII

HELL FIRE AND BRIMSTONE

I grab my phone and dial Jimmy as I drive with panic.

"Hello" a voice answers.

"Jimmy, it's me" I say relieved to hear the voice of my friend.

"Chris, you alright?" he asks with trepidation in his voice.

"Ya sort of I guess. You at home?" I ask.

"Uh, ya. What's up?" he asks confused.

"I'm coming over, we have to talk face to face" I say sounding like I'm not giving him a choice.

"Sure buddy. You know where I live?"

"No clue" I respond. "Text me the GPS co-ordinates but point me in the right way first."

"Uh, ya sure. It's just on the East outskirts of the city, rural property off of 150th street near range road 730."

"Ok, I'm on my way. Should be there in about an hour, see you then" I say.

"Chris?" he asks.

"Ya".

"You really okay or what?"

I take a deep breath and sigh "I'm not injured if that's what you're asking. I figured this shit out though, and it's ugly, I mean ugly man." Jimmy doesn't say anything, I know he feels responsible for everything and I don't want to add to the guilt that he must be feeling. "It'll be alright my friend, see ya in a bit" and then I hang up.

I haven't seen Jimmy face to face in over five years, but deep inside, I know he is my one true friend in life and I really never should have doubted him for a second. I thought that too about Tony until this went sideways, but Jimmy was never greedy, never wanted to be filthy rich and I know he would die before he ever gave up my identity. He liked money and nice things like anyone on this earth, but he was never obsessed with being rich like Tony was. I know his life has been threatened on many occasions by thugs and gangsters demanding he give up the identification of the contract killer that he was working with, but he remained loyal and true to me all these years. Even though for the last five years we have had a strictly phone relationship, I know that he treats me like he would a son with a genuine care and concern for me and paternal instincts. I don't have to see that in a person's eyes to know that, I can hear it in his voice when it comes through the phone. When we honestly ask ourselves which person in our lives mean the most to us, we often find that it is those who instead of giving advice, solutions, or cures, have chosen rather to share our pain and heal our wounds with a warm and caring hand. The friend who can be silent with us in a moment of despair, confusion or chaos, who can stay with us in an hour of grief and bereavement, who can tolerate not knowing, not curing, not healing and face with us the reality of our powerlessness, that is a friend who cares, that is Jimmy. I do feel guilty now for thinking that Jimmy was behind all of this, and although I am 99% sure he isn't anymore, I need to make sure he is safe. There is that 1% chance that he could be involved, heck, the last person on earth that I'd ever suspect put a knife in my back as soon as I turned around was Tony, but greed will make a monster and trader out of anyone and that may even include Jimmy.

This all still seems like a bad dream that I haven't woke up from yet. I can feel my disbelief about Tony was now turning to rage as I wanted nothing more than vengeance against him. Sad thing is, betrayal never comes from your enemies, it comes from the people you trust the most in this world, that's why emotions are so high when it happens. Just a few hours ago, Tony was someone that I considered my brother, someone I trusted, my family, and now, he is that one that I have the most detestation for on this planet, and soon he will get his. I don't know how, but his day of reckoning will be coming, and I will be the one bringing hell fire and brimstone his way. The bible does not condone revenge, by does state that wrongs need to be righted. *"I alone have the right to take revenge. I will pay back, says the Lord." Not defending yourselves, dearly beloved; but rather give place unto the wrath of God, for it is written, Vengeance is mine; I will repay, saith the Lord"*

Right now I need to focus on keeping Jimmy safe, then I'll deal with that no good two timing back stabbing son of a bitch later. I try to focus on my GPS making sure I don't speed or get noticed by the cops, for all I know, Tony may have a few of the boys in blue looking for me to help him out. I'm about a half hour from Jimmy's it looks, and then I take out my phone and call my Dad. The phone rings and rings "Come on Dad answer the dam phone!" I say growing impatient with each unanswered ring.

"Hello" a voice answers half asleep.

"Dad!"

"Christopher" he pauses to try to wake up. "You okay? What's going on?"

"I don't know where to start. It's Tony. Tony is the one behind all of this, he is the one who set me up to kill BOULDERDASH."

"What? Why the heck would he..."

"Money and Goddam fame and glory! He wanted to be the one to solve BOULDERDASH's murder to be the top cop in everyone's eyes, and he's gonna sell me to some dam mafia leader for ten million because I was responsible for eliminating his step son a few years back" I said getting flustered.

"Hold on hold on slow down here Chris." He pauses and takes a deep breath. "Are you fucking kidding me? Tony!" my Dad says getting angry. "I don't believe this shit! He was almost like a son to me and like a brother to you, and he's doing this out of pure greed!" he says now yelling.

"I know Dad, I know. Look, I'm going to get Jimmy, Tony has a price for him too." I pause. "Dad, I may need some help."

"Sure son what do you need?" he says trying to calm down.

"This won't end until either I'm dead or Tony is, and I for one have a lot more living to do. This may get bloody and violent so..." I pause again "you think some of your boys may have my back if I need some fire power or back-up?"

"The Hells Angels? Uh, ya. I could round some boys up to give you a hand" he says.

"You still have some contacts over there?" I ask.

"Ya, of course. Hells Angels for life, we always have one another's back when needed, and your back is my back. You let me know, and we'll crush that two timing bug into the ground."

"Thanks Dad. Not sure what kind of army he has, but I know he's got connections. May not need it, but it's nice to know I have some back-up if I do" I say.

"You got me too son. I may have not been the greatest Dad, but I'm still you're Father and you're still my son. You hear me? Don't ever forget that" he says.

"Ya Dad. Thanks."

"You let me know and it'll be one phone call away for some big ass bikers to come whoop some dirty cop ass, I'm sure they'll jump at the chance."

"Will do Pops, hopefully it doesn't come to that, but it just might, always gotta be prepared. Your knife save my life tonight by the way" I laughed.

"It's a good knife son and has always served me well. You take care of yourself, I'll be right here if you need me."

"Thanks. Gotta go, I'll keep in touch" and hang up. Right now I need all the help I can get, I need players on my team because I have no clue how many players Tony has on his side and I'll have to even the playing field. Never would have ever thought Tony would go dirty, he seemed like a good honest cop who loved his job and prided himself on his Dad and wanted to make him proud. That's enough thinking about stuff for now I thought as I turn on the radio and crank up some tunes. I have to just clear my head for a bit, not think of what is going on right now, just lean back, enjoy the music and enjoy the ride.

I approach Jimmy's house, a remote house in a rural location with large open fields and trees encompassing the house. It was an immense picturesque log house with a magnificent backdrop of a forest and a large gravel driveway. I pull my car around back of the house to make sure nobody sees my car. As I pull up, my lights illuminate a figure sitting out back with a smoke in his mouth and his head lowered in thought. Jimmy was about my Father's age, wore red framed glasses, thinning reddish hair, and a thick crimson soul patch. He used to be a heartless gang banger, but now he lives an unpretentious modest life. I step out of my car and Jimmy stands up as we look at one another for a few seconds without saying anything. We come together in an embrace "Chris, it's good to see you again" Jimmy says hugging me. I say nothing, just enjoying the embrace of my good friend. We let go and Jimmy grabs my arms and looks at me.

"Hey Jimmy, it's good to see you again too. It's been a while hasn't it?" I say.

"Too long." Jimmy turns around and says "Come inside, I'll fix us a drink and we can talk."

I follow Jimmy up the steps and walk into his house. He had bushy auburn hair sporting a plaid lumberjack black and red sweater with a pair a torn up blue jeans and work boots. "Sit down" he says pointing at his couch "What'll ya have to drink?" he asks walking towards his counter. He looks a lot thinner than when I saw him last and was walking with a sort of limp to his right leg.

I sit down while looking around his house and say "Rye straight up thanks." The house even smelled of wood, looked like a typical log cabin inside, wooden furniture and nice big fireplace.

As Jimmy pours the drinks he says "Fucked up situation we got ourselves into Christopher. I mean what the hell is going on?"

"Wanna hear the truth that'll blow your mind?" I ask. Jimmy hands me my drink and sits down in front of me waiting to hear what I have to say. "BOUCHER the guy who called you, was actually Tony."

Jimmy thinks for a bit. Then it sinks in "Tony? You mean your friend Tony?" I nod. "Are you kidding? That was Tony feeding me that garbage?" He rubs his hand through his hair, "I'm shocked."

"Ya. Kick in the teeth ain't it?" I say as I sip my drink and lean back in the chair.

"What the hell, I mean what in God's name is he thinking? Why?" Jimmy asks.

"Money and glory, isn't that what every greedy son of a bitch in this world wants? And get this, he was offered ten million large by ALVEREZ of the 88 Mexican Cartel gang for my head. Remember a while back we did a guy named TORRES who was part of that gang?"

Jimmy sips his drink, nods and says "Ya I remember. Rival gang ordered the hit, uh" he thinks. "RODRIGUEZ of the M.K Mexican cartel".

"Regardless, turns out this TORRES was a huge numbers guy for the 88's, did the books for them, kept the money in order and well hidden, made everything legit, kept track of every dime to make sure nobody was skimming, and kept away any scepticism from the Feds and IRS. Well, I guess RODRIGUEZ knew the right guy to take out because after TORRES was done, it crippled the 88's."

"Fuck me" Jimmy says under his breath.

"That ain't even the best part. The leader of the 88's ALVEREZ? TORRES was soon to be step son. TORRES was going to marry ALVEREZ's daughter and he considered TORRES practically his son already. ALVEREZ went on a rampage and personally executed five rival gang members trying to find answers to who was responsible for the murder of TORRES. The 88's were almost brought down completely by the Feds a few months later and several of the members were arrested for laundering and tax fraud. Tony saw this as an opportunity I guess and put it in his back pocket until the right time. Well, when I told Tony I was done with the whole contract killing gig, he figured he needed to play that card as soon as he could. He offered a bounty for my head to the notable gangs that may have interest in executing me, and eventually ALVEREZ put in the highest bid for my head and offered Tony ten million. Tony needs a public way to expose me by tricking me into shooting a US Senator making his killer public enemy number one. Tony gives me up to ALVEREZ and when my lifeless body is found later, Tony will make the connection and show me responsible for BOULDERDASH's death and he then is able to solve twenty two other unsolved murders in LA by pointing me out as the killer in all of them. Tony is a superhero cop and ten million richer and I'm dead and labelled the most evil scum that LA has ever seen."

I look at Jimmy who has his mouth open and speechless. He looks at me and finally says "Holy shit! That greedy two timing mother... what the fuck man!"

"Hang on Jimmy, here's another kicker for you to digest. Tony is gonna hunt you down and get a million for your ass."

"Are you kidding me right now? Am I actually hearing this? Tony? What the hell poison got into his blood and corrupted him? My God he was your friend, your brother practically?"

"I know" I say disheartened like my guts were being ripped out.

"I mean, I'm blown away! How'd you find all this out?" Jimmy asks taking a sip.

"Well" I say sitting up. "Tony decided to trick me into meeting him just a while ago so he could help me figure this mess out with the Senator. Then decided to duct tape me to a dam chair and deliver me tomorrow night to ALVEREZ on a silver platter with a big red bow on my head."

"Did you, did you kill him?" he asks in a whisper.

"No" I say. Jimmy looks at my hands which look a little red stained. I look down and say "Not Tony's blood."

"So, what do we do?" Jimmy asks.

"Well" I say "we finish our drinks and get you out of here in a while before that rat bastard comes looking for you." Jimmy nods. "You know Jimmy" I say softly "When all this was going down, I thought that" I hesitated "I thought that you were behind all this".

Jimmy looks at me with judgemental eyes "How could you even think that? You're like a son to me. We've been through a lot of shit together me and you, shit that nobody on earth could ever understand. I never once thought about throwing you under the bus for money. I'd rather die a horrible death that to expose your identity to some thug."

"I know Jimmy. But, realistically, I never thought for one minute that Tony would ever do this either. I know you're different, I see that now. You aren't about the all mighty dollar, you're about me and you, our team. I know you like money Jimmy, and heck who on this planet doesn't, but I know you'd never sell your soul to the Devil in exchange for a sack of money" I say with a smile. "That reminds me, speaking of money, what the heck have you got yourself into that you owe some bad dudes some big money anyway?"

"Ah Chris" he says pounding back his drink. "I'm just an old fool who got too deep into my gambling depts. I wanted to be a big shot playboy like the millionaires on T.V, call it a stupid vision, call it what you want, I wanted live that tycoon lifestyle. When a man wants to earn money in order to be gratified, his life then becomes devoted to the earning of that money. Happiness is forgotten; the means are taken for the end and before you know it, you are consumed in the pool of greed and keep descending to the bottom. I wasn't sure if I was addicted to money, gambling, the billionaire lifestyle or a combination of it all. You know the worst thing about gambling is? Winning. I won the first time I ever bet on a fight, four thousand I think, and from that moment on, I was addicted to win again. Heck, if I would have lost, I may have got discouraged and never gambled again. Sports, card games whatever, I was addicted to it and didn't know how to stop, like a runaway freight train."

I looked at him almost in pity and asked "Why didn't you ever tell me? I could have helped."

He looks to the floor "Not something that's easy to admit, like a person that's cheating on his partner, you want to tell them the truth, but are just too embarrassed and ashamed to do it." He looked at me and grinned "It is what it is you know. Anyway, we have more important things to worry about now."

I knew he was trying to redirect the focus on his problems, so I wasn't going to press the issue. I stood up and looked at some of the pictures Jimmy had up on a quaint little shelf. One photo caught my eye of Jimmy with possibly his son, looked like an old photo. I picked it up and smiled "This Clarence?"

Jimmy smiled "Ya, that's my boy. I'm so proud of that boy you can't even begin to imagine."

"Handsome kid" I put the picture back.

"Haven't seen him in a while. Last I know he was heading to grade eleven but I'm sure glad he isn't turning out like me. He's much better off living with his Aunt as painful is that is to admit, he doesn't need this world or a father like me. If it wasn't for me, his mother and sister would still be alive today. That boy has got his head screwed on straight and he is going to amount to something. He's much better off not growing up to be like me."

"Like us" I say sitting back down.

Jimmy grinned and said "You're a good kid Chris. It's weird how I say that about someone who kills people for a living, but it is true. Deep down I know you are a good person, unfortunately, we've become almost immune to taking a human life, doesn't even bother us anymore."

It's true in a way, and hearing those words made me feel like a soul less person. But I do care about taking a life. I mean I was devastated when I heard that the man I just killed was a US Senator rather than some former thug who killed a young boy. Morally there is a difference, you may think a life is a life but ethically one life is different from the other. And of course I was rocked when I heard I had killed Arina, a poor little girl that never had a chance at living a full life because of me. So in a way, I don't agree that I am immune to taking the life of another human, I guess it comes down to principle, morality, ethics and overall totalitarian of the situation and the person. But on the other hand, when I know I am getting paid handsomely for a hit, why is it so easy to pull the trigger at the person that I see in my cross hairs? I guess it boils down to logistic, when I kill a contract it's for a purpose, I mean I'm getting paid to take this person out so it's more like a job. Killing an innocent person without getting paid is a cold blooded heartless killing of another soul and flat out murder. I mean, let's go back when I killed for the first time for Cedric JONES, now a normal person would see that they had just killed another human and probably would be freaked out at that. Have nightmares, feel remorse, guilt, wouldn't be able to get that vision out of their head, and as a result either go crazy, turn themselves into the cops, or just take a gun and blow their brains out. But for me, it was almost a sense of pride, a sense of accomplishment, a challenge that I had conquered. I have always wondered that about myself, why did I feel that way? Why did I not go crazy? I mean, I've killed twenty five people including Arina, so that means I either don't have a soul, I'm a psychopath, or am just a cold blooded heartless killer? Pick one of them, it has to be one of those options right?

"I know you believe in the Bible and Judgement Day will soon come, Rapture and all that jazz" Jimmy says. "You know the Ancient Egyptians believed that upon death they would be asked two questions from their God and their answers would determine whether they could continue their journey in the afterlife. The first question was, 'Did you bring joy?' The second was, 'Did you find joy?' I can honestly say no to either one. I've brought death to this world and I'm not sure what joy even means because I'm not sure I have ever experienced it." He smiles at me "I know what lies for me when I leave this world, and I have accepted it. Nobody will shed a tear for me when I'm gone and why should they."

I look at his almost insulted and say "You're like a Father to me, you are one of the very few people that I call a friend. For the last five years Jimmy, you've been a crutch for me to lean on when I needed it, a person that I need in this world, not just for the contracts, but to know that there was someone out there in this world that I could trust with my life and will always have my back. I should have never doubted for a second that you'd be behind any of this, and I apologize for ever having that notion." I pause and asked him a question I have always wanted to ask him "Can I ask you a question?"

Jimmy nods and lights up a cigarette "Shoot."

"Why did you decide to do this? I mean what made you want this as a, well let's call it a career?" I ask. I was curious about other people's story about how they came into this so called occupation.

Jimmy smiles and takes a puff of his smoke "Well, I guess the way I got into it wasn't so different from the way you got into it. I rolled with a bad crowd growing up, one of my so call buddies introduced me to some members of the 18 street Grim Reapers gang. The boss of that gang, a guy named BUNDY really took a liking to me. We started talking and I mentioned to him that I was a marksmen shot and practiced for fun once in a while. Turns out, they had a big time hit that needed to be taken care of right away and their hitman was in intensive care as a result of a rival gang savage beating. So, BUNDY asked me if I'd be willing to substitute and take out this target today, offered me fifty grand for it, that was more money than I had ever imagined so I took it. Besides I was surrounded by big daunting bikers and BUNDY who looked like he could take on King Kong, shaved head with arms the size of my legs, I couldn't exactly refuse. I did it and, well the rest is history" he says taking another puff and looking at me for my reaction.

I smirk "Guess it ain't so different from my story is it?"

Jimmy looks at me and smirks "You know, I never could ever pin point the moment when my life went sideways, but that would be a pretty darn good jumping off point I'd say. When you're young you envision yourself married to the girl of your dreams, beautiful children, an honest job, big fancy house and just an overall wonderful life. Isn't that what the American dream has always been? It's an illusion though the American dream is, in part it's responsible for a great deal of crime and violence because people feel that the country owes them not only a life, but a good life. Still, the aspiration we have when we are young keeps those hopes alive. The young have aspirations that never come to pass, the old have reminiscences of what never happened. If I could push the reset button on my life Chris I would, but life isn't a Nintendo game, you can't just reset the game because you don't like the way your life has unfolded and want to start over fresh."

I look at Jimmy with surprise "Have you always felt this way? I mean, are you unhappy with your life and full of regrets?" It's weird because I thought Jimmy and I were living the perfect life. Well maybe not perfect, but we how can we complain about working a few times a year and bagging all this money for it? Until today, everything went pretty dam smoothly. "We all get second chances in life, God can make that happen and I believe that. God will fix, mend and save things that are broken. That means that no matter how hurt and defeated you feel, no matter how badly you've been damaged, no matter what mistakes you've made, God can repair you. God can give anyone a second chance, you just need to accept that and make the most of it. You said there isn't a reset button in life? I say there is and I'm gonna push mine right after this mess ends and start my new life all over again."

Jimmy grins "I like that. I've always admired that about you. You always see the glass half full, I always see the emptiness in a half a glass. And you're right, there is a chance for a new life and Goddammit I plan on...."

"Shhhh!" I say startled, perk up and look around. I whisper "You hear something?" I now get up and slink to the window to peek out. My heart drops as I see three vehicles pull up. "Fuck sake!" I look at Jimmy "Please tell me you're expecting company."

Jimmy then springs up from his seat with concern and saunters over to me and glances out "Not really."

I keep my eyes peeled on the cars as the doors nonchalantly creek open. Four people from each car get out and I see Tony is one of them. All of them are armed with some pretty dam powerful weapons, AK-47's, semi-automatic rifles, it looks bad and my heart starts to beat fast. "Well shit on me, how the hell did you find me you piece of turd" I say looking out the window at Tony.

"Christopher! I know you're in there" Tony bellows. He chuckles now and says "Dammit Chris, you are so dam predictable you make this too easy, where's the challenge? I mean come on, why didn't you just pack up and leave when you had the chance to? You could have set your course for Mexico and be drinking Tequilas with those little umbrellas in them tonight."

I look at Jimmy "Got any heat here with ya by chance?"

Jimmy smirks at me then walks over to his large wood coffee table. He stands in front of it and flips open the lid exposing a small arsenal "You dam right I do" he says and grabs a shotgun and rifle. "If I'm going down, I'm going down in a blaze of glory."

I walk over pick up two pistols and say "We ain't going down at all, this ain't our night to die. Maybe sometime in the future, but not here, not now."

Jimmy and I both take our place beside the window out of the line of fire. Tony speaks again "Come on Chris, the game is over. Just come out so we don't have to shoot up this beautiful house and turn Jimmy into a bloody corpse. I mean, I guess I'd be out a million bucks but at least I'd preserve my ten million in you. Or you can both come out now and take your chances with your buyers" he waits "Well? What's it gonna be?" I could see Tony looking at the houses in eager anticipation that we'd both just come out and willing turn ourselves over. "Come on guys, you're out numbered and out gunned, don't be idiots!"

I could see Jimmy getting infuriated and he stands up, breaks a part of the window with the barrel of his gun and sticks it out the window. He pulls the trigger of his shotgun with a deafening boom striking one of the guys outside directly in the chest as the bullets rips through his skin in a bloody explosion. The thug tumbles backwards and collapses as blood spills from the open chest wound. Almost simultaneously, everyone outside including Tony raises their weapons and returns fire on the house with a roaring explosion. Jimmy gets back behind cover as the windows get showered with bullets. The glass fragments spray everywhere as I look away not wanting to get any flying glass in my eyes. I could hear nothing but the sound of breaking glass being shattered by the storm of bullets. I then move to the window beside me and with both pistols in hand, I take aim and start unloading at everyone outside as I feel the kickback and echoes of my guns. I see one bullet strike a thug in the face as another one shatters the windshield of one of the cars. All the guys outside then move behind their cars and take cover and begin to return fire my way. I feel and hear the bullets wiz by my head as I look at Jimmy, take a quick shot outside then return to cover. All of a sudden all the shooting stops as I hear Tony yelling at everyone "Goddammit hold your fire you idiots, I need him alive, wound him if you need to, we can patch him up and still deliver him to ALVEREZ. That old bastard inside, blow his brains out if needs be, he's worth a million but it's worth it to see his head explode from a bullet."

Jimmy looks at me and says "Did he call me old?"

I chuckle and say "Ha, ya I think he did." I knew we couldn't just keep exchanging gun fire like this, we are badly outnumbered and eventually our luck is going to run out. "We gotta get out of here, we can't win this gun battle, we can only hold'em off for a bit."

"I know. I have two dirt bikes in the shed out back. If we get a chance, we can make a break for'em and get lost in the woods." Jimmy says.

"Ok, that ain't bad, it'll buy us some time at least. Just gotta hope they don't have anyone set up in the back waiting to ambush us, I'll go check."

As I stand up Jimmy says "No, I'll go" and runs to the back.

I crouch back down beside the window "Hey Tony!" I yell. "You better watch where you shoot, I felt a bullet come dangerously close to my head. Ten million bucks is a lot of money to lose if one of those bullets kills me."

"Don't worry Chris, I'll make sure I just cripple you or something, mangle your leg or arm, it's not like you're gonna be surfing or anything like that anytime soon. Just come on out and I'll only pistol whip you for a bit or smack you around, get you cleaned up, then you can make your acquaintance with ALVEREZ. What do you say to that huh?"

I stand up take aim and fire my gun at Tony and see the bullet demolish the windshield on the car Tony was ducking behind as he gets startled by the shattering glass.

"I take that as your officially no then?" he hollers.

"Eat shit Tony, I'd rather put a bullet in my own head than surrender to you and make you rich you greedy bastard" I yell.

"Ok, we'll do this the hard way I guess, your choice not mine" he says and the sound of thunder erupts from the guns outside as the house is peppered with bullets again.

Jimmy runs back beside on the opposite side of the window from me and says out of breath "Good news and bad news."

I shield my head from the glass as gun fire from outside sparks again and ask "What's the good news?"

Jimmy gets startled from a glass shattering next to him "Good news is there is nobody out back."

The gun fire stops and I get up and blast a few shots in their direction. I duck back down and ask "What's the bad news?"

Return fire comes storming back at us as I could hear bullets pelting the side of the house.

Jimmy says "Bad news is the bikes are locked in the shed and the keys are in my truck out front."

I lower my head with frustration and think. "Ok let me think, we can't do this much longer." I see Jimmy stand up in the mist of the gun fire and get two shots off at them. I try to think of something to do, how the heck are we going to get out of here alive. "Hey Jimmy" I ask him turning away from the shards of glass riddling the windows still. "Jimmy!" I yell as I wasn't sure if he heard me amidst the gun fire. I look over at my friend and observe his shotgun is down by his side and he's holding his stomach looking like he's in pain slumping over.

"Jimmy?" I ask now concerned not knowing what the problem was but fearing the worst. I look at Jimmy who was in obvious pain and was clenching at his midsection. "My God!" I scream in horror and crawl towards him. I look at him and he is hurt bad and I now see to my dismay, blood trickling between his fingers from his stomach. I remove his hand from his midsection and observe a gruesome gunshot wound that has penetrated his stomach. "No" I say in a whisper almost crying now. "Goddammit no!" It was a bad hit, a stomach wound in that area means you have about fifteen minutes or less to live. Looks like the wound hit near the liver or ruptured his stomach which would cause massive hemorrhaging and he'll be dead in less time that it takes to eat a meal. Even if the shot hit near lower intestine it would release bacteria fecal matter into tissue and the blood stream which is as toxic as a vipers venom giving him minutes to live before going into cardiac arrest.

"Dam it to hell anyway" Jimmy says as he looks at his wound and then his hand which looks like it has been dipped in a can of red paint. He looks at me with sorrow "I'm sorry for getting you into this. If I wouldn't have pushed you into doing one last job, you'd be in Mexico with Trina right now looking at a beautiful ocean sunset with sand between your toes."

A tear rolls down my face as I try to stay strong "It's not your fault old friend, it's that scum out there who did this to us. You hold on Goddamit you hear me?"

"Never thought I'd die like this" Jimmy says then smiles "Somebody should tell us right at the start of our lives, that we are dying, then we might live life to the limit and to the fullest every minute of every day. Life is just a brief intermission between the day we are born and the day that we die."

I smile and nod and say "Hang in there old friend, I'll get you out of here if it's the last thing I do."

"Forget about me okay, remember, I use to kill before back in the day, I know what this gunshot wound is. My stomach is on fire and it burns real bad, my intestines are ruptured and I have nasty poisonous shit filling up my body as we speak. I'll be dead before I step foot out of here and you know that" he says in a feeble dying voice.

"Dammit, it wasn't supposed to end like this, not here, not now. We were supposed to finally get to enjoy a normal life, get together every Christmas and reminisce, enjoy a sunset every night of our lives, swim in every ocean surrounding this planet and live till we are old can finally say that we accept death without fear. " I say with another tear down my face.

"We also have to know when our time is up. You know and I know that my time is right here right now. Not how I exactly pictured going out, always thought I'd always die peacefully in a calm sleep with a beautiful lady in my arms" he says as his voice starts to dwindle as blood now drips from his mouth.

"Dam you, this isn't fair!" I say almost annoyed.

"You listen to me" Jimmy says in a stern voice grabbing my collar "I'm not dying in vein, last thing I'm going to do before I leave this world is get you out of here. You got your car keys?" I check my pocket and pull them out. "Good" he says. "Make a run for your car out back, I'll hold'em off long enough for you to get the heck out of here."

"Jimmy" I say as I look at my old friend dying right in front of my eyes.

"Finish this Chris. Get out of here and finish this, bring that bastard out there down you hear me?" he says sternly. "Justice needs to be served, the bad guy can't win in this fairy tale. He needs to pay for this, justice needs to be served."

I wipe the tears off my face and say in an intense voice "Let's do this!"

Jimmy grins and reaches for his gun and says "Give me my gun" I pick up the shotgun and hand it to Jimmy. "Now get out of here, I got your back."

"You always did." I say. I put my hand on his shoulder and say one last time "Good bye old friend" I stand up and sprint towards the back not wanting to look back.

"Bye Chris, take care of yourself boy" Jimmy says.

I rush out the back door and into my car and hear "Tony he's in the back going for his car!"

I see the thugs and Tony all looking at me and turning all their guns in my direction. Just then, Jimmy comes storming out the front door with two shotguns in each hand letting off thunderous rounds at the thugs and yelling from the top of his lungs as the gun blasts echo in the night sky. All the guns that were pointed at me all turn at Jimmy. I slam the gas pedal to the floor and head towards the crowd and witness the grisly sight of my friend's body getting riddled with hundreds of gunshots as blood splashes and explodes into the night air. I see Tony point the gun at me as I drive past him as he pulls the trigger. I see the muzzle blast then hear my passenger window shatter as I shield my face. I wasn't hit and I drive off glaring at him now with Devil eyes.

I look back in my rear view and see Tony reach into his car, pull out a Molotov cocktail, light it and hurl it almost with joy through an open window of Jimmy's house. I witness what's left of my old friend and his house slowly go up in flames as the night is now lit up by an eerie mahogany glow. All of the cars quickly turn around and speed up after me as the engines roared. My adrenaline starts pumping and I say under my breath "come get me!" then slam it into fifth gear. I know the highway is a few miles from here as I press on the accelerator hearing the dirt underneath my tires kick up leaving a cloud of dust trailing me. I notice my speedometer start to climb all the way to over 100 miles per hour on this relatively straight stretch of partly paved road. The g-force and velocity sucks me all the way back into my seat as I have to extend my arms to grip the steering wheel as I rocket forward. I glance in my rear view and the pack is only about two hundred yards behind me, they must have powerful cars in order to keep up with me the way they are. I am moving so fast the world seems like a total blur, my adrenaline is pumping so rapid and I could see my knuckles turning white from gripping the steering wheel so tight. The highway comes upon me fast as I take a sharp left onto it and feel my back end fish tail as my tires screech. Not too much traffic and I know my way around this area pretty good so I'm not as stressed. Not even five seconds pass as I see one black car after another hit the highway and continue their pursuit in hunting me down. I see a red light approaching and I do a quick scan left and right then zoom through the intersection nearly hitting a car coming from my right which I hadn't noticed. All three of my pursuers fly through the red light after me with reckless determination. I quickly take a sharp left turn coming face to face with a set of headlights which blind me as they illuminate the entire inside of my car. My eyes widen as I quickly crank my wheel hard nearly avoiding a fatal devastating head on collision. I see one of the cars behind me clip that car with the sound of crumpled metal filling the air spinning it like a top. None of the black cars stopped, just kept on my ass like nothing happened. I notice an alley and take a tight turn down it. The alley was narrow and there was no room for error as brick walls enclosed me and there was no more than a few inches on either side of me. All three cars follow me down the alley as well not missing a beat and staying in the hunt. I'm hoping there is nobody down this alley or it may be ugly because at this speed there would be no way to stop which would result in a violent deadly impact. I stay focused on the road as my car jets down the alley like a torpedo. I see a chain link fence in front of me, I make the quick decision to bust through it hoping it's not too solid. The fence is upon me as I brace for impact, I fly right through it barely even feeling it as the metal of the fence scrapes my car as I zip past it. I look in my side mirror and notice an arm with a gun from the first car stick out and take aim in my direction. I hear the echo of a gun blast as my back window erupts in a crystal shower. I see the end of the alley approaching but I cannot see in either direction not knowing if any cars are going to meet me when I hit the road again at the end of this alley. I go for it with reckless abandonment and punch onto the street as my back end slams into an oncoming vehicle with a thundering boom. The impact spun my back end around but I was able to regain control and move forward. Two of the cars make it out but the final car is blind-sided by an oncoming truck that plows into the passenger side flipping the car over in a violent impact as the sound of exploding glass filling the streets.

"One down, two to go" I think to myself glancing in the rear view at the magnificent wreck.

Just then I hear my phone ring. I look at it, unbelievable! "Tony!"

"Hey Chris, don't you know you're endangering the lives of innocent motorists with this reckless driving of yours? Why don't you just pull over and give this shit a rest before you get yourself hurt or someone else" Tony says in a sarcastic cheerful voice.

"You killed Jimmy you son of a bitch!" I say with rage and fiery in my voice.

"Well if it's any consolation, you'll get to see him very soon, I'm sure he'd like to see you again."

I think for a moment not knowing what to say "You know what Tony, it ain't me who's going down tonight it's you."

"Is that so?" he asks.

"Come catch me you dirty pig" I say and hang up then pop the clutch and hit the accelerator. I look in the distance anticipating and facilitating two or three moves ahead. I whiz through another red light with unconcerned ease as my pursuers follow with recklessness and fortitude. I see the two cars behind me now break apart as one vehicle is now on my left and the other is on my right. I was curious about what they may be up to as I scan both of my side mirrors in anticipation on what their next move is going to be. I see the drivers of each vehicle stick a gun out and begin to blast shots at me, but I see their aim is low. They were trying to shoot out my tires! I quickly begin to zig zag back and forth trying to make it almost impossible for them to hit my wheels, I knew that if they shot out my tires, I was as good as dead. The gun blasts stop and the cars go back into "I" formation behind me. "I need to shake them, they won't give up" I say to myself. I have another insane idea as I see the sidewalk on the right of me. It looked empty so I crank my car over and ride the sidewalk as one car follows while the other remains on the road. I see a man on the sidewalk as I approach him fast and lay on my horn alerting him to move praying that he will get out of the way in time. The man looks as me with trepidation in his eyes and leaps out of harm's way. I smash into a mailbox and then crash into newsstands scattering paper and letters everywhere. Still, the car behind me does not give up and drives through the paper shower. I continue to rocket down the side walk dangerously, parked cars on my left, store fronts on my right as I blast my horn every few seconds to avoid a catastrophic collision with any potential pedestrians. I get another crazy risky idea as I look at the parked cars zooming by me. I see a small opening between two parked cars up ahead, I will try to squeeze through and get back on the road. It will be an extremely tight fit and risky at this speed, but I'll go for broke. I see my opening between cars and jolt the wheel as hard as I can to the left just clipping my back end on the front parked car and make it onto the road again. The car behind me was not anticipating that from me and instinctively tried to follow but slams into the back of the front car that I had just clipped with a roaring boom accompanied by the bloodcurdling sound of crumpled metal and shattered glass. I see my rear view mirror I have one more black car following and just know in my heart Tony is driving it.

As I look back onto the road my heart drops as I see a person pushing a shopping cart of cans crossing the street. I try my best to avoid him and intensely crank my wheel hard left but end up smashing into the cart causing cans to rain from the sky. "Wow, that was close" I said to myself glancing back and seeing to my relief the male just staring at me in utter shock. I see the cans bounce off of Tony's car as he begins to speed up and is right on my ass now. I could now confirm it was Tony as I see his devilish smile in my side mirror looking at me. I feel a jolt from behind as Tony's car rams me as my head whiplashes back. I take a hard right turn now almost drifting the car off the road but manage to regain control. Tony of course doesn't miss a beat as he drifts around the corner right after me with squealing tires. I look ahead to my terror see headlights coming towards me, I must have turned down a one-way street. I swerve to my right avoiding the oncoming car and ricochet off a parked car like a pinball and back onto the road. Very near miss! I know by now my car must be in bad shape and it may not last too long. I look in my side mirror as Tony quickly pulls out a gun and blasts the very mirror that I was looking through demolishing it. "Fuck me!" I say startled looking back in my rear view mirror of Tony laughing. "Real funny asshole" I say back to him in my mirror. I see another set of headlights coming straight at me but I see a side road to my left as a possible escape route. I quickly take the hard left nearly avoiding another oncoming car by a narrow margin. Tony slowed up to let the car pass before taking the left after me. I see Tony now speeding up and was now parallel right beside me. I look at him with resentment and he smiles back at me with a sinister grin. He then cranks his wheel and slams into my car with brutal force causing me to veer to my right clipping a parked car on my right jolting my head. I see Tony now swerving a little to the left then hard right again booming into me again nearly causing me to lose control. I knew I couldn't win this battle as his car was a whole lot bigger than my Porsche.

"We having fun yet" Tony yells laughing at me with his window rolled down.

I say nothing, just look at him with a blank stare as we continue to drive side by side.

Tony then yells "This is where you get off my friend" as I see him wanting to take another run at me. As he swerves his car to the left for momentum, I slam on my brakes as my tires squeal as the force of the stop jerks me forward into my steering wheel. Tony tries to come back right and sideswipe me, but, I wasn't there, I had stopped and Tony swerves in front of me slamming head first into a parked car with a roaring sickening impact and the tinkle of broken glass filling the air. I start to slowly accelerate again as I could smell the burned rubber from my tires. I casually drive around the wreck and I look back to see Tony's bloody face look up at me as I drive away staring right into his eyes. His face was red with blood but I could see his eyes were filled with fiery and undeniable rage.

I figured this may be my chance to pack up and get out of this country. I told you it would get bloody, I told you this would get ugly, and it may not even be over yet. More blood may flow, more lives may be lost, more death may come.

Chapter XIII

WAR IS UPON US

I race down the road and quickly pull out my cell to call Trina. The phone keeps ringing and ringing then eventually goes to her voicemail. "Shit!" I say and frantically try again. Once more it goes to her voicemail and I start getting worried. I try the house phone as it rings and rings "Come on baby pick up please" I say getting more concerned by each unanswered ring. I hang up then race home thinking the worse. "You better not have touched her you son of a bitch" I say gritting my teeth zooming down the highway to my house.

As I race home I try to flush out the bad thoughts about what could be wrong, maybe she is sleeping and doesn't hear the phone, maybe she's in the garage, anything to rationalize why she isn't answering the phone. I take out my phone again and try her cell one last time and once again, four rings and then her voicemail. This may be bad. I said it would get ugly and it may have got that way. Seconds seem like hours as I race through the streets almost in a panic now. I see my house up ahead and can't wait to get out. I pull up to the house and slam on the brakes as the tires screech.

I grab my two guns from the glove box and slowly approach the house ready for a possible war. My worst fears may be realized as I see the front door half opened, looks like it was kicked in. I cautiously enter the house with the barrels of my guns guiding me along as I manoeuver my way around. I look around and to my horror, I see chairs knocked over, a light smashed on the floor, and the coffee table knocked over, all aftermath of a struggle. I wasn't sure if the person responsible was still here so I needed to remain as silent as can be. My heart is racing so fast I could almost hear it beating from my chest but I need to control the rage brewing and stay focused. I creep into the living room and hear the deafening bang of a gunshot and I hit the floor behind the sofa in anguish. I look at my shoulder which is burning with pain, I've been shot as blood oozes out of my left shoulder. I pause for a minute as I hear footsteps approaching me and I remain behind the couch out of view. I look at the reflection in the television above me and see a man advancing towards me armed with a gun. I stick my hand under the sofa with gun in hand and see his feet approaching. I fire three shots under the sofa at his feet and witness the blood spatter from his ankle and shin as a result of my bullets pelting his skin. He screams in agony as I pop up with gun in hand aimed at his chest. He looks at me and takes aim but not before I put two shots in his sternum and he descents to the floor with a blood soaked chest. I hear more footsteps approaching from my right as I move towards the wall. I take cover and keep out of sight as another man with a gun enters the room discovering his partner's bloody corpse on my living room floor. I approach the man now with gun drawn at him, and he looks at me in astonishment and tries to raise his gun. Too late as I have the draw on him, two more bullets from my gun had already entered his chest as he drops like a bag of potatoes. I look at both men on my floor both with blood pouring from their chests and I wonder "Who are you?"

My focus turns back to Trina as I run through the house with blood dripping from my shoulder as I clutch it in anguish. "Trina!" I scream looking around. "Trina please answer me!" as I continue to frantically look for her all over. To my terror, I don't find her, she isn't here. With gun still in hand I grab my head "No, this can't be happening." Just then I am startled by my cell phone going off. I reach for it standing in my bedroom with blood dripping off my arm. It's Tony. "Where is she you son of a bitch!" I scream as I answer the phone.

"Chris? Well I see you are still alive and kicking huh?" Tony chuckles seemingly in pain.

"Where is Trina!" I yell.

"Goddam, my face really hurts from smashing into that car. Nice move by the way, that was some Fast and Furious type shit. My car is busted up and my beautiful face hurts like a son of a bitch" Tony says.

"Where is she Tony!" I demand.

"I take it you're at home huh? And I also take it that my two pals over there are dead?" he asks.

I was starting to get impatient "Enough fucking around, where is Trina!"

"Trina is safe. I had her taken a while ago, you know for insurance purposes in case things went a little sideways. Lucky for me huh? Always thinking ahead" Tony says almost in a cheerful voice.

"Let her go, she has nothing to do with this" I say trying to remain calm pacing back and forth.

"You're right she doesn't. So you are going to do the right thing here or that pretty little girl of yours won't be so pretty anymore you hear?"

"I will hurt you for this Tony. I don't know how yet, but pain will come your way soon. A moment will come when you think you're safe and happy, and suddenly your joy will turn to ashes in your mouth, your happiness will turn to terror and you'll know that vengeance is paid when I strike you down in a storm of violence." I say in rage as spit is flying from my mouth.

"Look, I have to call you back in a bit okay, gotta get some stitches to my face, I hit that car pretty good and probably have a concussion so I can't think too straight now. Let me recover from that and I'll call ya soon and I will give you your options" he says and the phone goes dead.

"No!" I say in a rage and hurl my phone on the bed. I drop to my knees almost in defeat. The adrenaline was wearing off and I could feel the burning pain from my bullet wound in my shoulder and the discomfort was getting overwhelming. I was feeling light headed now from lose of blood, I need to go somewhere safe, some place I can trust, with someone I can trust. There was only one place I can think of.

I stumble to my car in agony and speed away. Not sure which pain was worse, the one in my shoulder or the pain in my heart. I just hope he doesn't hurt her, she didn't need to be involved in this. I make my way to the Church, Father WHISTLER lives in the basement and right now, he's all I got. I pull up to the Church and almost crawl up the stairs in pain and exhaustion. I burst into the Church and scream "Vince! Vince!" I stumble a few more feet before I collapse on the floor and my world goes black.

I wake up slowly on a bed and see my shoulder wrapped up nicely in gauze. I look around taking a few moments to realize where I was. I was in the Church as I sit up and look around trying to regain my senses. My head was pounding, my shoulder was killing me and I feel like shit.

"Chris, are you okay" a concerned voice says and rushes to my side.

"Vince" I say in relief. "How long have I been out?" I ask in pain.

"Few hours, you lost a lot of blood." He says.

I quickly check my phone, no calls. "Dammit! No calls" I say.

"What the heck happened?" Vince asks like a concerned Father.

I rub my face "It's bad. Jimmy is dead and I don't know where Trina is. Worst part is, I figured out who was behind all of this."

"Really?" he says sitting next to me.

"Tony, my best friend and lifelong pal. Anthony Benedict Arnold BECHERELLI."

"What?" Vince says in utter shock leaning back.

"Yep, all for money" I say bowing my head.

"And Jimmy is..."

"Dead" I say completing the sentence. I look at Vince almost with puppy dog eyes and say "They killed Jimmy and took Trina Vince, the two people that I needed to protect in this world and I have failed. I feel so lost right now, I have no idea what to do."

"My God Chris" he says putting his hand on his cheek in amazement. "Sounds like this has got way out of hand."

"I knew it would get ugly, I knew it would get bloody, I knew it would get messy, but I didn't want Jimmy or Trina to get hurt in all of this chaos. This should have been between me and Tony, they should not have even been involved in this mess."

"I know, but when you seek revenge like you have, you should have graves already dug because it never ends peacefully. Do you know where they took her?" Vince asks.

I put my face in my hands and say "No. No idea. This is all my fault. Jimmy is dead because of me and now I don't know where my girl is or what they are doing to her. It wasn't supposed to go down like this for fuck sake, this isn't how I saw this day going down when I woke up this morning."

"Nobody can see or predict the future my son. I mean we all seem to have a visualization in our head about what the future may be, but trying to predict the future is like trying to drive down a country road at night with no lights while looking out a black window having no clue where you're going or where you are. *For I know the plans I have for you, declares the Lord, plans for welfare and not for evil, to give you a future and a hope."*

I look at Vince in awe and say "Wow, I've never heard that one"

"Jerimiah 29:11. It's a great quote meaning God makes huge promises and keeps them. He controls the future. He knows exactly what will happen and can foresee your future, but the only way to see your own future, is to create it." Vince gets up and hands me a glass of water.

I drink from it and say "You mean I control my own destiny and all that crap."

Vince smiles and says "Ya, something like that."

"I'm kind of at his mercy right now though, he's got me by the balls sort of speak" I say shaking my head.

"Well turn that around."

"What do you mean?" I ask confused.

"There has to be a way that you can get him to be at your mercy, figuratively speaking. You need to find that edge, that something that will turn this around in your favor. You said he seems to be one step ahead of you, I don't see any reason why you can't be one step ahead of him" he says.

I look at the knife my father gave me and got an idea "You're right."

"I'll never condone vengeance, heck, half the time I'm up at the podium I'm preaching to people to avoid it like the plague. But I also understand that your life cannot go on until this is finished. I'm not telling you to go out there and be Rambo and shoot up everyone, I'm saying, finish this without getting any blood on your hands."

I smirk and say "Easier said than done, but I hear what you're saying. Sometimes violence is the only way to solve things. As much as I wish this could end peacefully, I know that won`t happen, that only happens in fairy tales and children`s novels."

"You know, your brother always said you had this uncanny knack for solving problems no matter the magnitude. If you guys were in trouble, you were always the one to get you guys out of it, you had a problem at school, you'd always find a way to fix it. Just a while ago you told me there was no way to ever solve who was behind all this, but, you solved that didn't you? Now the Chris I know will figure out how to get out of this mess, get his girlfriend and high tail it outta here to a new life."

I look at my cell phone and have an idea, almost like a light bulb going off. I grab my cell phone, stand up and put my shirt on.

"Where are you going?" Vince asked with concern.

I say with confidence in my voice "To solve this problem and go get Trina back."

Vince smiles and stands up "Don't do anything stupid, please stay safe my boy."

I look at Vince while I button up my shirt "I will" I lean in and give him a hug "Thanks for everything, I really mean that. I didn't mean to bring this on you, I just didn't have anywhere else to go."

"You're always welcome here you know that. I will always be here for you" Vince says with a smile as he looks at me like a proud father.

"I have to go and create a new future. It looked a bit dark a while ago, but I think I can brighten it up a bit" I say with a grin. "This may be the last I will ever see you, please take care of yourself, and know that I am great full for everything that you have done for me."

"Thank you, I will say a prayer for you and have God watch over you."

"Father, God may not want to see this" I say and proceed to the exit. Just then two men dressed in all black enter the church and I stop in my tracks.

"Excuse me sir, are you Chris SLAUGHTER by chance?" one of the men asks. He was a bigger muscular male, scruffy beard, an earring in each ear and dark sunglasses with a brush cut hair.

I look at both of them very uneasy "Who the heck are you guys?"

The other male states "LAPD, there is a warrant for your arrest." He was chubbier guy with a bald head and thick black beard wearing a black leather jacket.

I step back and ask "Your cops are you? Let me see your badges."

They both start to advance towards me as I back away and the muscular one says "Make this easy on yourself Chris and come quietly with us and we'll get this taken care of. You resist then we'll have no choice to do this the hard way, you don't want that do you?"

Vince then jumps in front of me and says to the men "Now hold on a second here, what gives you guys the right to just burst in here and make these demands and not even show your badges? What's the charge and do you have a warrant to be in here arresting him?"

They stop and the bald one sneers "What he is under arrest for is none of your Goddam business, and second, this is a public place so we don't need a warrant to come in. I don't really appreciate being questioned by some wanna be messenger of God. Now if I were you Father, I'd move out of our fucking way before your face gets smashed in and your teeth rearranged!"

"Hold on hold" on the other male says to his partner. "Now look Father, we just want to do this as easy as possible, we'll just take Chris in to the station, deal with his warrant and then he's free to go okay? Now please, I'll ask you nicely to move out of the way and let us do our job, this man is under arrest and we need to detain him."

Vince then takes out his cell phone and begins to dial "I'm going to check this out if you don't mind gentleman" but the bald one swipes the phone out of Vince's hand onto the ground leaving Vince with a stunned look.

"I told you to butt out Father, don't demean us by trying to call in and verify what we have just told you. You try something like that again then I am not going to be a very nice person, now get the fuck out of my way" the bald one yells and shoves Vince to the ground. He then reaches into his jacket, pulls out a sod-off shotgun and jams it into my chest "now put your hands behind your back asshole!"

I remain calm and raise my hands "Is that a police issued sod-off shotgun or what? Wow, the LAPD has some really unique issued weapons now days."

"You couldn't have just gone quietly could you Chris? You had to do things the hard way and be a pain in the ass didn't you?" the muscular one says. "Tony said that you may be a handful and now I can see what he meant."

I look him up and down "You both are Tony's friends huh? Boy oh boy, he keeps some really good company now days I see. Still haven't seen your badges, you guys real cops or just playing cops?"

The bald one smirks and the muscular one takes off his glasses "We are friends of Tony's, so we're close enough to being cops" he says snickering.

"He's deputized us" the bald one says and they both chuckle.

"Let me ask you guys, what do you get out of bringing me in huh? Is he paying you, or are you just doing this for the thrill?" I ask looking at the gun jammed into my chest trying to figure out what I'm going to do.

"What does that really matter to you anyway?" the muscular one says gritting his teeth and eyeballing me. "From what I hear, you are going to die a very slow agonizing death. I know who ALVAREZ is, and let me tell you something, he is evil in a way that you can't even begin to comprehend."

"That right? Well fellows, hate to disappoint you, but I had no plans on dying anytime soon" I respond sarcastically.

The bald one chuckles looks at his partner and says "he's saying that like he has a choice."

The muscular one looks me in the eyes and scowls "don't even think about reaching for a gun or trying anything stupid because I guarantee you Chris, you won't win."

I look at him and give him a sarcastic grin "You gonna shoot me? That won't go over too well with Tony, putting him out ten million bucks. Better tell your partner here to be careful keeping his finger on the trigger or the gun may just go off."

The muscular one looks at his partner then back at me "Jesus Christ you are a wise ass aren't you? What say me and you dance right now, man on man?" and leans into me taking of his jacket wanting to fight.

"Wouldn't be a fair fight, there's only two of you, you'd better call for more if you want to make this fair" I said trying to be serious. My mind was now calculating what my next move will be as I try to play out what I'm going to do next.

"Just leave this house of God you no good thugs!" Vince yells still on the ground.

The bald one draws the gun to Vince's head and screams "You shut the fuck up old man or I'll put a bullet right between your fucking eyes!"

I saw my opportunity and snatch the barrel of the gun and deliver a viscous elbow to the mouth of the bald guy who stumbles back loosing grip of the gun which I swiftly grab and retreat. The muscular guys instinctively whips out a gun and fires a shot my way striking a wooden pillar next to me as I duck. "Come on Vince get up" I yell and help Vince to his feet and dive behind a pew as two more shots blast off splintering the pew we had just ducked behind. I stand up and fire a shot back at the muscular guy who now ducks and behind a pew as well. I see the bald one now retreat behind another pew with blood now oozing from his mouth.

"You okay?" I ask Vince who looks petrified.

"Ya, ya I'm fine" he responds almost as if he was in shock.

The church goes eerily silent as I couldn't hear anything besides the buzzing of the lights. "Here Vince, take this" I whisper giving him the gun.

Vince raises his hands and says "I can't Chris, no."

"Vince, take the dam gun alright!" I demand as he reluctantly takes the gun from me. I draw one of my pistols and slowly stand up to look around but can't see anything. My heart begins to race as I am not sure where these guys are or what they may be up to. I leisurely stay low and stroll over to the confessional booth and was greeted by a gun blast hitting the edge of the booth just missing my head. I get startled and duck into the booth as I did not see where the gun shot came from. I sit still and now I could hear footsteps ever so quietly advancing my way.

"Hey Chris" the voice says as it approaches me. "Come out and play Chris, we just want to talk that's all." The voice sounded sarcastic and possibly could be the bald one that's approaching me. "You broke my fucking teeth, you're gonna have to pay for that you little bitch!" I try my best to stay calm and think of a way out of this. The wood in this booth was thin, almost paper thin, if I could judge where he is at the right time, I may be able to shoot through the wood and hit him. Risky proposition I just presented to myself, but it's worth a try. I look at Vince who was still on the ground as I raise my finger to my lips indicating for him to stay quiet. I stand completely still and try to listen to the footprints and try gauge a distance. My ears pick up the sound of steps approaching, my guess, about ten feet from where I am. I take my gun and place it near one of the wooden walls of the booth and try my best to aim at where I think this guy may be in a few steps from now. My heart begins to race as I try to tell myself to be calm and control your heartbeat and emeotions. I stand ready, close my eyes and listen for two or three more steps before I pull the trigger. Five feet away now as I gently retract the trigger and let off a thundering shot as wood splinters fly in my face as I keep my eyes closed. I listen as there was nothing but silence as I remain perfectly frozen, and then I hear a thud as if a body that had just plummeted to the ground. I peek through the bullet hole that I had just made and see the bald one face first on the floor in front of me. I quietly exit the booth and creep back towards Vince who was sitting on the ground with the shotgun in hand.

"You doing okay Vince?" I asked.

Vince then points the gun at me as my eyes widen with shock. He lets off a deafening shot that I feel wiz past my ear. I gawk at him in disbelief then quickly look behind me and see the muscular guy clutching his mid-section which was seeping out blood. The muscular guy drops his gun to the floor in pain, falls to his knees while holding his stomach, then collapses face first onto the floor with a sickening thud. I then look back at Vince who had the gun still in hand with a smoking barrel and a look of disbelief. He then says "I got your back Chris" and grins.

I smile back at him and respond "thank you Father" extend my hand and help him up. I examine the two thugs and say "Cops my ass, these are more hired goons courteously of my good friend Tony."

"He needs you bad, he's desperate now. Tides may have turned" Vince says looking at the two thugs lying face first motionless on the church floor.

"This can't be the same person that I grew up with all these years, I mean how can I have been so wrong about someone? I never in my wildest dreams ever saw anything like this coming nor would I have ever fathomed that he would conjure up such sinister plans like this. How could

I have misjudged a person so bad and have been blind all these years?"

Vince shakes his head and simply says "Friends make the best enemies. They know all of your friends, who you'll turn to for help, who you care about and what your next moves will be. I too have misjudged Tony, I always saw him as a proud Police Officer always striving to be like his Dad. I haven't the slightest clue how a soul can just become so jaded like that overnight. A moment of opportunity can erase a lifetime of friendship and delete everything good that he has ever done."

I lower my head "It's sad Vince, I've lost a really good friend in Tony. Over twenty years of memories all come crashing down in one night. I just don't get it."

Vince puts his hand on my shoulder "You need to get out of here my son. This place will soon be swarming with cops and we don't know which one of them are on Tony's side." I look at the two thugs and Vince says "don't worry about it, I'll take care of it all, I won't mention your name whatsoever."

I simply hug Vince and he says "Get going and start that new future of yours."

I let go and saunter to the exit, I stop and look back "Thank you, from the bottom of my heart Vince, thank you" then leave the church.

I get into my car and drive off squealing the tires, I was on a mission now. My mind is filled with rage as I drive angry envisioning the face of my once friend now turned enemy. Best movie line and bible quote that I ever heard from Pulp Fiction was when Samuel Jackson quoted *"And I will strike down upon thee with great vengeance and furious anger those who attempt to poison and destroy my brothers. And you will know I am the Lord when I lay my vengeance upon you"* then unloaded his pistol at that dude. Awesome, simply awesome and very fitting. Tony will feel my wrath and will be at my mercy, think two steps ahead my father told me, I've already planned five moves ahead with plan B's lined up. That bastard Tony put his knife in my back, I'll put my gun to his head. You know that saying when people say, when life gives you lemons, make lemonade? I say fuck that, if life gives me lemons I'll squeeze them shooting lemon juice in your eyes and watch you suffer as it burns and stings. You took the woman I love from me, all bets are off. Trina is my true soul mate and one of few people in this world that I would die for.

I remember the first night I ever met Trina. I was at this high class extravagant night club with a few of my friends. I had only been in the contract killing business for just under a year and was living the high life already. Then I saw her, she was wearing this dazzling low cut violet dress, her hair was a flaxen rich blonde that flowed naturally in waves down to her mid back. Her skin was a flawless peaches and cream color which looked so soft and gentle I couldn't help but want to touch it. Her eyes, oh her eyes were a sparkling baby blue color that brightened the room framed with long gorgeous dark lashes. Her lips were a soft rose color that were in the perfect shape and had an elegant shine to them. I couldn't keep my eyes off of her as I watched her move through the room. Her smile almost took my breath away when I first saw it, seductive but welcoming, and when people around her saw that smile, they couldn't help but smile as well. She walked up to the bar right beside me. I needed to say something, something clever and witty. I opened my mouth and my brain went blank and all I could think of to say to her was "So, do you come here often?"

She looked at me with an amusing smile and said "Well, that's original" and chuckled.

I chuckled back and said "I agree, but I didn't have time to rehearse, or else I would have thought of something a lot better to say."

She smiled, turned to me and said "Oh ya? Well, why don't you try it again, I'll give you a do over."

Dam, she had put me on the spot and I needed to think quick. She looked at me with that charming smile of hers and I was hypnotised by her dazzling eyes and captivated by her enchanting scent. I smiled and said, "You know why the sky is so gray today?"

She smirked and said "No why?"

"Because all the blue vanished from the sky to be in your eyes" I responded and chuckled.

She bursted out laughing and said "Cheesy, but very creative."

I shared the laugh with her and giggled "And that was rehearsed."

As the night went by, we talked and talked and I never relished a woman's company the way I did hers that night. I couldn't take my eyes off of her, she was so gorgeous and I didn't want to miss out on one single expression that came upon her stunning face. We went back to my place and made love in the most passionate way I have ever felt before, almost like a fantasy come to life. Our bodies connected, and every time I touched her I got goose bumps as we were swimming in an ocean of pure bliss. Never did I feel so bonded to another human being the way I was with her that night.

After that seamlessly perfect night, came the next morning when she asked me the one question I dreaded she'd ask and I feared to answer.

"So, I never asked you, but what is it that you do for a living to afford a beautiful big house like this?" she asked.

It took me a few minutes to answer as I debated telling her the truth. If I told her that I kill people and get paid to do it, she may be disgusted or mortified and I will never see her again. Then again, if I lied to her, I'd pretty much have to keep up that lie for my entire time I'm with her telling her lie after lie after lie. I looked at her and she could see that I was struggling getting the words out of my mouth.

"Geeze it can't be that bad, I mean unless you're a lawyer or something" she said with a grin.

"Trina" I said softly, "I have no idea how to tell you what I do for a living and I'm not going to lie. It's is very complicated and not too flattering. I am" I paused and looked down asking myself if I'm doing the right thing? "I am a contract killer."

Trina looked at me with a blank stare, then erupted with laughter. "Oh my God Chris, you had me going, and you seemed so serious and genuine when you said it" she said and continued to chuckle.

I stood there not changing the expression on my face almost insulted by her reaction and said "Get dressed and come downstairs" and left the room. At that moment, I thought I was way over my head by telling this person that I had just met, something that I wanted to keep a secret from everyone and something that could land me in jail for the rest of my life. A secret like this should remain in the vault, sealed inside it forever for nobody to see. I just felt that Trina at that moment was the one and if she could accept this, it would confirm my feeling that we were meant to be together. She walked downstairs dressed in only a t shirt. She had a more serious look on her face now as she stood at the bottom of my stairs with confused and someone concerned draped on her face.

"Follow me" I said as I led her into my garage.

I saw her stroll in and instantly she was in awe of my three stunning exotic sports cars, a 2001 bright red Lamborghini Veneno Roadster, a sky blue Dodge Viper GTS, and of course my jet black 2004 Porsche 911. "Wow" she said admiring the beauty of my cars as they all glimmered and almost smiled at her with cockiness. I unlocked my cabinet and opened it wide up to reveal its contents which I am sure will get a stunning reaction. Trina looked at what was inside the cabinet which was now staring her in the face. I saw her jaw drop and her eyes widen at what she saw before her, my arsenal. Handguns, automatic weapons, sniper rifles, knives, and even a few grenades.

"Jesus Christ" she said astonished and looked at me with amazement. I couldn't tell whether reaction was horror, amazement, excitement, confusion, or just simply speechless. I saw her slowly move towards the cabinet and gently petted one of the sniper rifles, almost like it was a new born puppy. She moved her hand up and gently strokes the AK-47 with the softest of touch. "My Lord Chris, you weren't kidding were you" she said now almost in an approving voice, or so I hoped.

I stood behind her quietly letting her take it all in, letting her brain wrap around the idea that I get paid to kill people. It's not an easy thing to accept once it gets absorbed into ones brain, let alone let the realization set in that you are standing in the very same room as a killer. I was waiting with nervous anticipation on what she would say next, will it be approval or mortification?

She turned around and looked at me with a newfound intrigue. "So, how many have you killed?"

I quietly looked at her, raised four fingers in the air and simply said "Four." I was almost beside myself as I revealed all this to a complete stranger. Was I an idiot?

She looked me up and down and my heart beats faster than a racing horse anticipating what she might say next. She smiled and said "I always wanted a man who was mysterious, dangerous and unconventional."

I grinned and said "You should be careful what you wish for, may just come true. The stars up there in the heaven are all waiting for people to wish upon them ya know."

She approached me with a radiant smile on her face, wrapped her arms around me and kissed me more passionately than she did last night. It was a different kind of kiss, harder, more passionate and with more lust. We made love right on the hood of my Lamborghini in a more heated and sensual way than we did a few hours ago, it was magic and at that very moment, I confirmed that I found my girl and soul mate.

So, for the entire rest of that day, I told her everything, about how I met JONES who gave me my first contract to how I met Jimmy and became a successful tag team with him. It was weird at first telling her all that stuff, but for some reason I trusted her and felt a true genuine connection with her like I have never felt before with any other girl that I've been with. That single day thus far was the happiest twenty four hours of my entire life, I could never remember a time when I was more happier to be alive and more thankful for the gift of being able to feel such intense emotions. Trina moved in with me after two weeks and we have had the perfect relationship ever since, almost like a storybook.

Trina is one of the smartest people that I know, and I'm not just saying that because she's my girl, she is an extremely intelligent person. I have never met anyone so quick witted and filled with so much self-assurance as she has. In under a years' time she produced her own clothing line called StarLight which became an instant success getting contracts from major fashion stores to sell her line. She was studying to be a fashion major when I met her and I leant her the money to get her own business launched, and she was now running her own clothing line with her own label, and that was how I justified everything I owned to keep the Feds away. Her business was now my front and everything at that point was as perfect as perfect could be.

I'm not sure why I never proposed to her in all this time, I mean there was no doubt that I love her with all my heart, and of course I know I'll be with her forever, but I didn't have an answer to why I haven't popped the question. Apprehension? Procrastination? I have no clue, but I did plan on popping the big question once we crossed the Mexican border. I already had the ring custom made ready to go, a stunning bright black diamond stone as big as my fingernail in the shape of a heart surrounded by a border of 24 carat diamonds.

I wait now with nervous and eager anticipation for Tony to call as I have my head set in my ear. I could see the sun rise in a beautiful orange glow with a very calm breeze in the air. My phone rings, I know it's him as I press the ANSWER button on my head set and just listen.

"Solomon Grundy, born on a Monday, christened on Tuesday, married on Wednesday, took ill on Thursday, grew worse on Friday, died on Saturday, buried on Sunday.

That was the end of Solomon Grundy. Just substitute your name for Solomon Grundy" Tony chuckles.

"Brilliant, you think of that one yourself?" I sarcastically ask.

"Well I thought since you gave me a nursery rhyme about the gold hen I should return the favor. I betcha not too many people know that one."

"Goose" I correct him.

"Shit, ya ya I always screw that up. I thought of Solmon Grundy just for you buddy, I searched my brain for the perfect nursery rhyme for you since you came up with one for me."

"I'm flattered" again I say sarcastically. "Nice move by the way sending two of your henchmen to try to ambush me at the Church, classy move."

"Always have to have plan B's and plan C's buddy. I know you're a sneaky little bastard and I had to use every opportunity to nab you when I could. You being your predictable self, I knew you'd go see Vince at the Church, so naturally I knew where to find you."

I shake my head "Why didn't you come just get me yourself instead of making me kill two of your hired goons?"

"Okay enough chit chat, let's get down to business. It's real simple here Christopher, my boys have Trina right now as we speak with a knife to her throat, you turn yourself to me, I'll let her go. You don't and her blood will be spilled. Easy as baking a pie right?"

"How bout you let her go and I won't expose you to the world as the rat scum that you really are" I say in response.

Tony snickers and says "You have nothing to threaten me with, and that is a pathetic attempt of trying to blackmail me. You go to the cops and tell them some bullshit story about me, who the hell do you think they will believe?"

I pull out my Dad's knife, as I remembered it was also a recorder. I hold it to my mouthpiece and push play:

TONY: *I posed as Mr.BOUCHER and sent Jimmy a photo of good ole BOULDERDASH sporting his boys green hat and ordered the hit on him.*

I stopped and forwarded the recording a bit, then pushed play again:

ME: you mean you shot Tiger in the face?

TONY: Ha ha. Ya, fuck, I blasted him point blank in the head boom, thought it'd be one less piece of trash in this world if I put a bullet in his head. How the hell did he survive that? Dam Frenchman are tough to kill. Shit man, he must be all fucked up in the brain and have half a head or something eh.

I stopped the tape again and say, "You made a crucial mistake that no cop should ever make, you forgot to pat me down and search me. I had this knife my Dad gave me that was also a recorder, I switched it on the second I met up with you last night. Don't trust anyone my Dad said, words to live by."

I heard Tony turn away from the phone and scream from the top of his lungs "FUCK!!!!" He comes back on and says in fury "You sneaky Goddam little son of a bitch!"

"Might be tough getting that top cop award after ordering a hit on a US Senator and attempted murder of an unarmed Frenchman huh? Can't imagine what prisoners will do to a dirty cop in jail either, especially those gang bangers you put away" I said rather amused by how enraged he was.

"Ok here's the deal" Tony says trying to compose himself. "You give me that recorder, I'll give you my recording then you surrender to me, and Trina gets to live out her life. I mean, you always said you'd give your life for hers so here's your chance. And you will die with all of your secrets never revealed."

I think for a second to give him false hope "How bout this. You take that suggestion, roll it up into a nice little ball and shove it straight up your ass!"

"Dammit Chris, I'm giving you a way to save Trina. You don't take this deal then she's no use to me, I make the call to my guy and he slices her fucking throat so deep she'll be decapitated. Then I hunt you down like the animal you are and deliver you with a bright red bow to ALVEREZ and Trina would have died because of your stubbornness. How does that sound!"

"Remember that thing I told you about searching people?" I say calmly. "Thing is, I bet you didn't bother searching Trina and see that she has her cell phone with her. You also may not realize that her cell phone has a GPS device on it too."

Tony chuckles and says "You'll never get to her in time my friend, all I have to do is push send on my cell phone and her throat is sliced open by my guy who is waiting for that call."

"You got real good friends don't you Tony? I mean to call Lil Alonzo your friend? I mean, come on let's get real here" I say with utter amusement.

"Wait" Tony says baffled "How the hell do you know I have Alonzo working with me?"

"Because! I'm looking at him through my crosshairs" I say embracing Charlotte pointing her at Alonzo's head. He was with another guy and Trina was in the middle of them both looking frightened as could be. They were in an old junk yard and I saw the twinkle of the blade in Alonzo's hand as I sit perched in the distance.

I hear Tony say "Shit!" and hang up the phone. As I look at Alonzo through my scope and see him get startled by his phone ringing. He answers it and then brings the knife up about to cut Trina's throat but, he stops right in his tracks as one of my bullet's find's it's mark right to his forehead and a red mist of his blood flies out the back of his skull. I reload Charlotte quick in case the other thug has any bright ideas. I see Alonzo plunge face first onto the ground and drop his knife and cell phone on his way down. Sure enough, the other thug reaches for the knife with deadly intentions.

"Focus" I whisper to myself and ever so gently squeeze the trigger letting off another thunderous shot. I see the bullet hit the thug right in the ear as some of his blood exited the other side of his head and splashed onto Trina's pants. I see Trina stunned as she looks in the direction of the shot. I quickly dial her cell and see her pick it up.

"Trina baby are you okay?" I ask with a concerned voice.

"Yes, oh my God" she says bursting into tears overwhelmed with emotions. "They said they were going to kill me and that were going to expose you as the one who killed the Senator yesterday. What the hell is going on?"

"It's almost over baby okay. Trina I want you to head over to my Dad's house now on the double, you'll be safe there and he's expecting you. My car is just out front, the keys are in it, it's the Viper. Wait for me there, I'll come get you when I'm finished."

"What are you going to do Chris?" she asks.

"I need to deal with Tony once and for all. The showdown is about to take place and I'm the Sherriff" I say.

"Can't you just come with me? We can leave for the border right now and leave this all behind us?" she asks looking around trying to find me.

"Trina baby, please trust me, I need this to end right now. I know what I'm doing, that son of a bitch is going down for this, and he's going down before this day ends."

"Why is he doing this? He is your best friend?" she asked puzzled.

"Was my best friend" I correct her. "This will never end unless I finish this today. Trust me when I say this babe, we will be sipping margaritas tonight ocean side, just me and you, ok?"

"Okay babe. I love you so much" she says with emotion in her voice.

"I love you too babe. I will see you soon" I respond and hang up.

I need to finish this today or I will keep looking over my shoulders for the rest of my life. This story needs to come to an end, in life, every story has an ending, but to every ending, there is a new beginning that is just waiting to be revealed. Every story can have a happy ending if you want it to, all you have to do is just choose where to end it. I could easily just leave right now for Mexico with Trina, but unfortunately, that would not be the end of this story. It may be happy, but it won't be an ending.

Tony is sly and crafty but I will wait for his next move. He may either be on the hunt already trying to track me down, or he's thinking of a game plan in that evil malevolent mind of his. Either way, I am two steps ahead of him anticipating the move with his Bishop and countering it with my Knight. I walk back to my Porsche where a good friend of mine had dropped it off for me. It's a little worse for wear, but it cannot be mistaken as mine.

"Python hands me the keys to my car shaking my hand looking deep into my eyes "Whatever business you have to finish right now, remember what I said. Be calm, be methodical and outwit this motherfucker!"

"Thanks Ty. I have a game plan in mind already. I listened to your words man and it gave me an idea that may get me out of this" I respond.

Ty bumps my fist with his and says "You ever need any help Chris, you holla at me ya hear?"

I nod and say "Ya, I hear. Thanks bro."

I drive to a nearby coffee house to take a load off, have a cup of coffee and get some food in me before this whole crazy story is about to come to an end. I'm leaving it up to Tony to make the first move, I figure if I call him first, he'll feel like I'm the one coming to beg for a deal giving him the upper hand. He does have that recording of me admitting to killing Senator BOULDERDASH, but I have him on my recording putting out a hit on a Senator, so we're at stale mate. Still, I have to remain patient, even though I have the urge to pick up the phone and call Tony to get this thing over with, I need to be the one in control here. Besides, he may be thinking the same thing and waiting on me to come to him, so I need to remain patient and let him squirm a little. Patience is power and is not an absence of action rather it is timing. It waits on the right time to act, for the right principles and in the right way to do something to ensure it is done properly.

I slowly sip my hot coffee as I munch on a muffin and can't help ponder and envision how this may end today, bloody? Violent? Shootout? Who knows. My clothes are all dusty, my hair is a mess, probably don't smell too great and my shoulder is killing me, but I know even though Tony may be thinking one step ahead of me, I'm already thinking three steps ahead of him. I pop two Advil for the pain in my shoulder, lucky for me it was a clean shot through my shoulder so there will be minimal damage. Funny, almost two days ago, I was in a coffee shop not unlike this one, drinking a coffee with Tony as I was getting eager to start my brand new life with the girl of my dreams. Little did I know, the next forty eight hours would involve me shooting a US Senator, having a gun pointed at my head twice, be tied to a chair by my once best friend, see my true best friend get shot up, get into a high speed car chase, get shot in my own home, and shoot six thugs dead while saving my girlfriend.

I pick up my phone and dial "Room 223 please" I say to the receptionist on the other end.

"Hello."

"Hey Nate, how are you brother" I say with joy.

"Hey Chris, what's going on bro?" he asks seemingly with a smile.

"Nothing man, just had a rough fucked few days. Just need to chill out, relax and talk to someone that I know and trust."

"Everything ok?" he asks concerned.

"It will be, soon" I say with a little uncertainty. I didn't want to tell Nate about what has been going on, he really doesn't need do hear about all this garbage and the predicament that I'm in right now. "Just had one of those days you know" I say sipping my coffee.

"Ha, why, did you put a scratch on your Porsche or something?" he asks with a chuckle.

I look at my badly damaged Porsche outside and with a snicker and respond "Ya, it got dinged up a bit." I become more serious now, I couldn't be one hundred percent sure how this day will end for me, so in case this was the last time I got to speak to my brother, I better get some things off my chest "I really miss you brother, I mean I really wish you weren't in that dam hospital bed and you were out here enjoying life with me you know? Going on vacations with our families, partying it up in Vegas on a boys weekend, I just want my brother back. But no matter what, I love you man, you are my best friend."

Nate responds with a chuckle "I ain't dead yet."

"You know what I mean. The world just ain't fair sometimes Nate, you don't deserve this" I say trying not to get choked up.

"Well, I know I've been dealt a rather shitty hand in life, I sat down in the poker game betting on my life and got dealt an unwinnable hand. But rather than fold and walk away, I'd rather stick around a bit until the game is truly over. We can't choose the hands that are dealt to us, some people get good hands, some get risky hands, some get dealt a winning hand right off the bat, some have to work hard and try to get a winning hand, some are dealt a crappy hand, and then there are those that get dealt a hand that is unwinnable. You can't ask for new cards just because you don't like the ones in your hand, you just have to accept it and do the best you can with what you're given. I have been through all of the five stages of acceptance. You know what they are?" he asks.

"Mmm" I think "refresh my memory."

"Denial which is the first thing I did, convincing myself that the doctor must have made a mistake, anger which was aimed at God as I asked him how can you do this to me. Bargaining which again I've done with God trying to make some sort of deal with him, then depression where I felt sorry for myself and wanted everyone else to feel sorry for me too. And finally Chris there is the stage that I'm on right now which is acceptance, and it's not a bad or negative thing. Acceptance of my life has nothing to do with my resignation that I've handed in to God, it doesn't mean that I'm running away from the struggle or the road block in front of me either. On the contrary, it means that

I am accepting fate as it comes, with all the handicaps of heredity, of suffering, of psychological complexes and injustices" Nate preaches.

I listen with admiration as I hear Nate speak these words that I don't know if I could ever say. I take a bite of my muffin as I still felt in awe of Nate's positive outlook even in his darkest hour. "I still can't accept it thought bro, I don't know why but I can't. I think I'm stuck somewhere between denial and anger still. You're a trooper, you've always been."

Nate changed the subject and in a more cheerful voice said "Dad called a while ago, said you stopped over there last night and had dinner."

"Ya. Figured I needed to see him, he wasn't the perfect Dad, but he is ours and I do love him and he always loved us" I say while taking another sip and scanning the coffee house, just in case.

"I doubt Dad saw a future like this with his sons. One slowly dying and the other, ha ha, well does what you do" he says still in good spirit.

"Should have joined me, we'd make a good team" I say in joking way.

"Shit. I remember the day you sat me down and told me what exactly you got yourself into with Jimmy. I think I went through all five of those stages. Denial because I laughed my ass off when you told me figuring it was a joke. Anger because as your big brother, I told you that you could ruin your life by doing something so stupid. Bargaining, telling you I won't split your lip if you quit right now. Then finally I accepted it. Didn't agree with it whatsoever, but I accepted it. I still don't, but you know what, my mind is at ease knowing you take out the scum of society, something deep down we all wish we could do, fact is, you are getting paid to do it."

"I'm not proud of what I do Nate, I don't enjoy" I look around and mutter "you know, whacking people or taking someone's life, it's something I fell into and just didn't have the smarts to walk away from."

"You remember when we were small and Mom took us to the park that one day. She told us to write down on a piece of paper what our future was going to be like when we were adults and draw a picture of our house and family, then she buried it in the ground and said we'd all dig it up in twenty five years and see how close we came to actually predicting our lives. You remember that day?"

"Ya. Of course I do" I say softly as I remember my Mom.

"You remember what you wrote?"

I smile and look up trying to remember "I think I wrote that I was going to be married to Mariah Carey, I was going to be a doctor, and I was going to have eight kids. You?"

"Ha" Nate giggled "Oh I think I said I was going to be the quarterback for the Dallas Cowboys, be married to one of the cheerleaders, drive a Ferrari, and have two boys who will also be NFL quarterbacks because I'd teach them."

I smile "That was a great day. We went out and had ice cream and went home and watched movies all night together. We were a good family."

"I miss Mom. She was the perfect Mom wasn't she? I mean, she spoiled us rotten, but yet was strict in a way that we never got mad over it, dunno how she did that. God took her away from us way too early and I never understood why."

"We all die. The moment we are born, we are dying. But nobody in this world is immortal, even though as kids we always think our parents are. Believe in the good Lord, God always offers us peace in even the darkest of circumstances and we should remember that even God's son was not spared from death" I preach.

"Hey, that was nice. Wish I say bible stuff like that and sound spiritual" Nate chuckles.

"Gotta read the book first."

"Ha, ya, guess that would help." He pauses "I'm looking forward to new scenery in Mexico, just want to see that big beautiful ocean one last time before I pass, and a few little Mexican senioritas would hurt either."

I bow my head hoping that I can keep this promise I was about to mutter "You will Nate. It will be a nice change for all of us."

"Ya it…shit, nurse is here with my breakfast. Hey bro, gotta go, call me later okay?" Nate says.

"Will do brother, I love you man, you are the best brother anyone could ever have."

"Love you too bro, and, you ain't so bad yourself" Nate chuckles.

I hang up the phone with a smile and sip my coffee. For those minutes I was on the phone with Nate, I escaped reality and this world for a bit. I almost didn't want to get off the phone and have to face the rest of this day. I grit my teeth at the thought of Tony kidnapping Trina and quote to myself in a bitter whisper as I rehearse one of the greatest bible quotes of all time, Nahum 1:2-8, *The Lord is a jealous and avenging God; the Lord takes vengeance and is filled with wrath. The Lord takes vengeance on his foes and vents his wrath against his enemies. The Lord is slow to anger but great in power; the Lord will not leave the guilty unpunished. His way is in the whirlwind and the storm, and clouds are the dust of his feet. He rebukes the sea and dries it up; he makes all the rivers run dry. Bashan and Carmel wither and the blossoms of Lebanon fade. The mountains quake before him and the hills melt away. The earth trembles at his presence, the world and all who live in it. Who can withstand his indignation? Who can endure his fierce anger? His wrath is poured out like fire; the rocks are shattered before him. The Lord is good, a refuge in times of trouble. He cares for those who trust in him, but with an overwhelming flood he will make an end of Nineveh; he will pursue his foes into the realm of darkness".*

Just as I was gritting my teeth with rage, a young lady stands next to me and says politely "Having a bad day already?"

I look up and her startled. She was very attractive and had a glow to her while she was standing there with her coffee smiling at me with dazzling cherry lips and beautiful flowing jet black hair. "Oh, uh, ya guess you could say that."

She gives me a breathtaking smile and says, "Do you mind terribly if I sit down, there are no empty tables and I see you have an empty seat," she looks around "unless you are with someone?"

I chuckle and say "No." I point to the chair and say "please by all means sit."

"Thanks" she says and sits down. "I'm Jillian" and reaches out her hand.

I smile and say "Chris" and shake her hand, her skin was flawless and she had the softest hands I've ever felt.

"Rough night or rough morning?" she asks and sips her coffee.

"Both" I say. She smelled enchanting and was dressed up in a business blazer and skirt. She was definitely easy on the eyes and I immediately could tell she was well educated or at least very successful. I look her up and down and ask "Let me guess, lawyer?"

Jillian smiles in delight and says "Far from it. I'm a psychiatrist, my office is on 50ᵗʰ." She looks at her coffee "I always start my day with my coffee, somehow it's just become psychological that I can't start my day until I have my first cup of coffee. Not really sure I even need it, but I've become so use to the habit, it would be just weird to not have a cup. I mean did you know that over sixty percent of Americans say that they need coffee to start their day in order to feel like themselves, and over seventy percent say they drink that cup within the first hour of waking up." She pauses and almost blushes "I'm sorry, don't mean to bore you or sound like a nerd."

My eyes widen and I say "No no, not at all. I guess I have a morning ritual, not really sure if is considered a ritual."

She sips her coffee and crosses her legs waiting to hear what I have to say.

"I have to look at myself in the mirror every morning, I mean I need to do it before I can consider starting my day. Not sure why, maybe it's to reassure myself that nothing changed while I was asleep." I look up at her and grin almost like a kid "I mean, for eight hours or so, I'm not sure what my body is doing during the night, so, every morning I need to saunter over to the mirror and give myself a once over from head to toe to be sure I'm the same person that I was last night. I mean I'd dread the thought of not looking in the mirror and something be out of place and me walking around not knowing about it" Jillian smiles and chuckles a bit and I join her chuckle "Stupid isn't it?"

"Not at all, it's actually a very common thing. There is a deeper meaning of why someone does that every day. Sometimes it's to reassure one's self that they still look appealing as ever and need to see that first hand for themselves every morning, or maybe they feel ugly or less attractive and want to see if they perceive themselves that way every time they look in the mirror. Funny thing is, whether we know it or not, we see a different person in the mirror every day. One day we may be ugly, one day we may be fat, one day we may be as handsome or as pretty as ever, and other days we just stare blankly not knowing what to think" Jillian explains.

I think to myself and say to her "Not sure if that's why I look in the mirror every day" and sip my coffee.

"Well" she says "other people look at themselves in the mirror to make sure that they are able to look at the person staring back at them by looking deep down into their soul and asking themselves if they are truly proud who they are" she preaches.

"Huh" I say looking down with a disappointing realization "I think you just nailed it right there Jillian."

"Call me Jill. You have demons in your closet Chris? Sorry I don't mean to pry." she asks sounding genuinely concerned.

"More than a closet full, more like a mansion full."

"Do mind if I give you some advice and knowledge?" she leans in and asks.

"Free advice from a psychiatrist? I'm all ears."

"You are not the physical body that you see in the mirror every day, that is just a sort of a temporary suit that you are renting to walk around in while you live your life on this earth. The actual you is your soul that is dwelling inside of that physical body of yours that you are renting. Your physical body is temporary, I mean one day it will cease to exist and it will die, your body will decompose, rot and be no more, but your soul is eternal, it is forever and nothing can destroy that." She put down her coffee and looks into my eyes "When your physical body dies, your soul will come out of it and move on to one of two eternal dimensions. The undesirable one is an evil place called Hell. Hell is like a jail you can never get out of because there is no key and is the place where all the enemies of God end up. Only God can save your soul from going to Hell. Why would God want to do that? Because God loves you, even though you've done nothing to earn His love, He will just loves you unconditionally. So no matter what your demons are, God looks deeper inside of you and sees the true soul of a person and that is how one is judged after death and that is how He will decide if he wants to save your eternal soul or not. Don't just look at the body or exterior when you look in the mirror, look at your heart and your soul" she says.

I look at her in amazement and say "Wow. That is the deepest darkest explanation that I have ever heard."

She now looks at my eyes with intensity and says "You know how they say eyes are the windows to your soul? Eyes can tell a lot about a person. Take you for instance, when we were talking about you and yourself looking in the mirror, your pupils contracted telling me it was an issue you were not comfortable in discussing. But, when I just gave you that explanation, your pupils widened meaning you were interested and wanted to listen to what I had to say. That tells me you are battling your eternal soul but want to hear the explanation on how to cleanse it and become a better person. You also avoided eye contact when I asked you if you had demons in your closet which tells me you are ashamed or not proud of some previous things you've done in your life and maybe now you were looking for a change or fresh start, wipe the slate clean as they say."

I noticed my mouth was open with amazement and I said "Holy shit." I paused and looked at her and said "You're good. I mean, you pretty much summed me up within five minutes of talking with me, I'm blown away." I smirk and say "Imagine what you could do for me or reveal in a few sessions. Geeze, kinda scary to think about."

She reaches into her purse and hands me a card and politely says "Call me and we can try it out, no pressure or anything, just whenever you want to let those demons out and talk about it, let me know."

I take the card and she asks "You battling those demons today? Just asking due to your clothes and wicked wild hair due."

I smile and rub my hair "No, just battling an old friend turned enemy that's all. Guess you can say he is the demon sort of."

She sips her coffee and says "Bummer. You know they say the best revenge is living well, I say that is a load of crap. I can see that you seek revenge so can I give you one last piece of advice before I take off?"

I look at her and say "Shoot."

She looks deep into my eyes, almost into my soul and says "It isn't the strong or fierce who get the greatest victories in life, it's the smart and cunning that truly reap their rewards and come out victorious. Out think him Chris, don't out try to out power him. Know why Muhammad Ali was the greatest?"

"No" I asked softly hanging on her every word.

She stood up and said "Wasn't because he was the strongest, or faster, or toughest, it's because he was the smartest, that's why he was successful" and she walks towards the door. She takes one look back and me and says with a beautiful radiant smile and says "Food for thought. Nice to meet you Chris."

I just stare at Jill with awe and softly say "Bye Jill." I thought for a moment and really try to absorb her advice which made perfect sense and logic. I truly put some thought into the advice she gave me about revenge, I mean every fiber of my body wants to put a bullet between Tony's eyes, my friend turned instant liar, betrayer, back stabber, and all round demonic person, not at all the person that I had grown up with my whole life. But at the same time, I do not want to get rid of Tony by blood shed from my own hands but he needs to be destroyed and I need to destroy what wants to destroy me.

CHAPTER XIV

DESTROY WHAT WANTS TO DESTROY YOU

I close my eyes at the table and slowly fall asleep. Wish I could wake up and still be in the coffee shop two days ago and realize that I had dreamt this entire insane past forty eight hours. Or better yet, not wake up and just be at piece for a while having no drama in my ever so pleasing semiconscious state. I get startled when I hear my phone ring. I look at it, it was Tony. I figured I'd let it ring for a while, make him a little uneasy, make him sweat it out a little. Finally after seven rings I answer "Ya, I'm here."

In an almost defeated voice Tony responds "You know Chris, I never thought it would turn out this way, not really the way I envisioned it going down. I mean me being so gluttonous and greedy that I'd sacrifice my friend to a callous gangster like ALVAREZ all for the mighty dollar. My Uncle once told me a saying, he said: to get what you want, you must stop doing what isn't working. I wanted money and glory and what I was doing just wasn't working in my life, and it would never get me there. Day after day just making enough to get by and watch my days pass by and dreams dwindle away."

"At least it was honest" I responded.

"The successful people in life don't achieve their success by being honest, they lie and cheat and would willingly sell their soul to the devil for success or crush anyone that gets in the way. You know where nice honest guys finish Chris? Last! Are you an honest person Chris? Truly honest?" he asks me.

"I'd like to think of myself as an honest person ya."

"Oh ya? I'll bet When Trina asked you some years back how Russia went, you didn't tell her about that little girl did you? You probably told her everything went okay and was successful without a hitch. Seems like that was being deceitful to the woman you love more than anyone in this world. You think she would be more hurt by the fact that you murdered a little girl, or that you kept it hidden from her the entire time and lied to her when you said everything went smooth in Russia that day?"

I lower my head and ask sympathetically "What are you getting at?"

"I was given the opportunity by ALVAREZ to better my life, become rich, become famous, and make my life a little easier and Goddammit I took it! Same way you took it with JONES" Tony yells.

"Money isn't everything."

"Fuck that!" he screams. "Wealth makes an ugly person beautiful, a poor person famous, and with wealth alone we can enjoy endless decadence even in sickness and it can conceal all of our miseries despite how corrupt or how many. Money makes you happier, money makes your life easier, money brings you success, money gives you power, money takes away your worries, money runs the bloody world Chris and I dare you to tell me that I'm wrong. If you were given the opportunity to take me out for ten million you Goddam know you would pull that trigger in a heartbeat. You'd be rich, live wherever you want, buy an immense exquisite house, not have a worry in the world and all your problems would go away. You tell me right now, you wouldn't take it?"

"No, not even for one hundred million" I say.

"You know why it's easy for you to say that? Because I just gave you a 'what if' scenario, it's not real. But mark my word, someone shoves ten million in your face and then asks for your answer again, you'd take one look at that money, smell it, touch it then find me and put a bullet in my head."

"I learned a long time ago how precarious and dangerous greed can be. Money is like a beautiful thoroughbred horse, very powerful and always on the go, but unless that horse is trained properly, it will be an out-of-control dangerous animal and will hurt anyone it loves." I say.

"Money is the root of all evil? Is that what you're preaching?"

"Money isn't the root of all evil, it's the lack of money that is the true root of evil" I explain. "The greedy dog."

"What?"

"Never heard that one either huh? Well, there once was a greedy dog, let's call him Tony. Tony vowed to not be greedy any longer. One day he was walking home and saw a bone. He was very hungry so he walked over and snatched the bone up, but being afraid that another dog will try to come take the bone he decided to walk home with it and eat it there. So, while he was crossing the bridge he looked in the water and thought he saw another dog with a bone starring back at him. He thought that two bones were better than one so he dove in after it trying to steal the other bone not realizing that the other dog was actually just his reflection that he was looking at. After all this the greedy dog dropped his bone in the river and walked home hungry with nothing."

Tony takes a big sigh and I can hear him lighting a cigarette. "So I'm a greedy dog huh?" he puffs a cigarette "What do you want me to say huh? I screwed up? I saw an opportunity to better my life and I took it. I threw all my dignity, loyalty and honesty out the window just for a big payout. I'm scum, is that what you want to hear?"

"What happened to you man?" I ask with concern. "I mean, you were my best friend ever since we were little kids, heck I considered you my brother. And you were ready to hand me over to ALVAREZ for him to butcher me, all for money? Never thought in a million years you'd put a knife in my back as soon as I turned around, or that you could do it so easily" I said in a disappointing voice.

"You're right ok, I don't know what more to say alright. I was consumed by greed, I was blinded by the possibility of prosperity and power and I was in awe of being the best cop in the land and making my Dad proud, am I a bad person? Yes, is that what you want to hear? Huh?" he asks almost pleading.

"How do we end this?"

I can here Tony take a puff of his cigarette and says "Look, why don't we meet up, we destroy the recordings, we shake hands and continue with our lives and put all this in the past like a forgotten nightmare. You go your way, I go my way."

"I ain't gonna shake your hand. You had me kill an innocent person, you were about to sell me to ALVAREZ so he could slaughter me, you killed Jimmy, had one of your men shoot me, kidnapped Trina and ordered your guys to cut her throat. And you have the nerve to ask me to shake your hand? If it was up to me, I'd walk up to you and put a bullet right between your fucking eyes. But I am done with killing, I will never take another person's life as long as I am alive so help me God. You will get what is coming to you, karma is one nasty bitch." I say with resentment, pause then ask "Okay, where do you want to meet up, I want to destroy the recordings as bad as you."

"How bout 124th and main, there is an alley there. Probably best if nobody saw me and you together with all this shit going on ya know. We'll destroy the recordings and go live our separate lives" Tony says.

"Fine" I reply almost annoyed. "I need about an hour to get there."

"Okay, let's make it for nine o'clock okay?"

"Nine it is" I say and hang up. I wasn't sure if I could trust him, he sounded sincere, but once a back stabber, always a back stabber. I look at my phone, there was one last phone call I needed to make.

Could I ever trust Tony again despite that sincere sounding plea he just made? I'm not sure, but all I know that by nine this will all be over one way or another. Friends unfortunately make the best of enemies, they know who you are, know your fears, know what makes you venerable, know how to hurt you and know what will break you. Never fear the enemy that is charging at you to attack, fear the false friend that embraces you with a hug. When they are hugging you and you feel safe, that will be the time that they will see the opportunity to jam the knife into your back. Tony valued money over our friendship and I truly believe that other people including me just value friendship over any amount of money. People have a different perception of what it means to be rich in this world. Some people feel that to be rich means you have an abundance of wealth so who would needs friends if you are rich. Some people put no value on money at all thinking that you can have no money at all but if you have close friends and family, then you are truly rich. Then there are those like me who feel that you are rich by having a little of each, some good family and friends and have enough money to live a good life. Tony of course would be the first choice having no value in a lifelong friendship versus a dump truck of money. It's sad because people like that will get consumed with greed making them do unthinkable things for money and often leading them down a dark evil path which can ultimately lead one to their doom.

Do I trust him right now? Hell no. Do I want this shit to be done and over with? Hell yes! I am anticipating that he has something planned at this so called meeting, I can't see this going as smoothly as he is trying to assure me it'll go. Still, what choice do I have? If I don't show up or am not there, where is that going to get me? He will have the recording and I'll be a wanted man, looking over my should for as long as I live, having anxiety attacks every time I see the Police, and not knowing if he'll strike up another deal and come hunt me down. Tony is clever and I will never take that away from him, but I need to go in unarmed, I swore to never shed any more blood so help me God as long as I live. I am fully aware that I may lose this battle and maybe there is a chance that he has thought of something that I would never anticipate. I just have this feeling coursing through my veins that Tony won't go out this easy, he won't accept defeat especially by my hands, this may end up in a violent shootout and when the dust settles, we will see who will be the last man standing is. I had no idea what was about to go down in the alley but, neither did he.

1 week later in Mexico...

I am on the beach now lying next to my beautiful new fiancé on a blanket of picturesque white sand in Mexico. Ya you heard me, I popped the question and she said yes. I am the luckiest person on earth, I had everything I could ever ask. I remembered what Jillian told me, it ain't the strongest who survive, it's not the skilled who win the game, and it's not the baddest who conquer it all. No, it's the smart, the cunning, the crafty, the quick thinking who last in this world and get ahead. But what does it mean to win anyway? For every person out there, they have a different meaning for winning. Websters defines winning as; gaining, resulting in, or relating to victory in a contest or competition. The gain you get could be anything from wealth, a trophy, a good life, a promotion at work, a battle with an illness or simply getting what you set out to achieve in life. And of course the competition that you have achieved this gain from can be numerous, a game, a bet, a project, a life goal or simply just winning at life itself. I'm not sure exactly if I considered everything that has happened a victory or a win, but really, in the grand scheme of everything, I came out on top. Good people's lives ended, blood was spilled, innocent people were hurt and killed and I lost a lifelong friend that I will never see again. Is that really a victory?

I get a text message on my phone. I look and it was from T, it reads "THIS PLACE IS GREAT MAN, I AM LOVING IT HERE. THE KIDS HERE ARE REALLY COOL

AND LOOKING FORWARD TO GETTING BACK IN SCHOOL NEXT WEEK. THANKS FOR EVERYTHING MAN- T" I smile as a serge of warmth runs through my body from the words.

"Hey you, you okay" Trina asks me.

I am gazing into the ocean in awe of its majestic wonder and appreciating its beauty and just listening to it speak to me. I look at her and smile "Of course babe, how could this not be perfect? I have the love of my life beside me, magnificent ocean in front of me and best of all, we have our future to look forward to. What more could I ask for?"

"It's been a week and you haven't mentioned it once" she beams.

"That part of my life is over, I left it in LA and as far as I'm concerned, it never existed or happened. I pushed the reset button exactly a week ago and have started my life all over." I glance out into the ocean again "I am a new person babe, I feel like a new person too you know. Not really sure how to describe it, it's just I feel that I've closed the book on one life, and decided to end the story at that point a week ago. And now I have begun a new book which is completely different from the old one with a new setting and a new story line. Thing is I have a lot of blank pages that need to be filled and I can't wait to fill them up." I look at her and grin "We have a life together that we need to live and enjoy."

Trina just smiles at me and holds up her glass in a toast. I grab my glass and hold it up to hers and she says "To the new book" and we clang our glasses together.

What went down in that alley that day a week ago? Well, this is how I pictured it going down:

My beat up Porsche probably rolled up to 124th and parked beside the alley right at 9:00 sharp. I have known

Tony for almost twenty years and I guarantee when we agree to meet a 9:00, he would have been there at 8:45 just to make sure that he could see everything so there wasn't any surprises. Tony is a complicated person, nothing is black and white with him, there will always be every shade of grey you can think of with him.

Tony would have seen me stroll into the dark alley with my hood up so I wouldn't be exposed or let anyone know who I was or what I was doing there. I'm sure Tony would have been somewhere in the area surveying my car as it pulled up and saw me walk into the dark dense alley. Knowing him, he would have quietly snuck up behind me so he'd catch me by off guard and by surprise, not face to face like a real man. Tony never goes anywhere unarmed so Tony would have jammed a gun into the hooded persons back thinking he was going to stab me in the back and renege on our deal. Tony doesn't like to loose and no doubt he would have never just turned over the recording that easy and walked away with nothing, in his books that would have been a defeat. He'd rather die than admit defeat or accept the fact that he was outsmarted or outwitted by me, so he'd would have wanted to turn the tables and would have tried to outwit or outsmart me that day. But oh how he underestimated me and tried to take me for a fool, I didn't get as far as I did in life without being street smart and street savvy knowing how the mind of these scumbags work, let alone someone that I've known for close to twenty years.

Tony would have thought he had the game won when he approached the hooded man and demanded the recording at gun point squashing the deal and serve me up to ALVEREZ just he originally planned. I would have paid a lot of money that day to be a fly on the wall to see the look on Tony's face when the man he thought was me in the hood turned around, lowered the hoodie and exposed himself to Tony with that unforgettable scar underneath his left eye from the bullet of Tony's gun. The hooded man that Tony thought was me, was actually someone from his past who has probably waited for a confrontation like this and finally get his revenge on the man responsible for the nasty scar on his face, the hooded man was no other than Tiger St. Pierre, and I for one was glad to do this favor for him.

The horror and sheer terror that would have been on Tony's face when he didn't see the face of the person he was expecting to see. The panic that would have been running through his body as he gazes upon the face of the devil that has come to seek out his revenge on the person responsible for trying to kill him in cold blood.

My phone rang shortly after that encounter and I answered "Tiger."

Tiger said to me "Thank you my friend. This city doesn't need a person like him on the streets anymore, he is a cancer to this great city and law enforcement everywhere. And more than that, you have given me closure on something that has haunted me for all this time. My men ambushed him and we were able to take care of him."

"Figured you enjoy it more than I would, besides, I knew you needed closure and I know all about closure. I made a vow to never kill another soul for as long as I live. So, I just have to ask, what was the look on his face when you lowered the hood and he saw your face instead of mine?" I asked.

"Oh my friend, it was a look of pure terror and panic, and that look in someone's eyes you see when the person knows that he is about to die. That look of fear that makes any man's soul disintegrate and his insides turn, that was the look that he gave me as I gazed soullessly into his eyes" Tiger explained.

"I wish I could have been there to see that look. I knew that he would try to backstab me and renege on the deal, so I figured this was the perfect opportunity for you to execute your revenge. You did the LAPD and the world for that matter a colossal favor" I congratulate him.

"Thank you my friend, I could not agree with you more. I will mail you your Father's knife, and I have already destroyed the recording that I found on your friend here."

"Uh, about that recording, I can explain…" I said as I didn't want Tiger to hear what was on that recording.

"I never listened to it. It's not my business, what's your secret will remain your secret my friend" Tiger explains.

"Thanks Tiger. You can keep the Porsche too, just a part of my past life anyway that I don't need" I say.

"Thank you my friend, how can I ever repay you for this?"

"I'm pretty sure we can call it even. Take care Tiger, and thanks" and I hung up. At that moment, the story of my past life was over and I could finally move on. I sold my house in LA and told the realtor to send half the money to Sherman SLAUGHTER (*My Dad*) and the other half of the money to the boys community shelter so they can upgrade it and welcome every kid in that needs a place to stay.

As for Tony, well let's just say that Tiger told me that his piranhas were very well fed that night and they appeared to like Italian.

Present day in Mexico…

I stand beside Trina and just stare at the impressive turquoise blue ocean with a backdrop of a mystical tangelo coloured sunset. And there in front of us taking it all in was my big brother Nate in his wheelchair.

"Unbelievable. I could just sit here and admire this beautiful portrait forever" Nate says in wonder.

I put my hand on his shoulder and say "I made a promise to you that I would make sure that you witnessed this awe inspiring masterpiece again. I always keep my promises."

"The sunset just glows as if it's illuminated by thousands of tangerine colored diamonds, the waves sound like thunder as it crashes onto land, and the smell of the fresh ocean air with that hint of cool sea breeze, this is what heaven should be like" Nate says closing his eyes.

I am so moved by the way Nate could see the beauty of the world that we all take for granted every day. The denim blue sky, the shamrock green grass, the majestic trees and forests, the magical waters surrounding us, and the beauty that is life itself, things we take time to really appreciate.

"It's just perfect Nate" Trina says now also putting her hand on his other shoulder.

With his eyes still closed Nate extends him arms like a bird and says "Sometimes I feel like if you just admire the world, just sit perfectly still and let it just exist in front of your very eyes, sometimes you can make time freeze and the world pauses for a brief moment. And if somehow you could find a way to live in that particular moment, you could live forever. Maybe the elegant dream catcher above my bed can make that wish come true one day because I don't ever want leave this moment."

"We have all the time in the world brother, we will stay out here with you for as long as you want" I say with emotion in my voice.

We stayed out till the morning hours until Nate was able to experience once again the sunrise. All night long he sat there in awe and was almost hypnotised by the smell, the sounds and of course the view of the moonlight illuminating the dark waters of the ocean. We all talked the entire night, Trina gave me a few hours to be alone with Nate and bond as brothers do. Nate and I had a great relationship and he was not only my brother, but my best friend.

Nate passed away shortly after that, we never made it back to the hospital with him and he died peacefully in the back seat of my car. His lungs stopped working on the ride back and there was no chance of resuscitating him, he was gone, my brother was gone. I knew Nate died happy with a peaceful smile on his face because God let him hang on just long enough so he could experience what he wanted to before he passed and left me forever. I will never forget my brother and somehow I will try to forgive God for taking him away from me so early in life. That very same night Trina told me that she was two months pregnant and I was going to be a Father. She told me it was going to be a boy and asked me to pick the name, which I had no hesitation in choosing.

"There is only one name that comes to mind, Nathaniel J SLAUGHTER." The J was for of course for my pal, Jimmy. R.I.P my friend."

"He will wipe away every tear from their eyes, and death shall be no more, neither shall there be mourning, nor crying, nor pain anymore, for the former things have passed away"- Revelation 21:4

CHAPTER XV

RUSSIA REVISITED

(chapter closed)

1 month later in St. Petersburg Russia...

There was one more chapter that needed to be closed on my old life, the story that was not yet finished; Russia.

I hike down the wintriness snowy streets of St. Petersburg wearing a big heavy winter jacket as the cold artic air hits my face and spears through my coat. I look for the address that I have written on a piece of paper, the address that I have known in my head for a very long time. I keep looking up at the house numbers and finally stumble across my destination and my heart jumps in my throat as I feel the air rush out my body. I have replayed this moment a thousand times in my head and rehearsed every word that I will say but it still cannot prepare me for this face to face meeting.

I approach the house and hesitate for a few seconds as I bow my head. "Come on Chris, you've come all this way, don't chicken out" I mutter to myself.

Finally I look up and knock on the door and wait with anticipation. I stood in the porch of the resident almost trembling with fear, anxiety, and apprehension but this is something that needs to be done. I knock again and whisper again to myself "Please answer, I want to get this done."

Finally the door creeks open and a younger stunning female peeks out through the opening. "Yes?" she curiously asks.

"Hello ma'am, I am looking for Maria FINAGOV?" I politely ask.

She examines me up and down and asks in her Russian accent "Who are you?"

"Sorry, my name is Chris, I am an American."

She stares and me and begins to close the door and says "Sorry I don't know who you are."

I swiftly put my hand on the door preventing it from closing and quickly say "I'm here to talk to you about your sister Arina." I look at her with puppy dog eyes "Please, I have come a long way to come and speak to you, all I ask is for a moment of your time and I'll be out of your hair."

She hesitates and looks up and me "My sister is no longer here."

I lower my hand and softly say "I know, that's why I'm here, you'll understand once I tell you what I have to say."

Maria looks at me and asks in a rather stern voice "What could you possibly know about Arina?"

I gaze deep in her eyes and say "Please, may I come in and explain, it's rather cold out here?"

Maria looks me up and down once more then opens the door letting me in. "Thank you" I say.

She closes the door behind me and softly points to a dining room chair and says "Please sit down. Would you like some tea?"

I sit down and say "Uh, sure that would be nice thank you."

She pours two cups of tea, hands me a cup and sits down "Thank you very much" I say.

Maria was a beautiful girl, vast striking liquid sienna colored eyes, rich sunglow shoulder length hair and an innocence on her face. She couldn't be older than eighteen years old and had the most eloquent sounding voice mixed in with her Russian accent along with a dazzling body with curves in all the right places.

"So, how did you know my sister may I ask Mr....?"

"Please, call me Chris. I'd like to talk to you about how she died if that's okay?" I ask softly looking at her.

She bows her head and says "She was killed by a monster name Victor BRESHNEKOV. He was a merciless cold-blooded demon who had no business being on this earth, I mean how can God create a human being that despicable and malicious? I don't like to say this, but I was glad he died, he deserved it after he killed my little sister." She now looks up at me "But I don't understand what you have to do with any of this?"

I look at Maria directly in her copper eyes and try to speak the words that I have wanted to say for years, but I struggle "Maria?" I finally say. "I was hired by the Russian mafia to kill BRESHNEKOV that day. They put a contract on his head and asked me to come to Russia and kill him to make this world a better place. I am a hitman, was a hitman, and the Russian gangs in Los Angeles were the ones who gave my name directly to the big bosses in Russia saying I would be the perfect person to do the job with no ties leading back to them. Russian mafia at that time were being heavily watched by Russian Intel and they couldn't afford to take BRESHNEKOV out on their own despite how much they wanted to. When they told me what BRESHNEKOV had done, the horrendous unforgivable things that he did to these girls, I gladly accepted the contract and agreed to take him out. I remember that day like it was yesterday, the sky was a dim grey color, the rain was cold, the wind was soft, and all the emotions in my body left for a while."

I pause and see Maria hanging on my every word. I lower my head and begin to tear up "I had no idea Arina was in the next room. I took that son of a bitch out with a bullet to his head, but I had no clue there was an innocent little girl on the other side of that wall, how would I have known?" as a tear ran down my face I looked up at Maria who was staring at me with her eyes filling up with water and now put her hand to her mouth. "I swear on my Mother's grave I never knew that she was there, I pray to God every day to let me do it over again and spare her life. This has plagued me with demonic nightmares for five years, and there isn't a day that goes by that I don't regret doing what I did to her."

I look at Mariah who now had tears streaming down her face as she closes her eyes and sobs.

"Words cannot tell you how sorry I am, the remorse that I have built up over these years is enormous. This has tugged at my soul, has infested my dreams and has gutted my heart for all this time and there is nothing on this earth I can do to bring her back."

Maria takes her hand away from her mouth and asks me "Why? Why would you tell me this?"

I look her in the eyes then sink my head almost in shame "I thought you had the right to know. I thought your family should know the truth. I held this dark secret inside of me for five long years and I needed to tell you. I have replayed this moment over and over again in my head, the day that I would meet you and have the courage to tell you this, and even in my mind it never gets easier to play out."

I was anticipating Maria at any second to be overcome with rage and strike me or even call the Police. She gazes at me with melancholy eyes and wipes her tears. "Arina was a good person, she was going to school and was always courteous and kind to everyone. She was considerate to everyone she met and was a true gift to this earth. When they found her, the autopsy revealed that she had been raped by BRESHNEKOV several times and beaten almost beyond recognition."

"My God, I'm so sorry."

"You wonder if a person could have ever recuperated from something like that, or would they ever be the same. Would she relive that nightmare every time she sleeps, would that revolting day taint her soul forever? Some of the other girls that he had apparently done this to were scarred emotionally for the rest of their lives unable to even function properly in society and wake up with blood curdling screams from the night terrors. I for one am thankful that you put a bullet in his head and maybe you did Arina a favour and mercy killed her as painful and difficult as it is for me to say something like that. I miss my sister every single day and I could never understand why anyone would want to hurt such a wonderful person like her" she explains.

"That doesn't vindicate what I did and certainly doesn't justify it. I am glad that I was able to rid this world of a dreadful human like Victor, but it should never have come at the expense of a young girl's life." I say.

"You kill people for a living yes?" she asked looking at me with scrutiny in her eyes.

"I used to. I don't anymore, I couldn't take it, I wanted a new life free of sin. It takes a certain person to be able to pull the trigger knowing that it will kill someone when you do. I guess it just got to me psychologically, knowing how many people have died by my hands, and the fact that I have killed two innocent people while doing this just was too much for me to bear. I have a wife and a baby on the way, and I can't live like I used to anymore, but I couldn't start my new life without closing the book on my old one. This was the last page that had been unwritten for five years."

"You need this to close your book, is that why you have come here today?"

"No I needed to do this for me, for you and most importantly for Arina. I needed to have my soul purified, and you deserved closure and the truth. I feel like I practically knew her as weird as that sounds. After I found out what had happened, I researched and dug up every piece of information about Arina that I could so I could get to know her, and you are right, she was a beautiful person inside."

"What do you know about her?" she asks almost sarcastic.

"Arina Olga FINAGOV, born August 13th, 1990 in St. Petersburg at Pokrovskaya Bolnitsa hospital at 2:37 a.m. She was named after her great Grandmother Arina SLAVIKOV and her middle name was her mother's name Olga SLAVIKOV who died last year of breast cancer. Father was Igor FINAGOV who died when you both were very young from heart complications. Arina attended St. Petersburg International Christian School for ten years and was attending Gunzburg High School where she played basketball and had hopes of attending Herzen Univerity in four years to become a science major." I began to tear up and continue "her favorite color was baby blue because it was the color of your Father's eyes, her favorite movie was The Green Mile, her best friend was Elsa BURE and she loved her sister Maria very much."

Maria teared up as well and looked at me almost with admiration. She then reached out and put her hand over mine and said "I loved my sister very much and when she died I felt like I had so much more that I should have said to her. I realize no matter how much I loved her, how much I appreciated her, it never seemed like it was enough. Death leaves a heartache no one can heal, but love leaves a memory that no one can steal. I have lost so many people close to me Chris you will never know."

I grab her hand and say "I do know all too well. I lost my Mother when I was very young and I recently lost my best friend and my older brother. My Mother was taken from me before I really got to know her, my friend was taken from me as I was getting to know him, and my brother was taken from me as someone I knew better that anyone on this earth. So yes, I do know the gut wrenching pain you feel when you lose someone close to you, but you will never understand the heartache someone goes through when they are the one responsible for killing someone who should never have died. You'll never know the anguish that I have carried and will continue to carry my whole life, the guilt I feel, and the nightmares that constantly remind me of what I have done and the blood that will stain my hands forever. I won't ask for your forgiveness, but understand that this is something that I had to do, I had to tell you the truth about your sister so that maybe I will be able to sleep at night without those sadistic horrifying dreams waiting for me every night when I close my eyes."

"I can see that you are truly sincere, you have caring eyes and genuineness in your face. Nobody would go through that much trouble to really get to know the person that he has taken from this earth if he wasn't authentic in his sorrow." She looks at me deeply puts her hand gently on my chest and says "I do forgive you, you never meant for your bullet to hit my sister, it was an accident, I realize that and I also realize that it has affected you very deeply. You tried to do the world a big favor that day and by all accounts you did, unfortunately my sister was an unexpected collateral damage. You have come half way across the world to tell me this not knowing how I would react or if I would immediately call the Police to report to them what you have just told me." She now puts her other hand over mine and says "I believe you are a good person Chris, I really do mean that."

"You don't understand how much your forgiveness means to me. I have hurt and killed a lot of people in this world in my life, and I do not believe that I am a good person, but I am trying to change that and this was a good step in that direction" I say. I then pull out a cheque "I understand that you run a charity dedicated to abused teenaged girls in honor of your sister is that right?"

She nods and says "I started it right after Arina was found, and I mostly did it because of all the girls that Victor had abused but I realized that there were so many others out there who needed help and professional guidance. Girls out there need to know there is hope and have to realize that there is a set of open arms waiting for them and ready to embrace and support them."

I put the cheque face down and say "This is my donation for your charity, it is the very least I can do" she goes to turn it over and I stop her "Please, don't look at it until I leave. This is to help girls that have been abused like your sister and maybe help them recover properly and get the help and support they need."

"I don't know what to say, thank you."

I got up and couldn't help notice a photo of Maria and another girl. I pick up the photo and ask "Is this her?"

Maria nods and says "That was when we went to Italy six years ago."

I stare at Arina's breath-taking smile in the photo "She's gorgeous and looks so happy and blissful. She looks like she just loves life and is grateful for everything that she has, I can just see it in her smile."

"She was always a happy person, didn't seem like anything could make her depressed, she always walked around with a smile of her face, almost like she just appreciated every breath she took. The worst part about losing her was the fact that I never told her how truly wonderful she really was and how much she means in my life."

"I understand that. I guess I never got the chance to say that to my brother before he passed. But then again, we never anticipate that our loved ones would ever leave us either. Besides, I think my brother and your sister probably knew how much they meant to us even though we never actually spoke those specific words to them before they passed" I articulate.

"You're right I suppose. Arina had such a radiant soul and a peaceful smile, I try to remember all the good things about her and that sometimes makes me smile and eases the pain a bit."

I put the photo back and turn to Maria. "She sounds like a truly special person." I look at my watch and say "I should get going, I don't want to keep you any longer, you've been more than hospitable."

Maria stands up and says "You are more than welcome to stay for dinner if you like?"

I smile at her and respectfully say "That is most gracious and kind of you Maria, but I need to get home, my wife may think I'm up to something" I smirk.

Maria grins and I extend my hand to her. Maria moves close to me and wraps her arms around me with a hug. "Thank you for coming here, as painful as it was to relive my sister's death, I am glad you came, it gave me closure and I now know the truth."

I hug her back and say "I'm glad I came too, this was much needed for both of us I think. It was so hard to tell you what I have just told you, but I'm glad that I did." I look at Arina's photo again and ask "Do you mind if I keep that photo of you and Arina?"

Maria takes the photo out of the frame and says "I insist you have it, I have tons of photos, you keep that one."

I take the photo and stare at it again. "Thank you for everything and mostly for your forgiveness, I think I may be able to dream pleasant dreams now." I walk towards the door, I look back one last time at Maria "Goodbye Maria, God bless you" and leave.

Maria will be shocked and utterly surprised when she sees the cheque that I left for her. It was for two hundred and twenty five thousand dollars and I know that she will put that money to good use helping hundreds if not thousands of young girls that need it.

I am taking all the right steps I hope to counteract all of the death that I have brought to this world. I think I am on the right path, but I know I still have a long road to walk before I can get back into the good books of the Lord.

One day I will, and everything I do will one day be forgotten by this world. Life will go on and it will be as if I had never existed, just a mere speck in the grand scheme of all that has existed. Nobody will ever care when I am gone and no longer subsisting on this earth. Just like right here and now, almost nobody cares what I am actually saying or doing with my life at this very moment. Just think, over seven billion people on this earth, what percentage of that population actually gives a shit about me or what I am doing right now? Less than one percent? And this is actually really good for me in a way, it means I can get away with a lot of stupid mistakes and seven billion people will have no idea of what I have done, nor will they care or remember. It means there's absolutely no reason why I shouldn't be the person that I want to be, and all of my mistakes that I have made in my past are now a distant memory that are done and over with and cannot be relived for as long as this earth exists. All my future mistakes will also soon fade away as time slowly passes. The pain of un-inhibiting myself will be fleeting and the reward will last a lifetime. I think when we are kids we have all these ideas that we have to do this one big thing that is going to completely change the entire world. We dream so big because we don't yet realize that we are only kids and that that "one big thing" is actually comprised of thousands of daily small things that must be tentatively and cautiously maintained over our entire life time with little or no rewards. When you have lived your life and take a few steps back to observe the big picture that you have painted for yourself with those thousands and thousands of daily brush strokes, that's when you can truly see your whole life in front of you. If you can look at your masterpiece and be truly content with what you perceive in front of you, then who gives a shit what others think of it. Beauty is in the eye of the beholder, look at your exquisite life, and if you don't like it, change it, fix it, mold it into the center piece that you want, not what you think everyone else will want. Live your life the way you want to live it, it's yours, you only get one, do as you wish with it. Live out loud, live care free, live bold, live unbothered, live animated, live spontaneously, live on the edge, and most of all live with so much confidence it spills out your pours.

If God never forgave sinners, then heaven would be empty.

Printed in the United States
By Bookmasters